RAPTOR'S REALM: PROTECTOR OF THE VOICELESS

A Fantasy Tale of Faith, Courage, and Destiny in the Face of Evil

D. M. Harold

Cover design by:
Hampton Lamoureux of TS95 Studios

ISBN-13: 979-8-9920089-1-3

Contact the author:
www.joyfulscript.com

I dedicate this book to the Great One, who has been my help, and in the shadow of His wings, I sing for joy.

CONTENTS

CHAPTER 1

The osprey glided in a circle one hundred feet above the freshwater canal, the rising sun tinging his white head and chest to a glowing soft pink. Oz's shoulder ached from the effort of three failed dives, but he couldn't give up. Preya was back at the nest, heavy with eggs and hungry. Suddenly, below him —a ripple. Oz hovered, calculating speed and trajectory. With a few wing beats, he dove at a near-vertical angle. A split-second before crashing through the surface, he extended his legs forward and spread his feet open to grab the mullet with his talons. Submerging, he grabbed for the fish but pulled back as the familiar knifing pain shot through his shoulder. The fish was gone. He had failed again. Ignoring the pain, he thrust his head above the surface, forcing his wings upward, beating just above the water level and lifting skyward. He would have to start over.

Landing on a gnarly limb of a southern pine, Oz battled against a rising sense of failure and panic. How would he provide for a brood of chicks if he could not even feed Preya and himself? He rubbed his shoulder to ease the pain and looked east over the canal. The sun had broken away from the horizon and reached into the clouds, stippling their rippled underbellies with deep shades of orange, red, and purple. Oz turned to the west.

A few far-off clouds had already lifted their bulk high into the heavens and had grown dark. A streak of lightning flashed in the heavy shades of gray. Several seconds passed before he heard the rumble. He wondered if the storm would come this way.

Forty feet below, the water clapped the sides of the cement seawalls. Be calm, he told himself. It may take you more attempts than others, but you always, well, usually, bring home food. Oz sighed. What would it be like to fish without this shoulder impeding his efforts?

A movement in one of the backyards lining the canal caught his attention. A brown muscovy duck with white wingtips emerged from underneath a hibiscus bush. Oz recognized Bertha. Toddling behind her were thirteen baby ducklings, or maybe fourteen; Oz lost count. They were tiny, each about the size of a mouse, but he could clearly hear their peeping. They probably had hatched yesterday, and this was their first lesson in life. Swim. Following the group was Brun, also brown with white wing tips. Oz waved to Brun, but the large male was too busy shepherding his brood to notice him. It amused Oz that the muscovies usually choose mates with the same colorings and markings.

The family walked along the seawall, and Bertha jumped into the canal. One by one each of the ducklings plopped in beside her. The last was not so brave. Oz chuckled watching him run back and forth along the seawall peeping at his mom. The little guy was unsure about the two-foot drop into the water. Brun waddled up to the stray hatchling and lightly tapped his butt with his beak. Encouraged, he took the leap and joined his mom and siblings. Brun fluttered down to the water, and the family paddled off together.

Oz resumed scanning for fish. A warm breeze carrying the smell of fermenting sea grass ruffled his dark brown pinions. Shifting his weight from one leg to the other, he stretched out cramps. He worked his left shoulder again, trying to ease the ever-present pain and stiffness. For whatever reason, the fish were eluding him. This gave him time to think. And there was a lot to think about. And worry about. The hollow pain in his gut was not just from hunger.

Preya should start to lay her eggs any time now. This should be a happy time, but Oz was struggling in a quicksand of sorrow. Anxious fears threatened to grab hold and pull him under. His thoughts focused on his father. Oz missed him so much. It had been just three weeks since Otto had gone to fly with his fathers.

Otto had been the leader of the Council of Protectors of Havenport for well over a decade. He led with compassion and wisdom, extending justice and protection to all birds of Havenport and, against a few of the other council members' wishes, to the other animals sometimes. In the past year, however, Otto would forget recent conversations with council members or family and get confused about simple details. He'd miss a meeting or show up at the council post when nothing was scheduled. Obsolom, Otto's first-born son and Oz's older brother, was the chief elder of the council. He had taken over most of Otto's duties along with Huldah, Otto's sister, who also advised on spiritual matters. While only being a figurehead, Otto still maintained a culture of caring and justice.

Otto always had a quest to catch Mulahyay, the legendary king of the mullets. At almost two feet long and weighing three pounds, he was twice as big and twice as fast as any of the other mullets in the Havenport canals. Mulahyay was seldom seen, and no osprey had been able to get close to him. Because of Mulahyay's size and speed only the strongest and most skilled fisher could ever hope to catch him. Otto was large for a male osprey at just under four pounds and was a magnificent fisher. But that had been in his younger days.

One morning, three weeks ago, when Huldah and Otto were flying over the lake, Otto spotted Mulahyay. Huldah called out to Otto but could only watch in terror as Otto soared to a height of 150 feet to get the required force and then dove at a speed topping eighty miles per hour. Spreading his wings back, he pounced on top of the fish, sending sprays of water ten feet high. His front and back-facing talons had hooked his quarry, and Otto immediately began flapping his great wings to take himself and Mulahyay out of the water. But instead of rising out of the water, Otto, unable or perhaps unwilling to release his grip on his writhing prize, was pulled into the dark depths of the lake by the mammoth fish, where they disappeared among the eelgrass.

Later that morning, Huldah found Otto floating on his side next to a sea wall; his right front talon had been torn off. The way of the air and water and land. All return someday.

Still on the pine limb, Oz again shifted his weight. His musings turned to his older brother, Obsolom, who had succeeded their father as the council's leader. Obsolom. Beautiful Obsolom.

His brother was two years older than Oz, and in all Havenport, there was not an osprey so highly praised for his handsome appearance as Obsolom. From the crown of his head to the tip of his tail, there was no blemish in him. Like his father, he was large for a male osprey. Filling out at four pounds and having a wingspan of almost five feet, he was larger than any other male and many of the female ospreys in Havenport. His keen yellow eyes were set against a wide black eye stripe that extended from his sizeable hooked beak, around his eyes, and down the sides of his neck. While all ospreys had this marking, Obsolom's head and neck were an unusual pure white, giving him a regal appearance. But everyone agreed his most appealing feature was the long, silky feathers of his wings and tail. When Obsolom molted one, the unmarried male ospreys would fight over it so they could give it as a courting gift to their desired bride.

Oz had not been blessed with any of these attributes. Smaller and common in appearance, the only things that made him noticeable were a persistent slouch and his hampered flight from a shoulder injury when he was a chick. At least the disability caused people to have no expectations of Oz to be like his brother, and he had long ago shed his adolescent jealousy. Oz was happy to have his brother take all the praise and attention; the only important thing was Preya and their expected brood.

Highly revered, Obsolom was an eloquent speaker at the council meetings and carried out his duties effectively. Aunt Huldah, however, did not seem to trust him fully. More than once, Oz had seen her speaking in hushed yet authoritative tones to Obsolom after meetings. Perhaps, Oz thought, it was because Obsolom was abrupt at times, not allowing more than one or two opinions to be heard before making decisions. Like the other council and community members, Oz would rather think his brother was being efficient. Heading the council and leading the thousands of birds in Havenport was a big job. Of course, Obsolom was the obvious choice to fill the position of leader when Otto went to fly with his fathers. Who else was there?

Oz shook himself out of his thoughts and checked the sun's position. He had been gone over two hours. Fishing was over for the morning. In his mind, jeers of defeat taunted him. He would return later today. He needed to get back to the nest to check on Preya.

As Oz flew toward his nest, he looked to the west. The storm cloud he had seen before had rained itself out and was only a mere whisp of what it had been. Now, closer ones in the south had begun stacking themselves up in menacing heaps.

CHAPTER 2

A few streets over from where Oz had been fishing, Sophie muttered to herself as she opened every cabinet in the outdoor kitchen on her lanai. "Do I have an extra pair of those purple gloves?" Standing up from peering into the lower cabinet, she grabbed the small of her back and rubbed it hard. The rheumatoid arthritis was acting up again. As her mother used to say, aging was not for sissies. Copper, her cat, had followed her and was sitting on the stone bench in the corner of the lanai, tracking a family of squirrels that had arrived on the pool cage above. Copper's one good ear lay flat against his head, chagrined at not being able to get close to the squirrels. The other ear had been ripped to shreds, maybe by a coyote, and had to be removed. Sophie remembered her husband Jeffrey calling Shannon one night about a year ago to bring over her veterinary bag when he found the mewing kitten bleeding and cowering in their bushes.

Sophie stepped over to the screen door to look out by the hose reel where she had rinsed out her cleaning bucket and laid her gloves over it earlier this morning. Those nitrile exam gloves worked as well as the expensive rubber gloves and lasted almost as long. She would have to ask Shannon for another pair.

Just then, Shannon came walking around the corner

of the house with her phone in her hand. "Shannon, someone took the purple gloves you gave me." Sophie opened the screen door for her neighbor. Even though they were a generation apart in age, the two women had bonded over their love for animals.

Shannon hugged Sophie. "Is Jeffrey home?"

Sophie started opening each drawer. "Can you give me another pair of purple gloves?"

The family of squirrels were now chattering as they jumped and clamored over the screen to annoy Copper.

"Sophie, Is Jeffrey home? You both need to look at this!" Shannon glanced up at the noisy squirrels. Their racket and bouncing around on the screen made it hard to focus on anything else.

Finally hearing the urgency in Shannon's voice, Sophie turned around. "Shannon, what's the matter? Jeffrey took Duke for a walk." Sophie pushed a loose strand of gray hair off her forehead.

"Read this email I just got from the Havenport HOA. You probably got the same one." Shannon held her phone out to Sophie.

Sophie turned her head toward the noisy family of squirrels and waved her arms to get them to scamper away. "Quit the chattering, you silly bushy-tailed rodents!" Her attention now fully on Shannon, Sophie took the phone and started reading. "I can't believe this! Why would they do this? I know there are lots of ducks here—but what do they expect in a neighborhood with freshwater canals and lakes?"

Sophie swiped the screen to move the text. "So, they say there are too many of them and that their dung spreads disease? Really? What about all the dog poop that people don't pick up?"

"Keep reading. It doesn't get any better," Shannon noticed that, thankfully, the squirrels were no longer making a ruckus. They were now perched on the screen above Shannon and Sophie and seemed to be listening. Copper had also moved closer and sat at their feet, looking up at them with his one ear perked.

Sophie drew in a sharp breath and put her hand to her mouth. "We should shake the eggs if we find them?"

"Yes. Shaking the eggs is called addling. It kills the embryo, but the mother duck will still lay on them, thinking the eggs will hatch. If the eggs are just removed, she would lay another batch, just like a chicken does." Shannon folded her arms across her chest. It angered her that the muscovies were being targeted when the other birds made just as many messes and made much more noise. But unlike other bird species protected by the state, the muscovies were non-native to Florida and could legally be removed by anyone. Many people didn't like the large ducks and thought they were ugly with the red wattle around their eyes and head.

Sophie put her arm around Shannon. "I know you love all the ducks. I hear them every morning honking at your back door to be fed. Are you going to stop feeding them?" Sophie was always amazed that Shannon had named so many of them and knew each by their different characteristics. "I know feeding them keeps them around the yards, and they do make messes everywhere. Jeffrey is always getting the hose out to spray off the boat and the dock. But I would rather clean up their messes than not have them around."

"Me too. And I don't want to stop feeding them; I get so much enjoyment from seeing them every day. They are fun to watch and to see how they interact with each other and care for their families. Did you know they mate for life? I'm always sad when one of them doesn't show up anymore. I think about what might have happened to them. But to know people will be intentionally removing them or addling their eggs; it just does not seem right."

Sophie continued reading the article. "It says the company they hired is supposed to trap them and release them somewhere. They don't say where."

"No, and I am unaware of any muscovy refuges close by. There is one about thirty miles south of Sarasota, but that is over a two-hour drive from here."

"Jeffrey is going to make some thunder when he hears about this. That HOA president better get ready to answer some questions instead of spending so much time washing his Tesla." Sophie hugged Shannon and took her hands in hers. "Let's pray about this. The Bible says God cares about sparrows and ravens. I'm sure He cares about the muscovies."

As Sophie prayed, the squirrels resumed their chattering, and, bounding across the screen and up the roof, they disappeared into the oak, pine, and palm canopy that lined the street and covered most of the neighborhood.

Up in the palm that grew twenty-five feet over the pool cage, a crow called to her neighbor across the canal. "Kwok, Kwok, Kwok. Uh-oh, uh-oh."

A hundred feet above the crow's nest, an osprey gracefully glided in circles on the thermal updrafts, exclaiming, "Fweep! Fweep! Fweep!"

"I sure would like to know what those animals are saying," Shannon said as Sophie ended her prayer.

CHAPTER 3

C hatty bounded up the branch behind Skamp as they jumped in tandem from the oak to a pine, using their bushy tails as rudders to maneuver through the air and land safely on the nearest outstretched branch. "Are you sure we heard what we heard when we heard it? Hearing can be tricky. I hear one thing, you hear another, and maybe what really was said was something else."

"Chatty..."

"Remember last week, when you thought you heard Scramble telling Chit-Chat that he was fired from his job and what he really said was that he was *tired* of his job, but by then, it was all over the neighborhood, and his boss found out, and...."

"Chatty—you, me, and the kids heard those ladies talk about the decree from their Ayechoe-aye, which must be their high council, about capturing and exiling the muscovies." Skamp looked behind him to make sure Chatty was still following him closely through the trees. She tended to get distracted when nervous, and what they heard had given them both the jitters. They must get to their own council leaders as quickly as possible to inform them. The treetop route was the shortest, but it was still about a half mile from the lady's house to the conservation area behind the retention pond. There was usually at least one council member on duty.

Chatty suddenly stopped on top of a palm and was chittering away, attempting to groom her tail, which swished up and down, evidently out of her control. "This is not right, I don't think. I mean, will the humans exile us next and shake our babies? What would we do? I just can't imagine." Chatty's whiskers twitched nervously as she looked toward Skamp.

"Chatty, let's not go nuts about this." Skamp jumped over to Chatty, put his paw on her shoulder, and looked into her soft black eyes. She was the most beautiful squirrel he had ever seen, even after two litters, and it pulled at his heart to see her so upset.

"And I didn't understand about this human that is going to rescue them. And did you hear that lady call us rodents?" Chatty stood on her hind legs with her paws on her hips.

"Come on, let's get to the council. We're almost there. They will know what to do. Their mission is to protect." Skamp bounded ahead through the trees.

CHAPTER 4

Obsolom preened his feathers and sharpened his talons with his hooked beak as he listened to Crete. They were perched thirty feet up on the gray skeleton of a cypress which jutted out from the middle of the marsh brining below them and had long past succumbed to the brackish water. The old snag served as the council's post during the day and was also where they held council meetings. It was now high tide, and all the ground hunters had left. Even though Obsolom and Crete were surrounded by silence, they huddled close and spoke in hushed whispers.

"You are the new leader, and it is in your wings to have the Great Blues supporting you. Or not." Crete towered above Obsolom with his long legs and neck. His plumed head, chest, and wings gave him a graceful appearance that belied a friendliness. However, one look into Crete's yellow-orange piercing eyes was a chilling experience and would confirm that the heron was anything but friendly.

Obsolom stopped preening and peered into Crete's eyes. "Whether the Great Blues support me or not is of no consequence. Your threats have no substance."

"A new leader is always in such a precarious position. Especially one who aspires to rule with absolute control." Crete looked down his long bill at Obsolom.

Obsolom hunched toward Crete and sneered. "What do you know of my aspirations? My superior capabilities have finally been recognized; I should have been made leader years ago when my father started making a fool of himself. The vote of the people was unanimous for me to be leader."

"Unanimous because you made sure you were the only candidate. And, as you and I both suspected, your brother was wise enough not to contend with you."

"Why would he? He prefers to remain crippled in the background whimpering over the past."

"But you do not fool me, Obsolom. It is obvious that you intend to turn this weak democracy into a formidable monarchy." Crete paused for a few seconds. "A noble cause long overdue."

Obsolom stood in silence, grinding his beak.

With lightning speed, Crete snatched an unwary lizard off a nearby branch with his daggerlike bill and swallowed it whole. "I'm simply stating that you will need fearsome backing to make this happen."

Obsolom puffed his chest forward. "And you propose yourself to be that backing?"

"The people will follow you blindly until you have to lead in contentious times. From the news you heard this morning, those times have dawned."

Obsolom raised his eyebrow. "This news does not strike me as causing contention."

Crete grunted and pointed at himself. "*I* know your manic desire for absolute submission from your subjects. I also know the other council members are mired in their delusion of fulfilling what they see as their calling to be protectors of all the birds."

"Get to the point, Crete. I'm tired of your clucking."

Obsolom resumed preening his pinions.

"You heard that the humans are going to destroy the muscovies. If you and your council vow to protect the muscovies, won't you violate the higher law from The Order that humans maintain dominion over all animals?"

Obsolom turned to look Crete again in the eye. "Go on."

"By protecting the muscovies, you have declared war against the humans. Wouldn't the Great One retaliate?" Crete had lowered his head to Obsolom's level. "Now, on the other wing, by supporting the humans, you are establishing your strength by holding to a higher law, and who can disagree with that?"

"You know that the people view the council as protectors."

Crete continued. "It is all hinged on how the news is shared. The people may squawk about it a bit, but no one really likes the muscovies. They are refugees from farms where they were being bred for food. They have escaped to Havenport and have taken over the best nesting areas."

Obsolom slowly nodded, keeping his eyes in line with Crete's. "That is true; ask any mallard."

Obsolom began to tap his right fore-front talon on the branch. "Your reasoning against protecting the muscovies has nothing to do with some higher law. I know you have no love for The Order or the Great One."

"Nor do you." Crete darted his head toward Obsolom.

"What is your real reason for supporting the humans, Crete?" Obsolom stretched out his mighty wings and thrashed them, almost knocking Crete off the branch.

"You stupid fish hawk!" Crete regained his balance and jabbed at Obsolom's chest with his beak. "You would serve yourself well by convincing the council to lift the muscovy duckling limit on the Great Blues immediately and permanently. You should have acted on my advice before."

Obsolom leaned forward, thrashing his wings again. "You know my views were overruled. Besides, if your kind had not been so greedy by devouring entire clutches, the limit would not have been necessary." Obsolom's knuckles were white from his stronghold on the branch.

"You will tell the council that by lifting the limit, you will please the Great One by letting the Great Blues assist the humans in removing muscovies." Crete pushed his beak toward Obsolom's face. "When you get the council to agree, the Great Blues' support of your monarchy will be ensured. You will have a secure reign, and the Great Blues will have unlimited muscovy ducklings."

"Who are you to give me orders?" Obsolom screeched.

"Your dynasty will topple without the strong support of your aspirations," Crete shrieked back.

Suddenly, Obsolom turned his head around. "Hush! I hear something."

The birds turned toward the rustling sound to see two squirrels bounding through the trees. Obsolom knew why they had come.

CHAPTER 5

"Look, Chatty! Obsolom is at the post. He will know what to do."

"Why is Crete with him? He's not on the council. Maybe he also heard about it and is asking for Obsolom's wisdom."

Skamp hoped that was true, but seeing Crete hunched over, having what looked like a sneaky argument with Obsolom, made him uneasy. The Great Blues were excellent hunters but were not particular about their diet. Baby squirrels and even smaller adult squirrels could be on their menu.

"Who approaches?" Obsolom called out with a tone of warning.

"It is Skamp and Chatty, Obsolom," Skamp said as he and Chatty jumped over to the snag and climbed up to a branch across from Obsolom and Crete. As they neared, Skamp felt a pinch of fear. Both birds towered over them and were at least ten times their size. They were armed with beaks that could slice flesh and talons that could strangle and puncture. He tried to give himself solace in Obsolom's oath as Leader and Protector.

"You may call me Leader. Why are you here? You were not sent for." Leaning toward the squirrels, Obsolom jerked his head sideways and peered at them with one eye as though they were being interrogated for raiding a bird feeder.

Chatty's tail swished rapidly up and down, and her whiskers twitched erratically. "We need to tell you about what we heard today when we were teasing the orange cat, and then the ladies were talking and..."

Skamp noticed Obsolom's beak clenching and reached over to touch Chatty, hoping she would calm down.

"And the ladies, there were two of them, and one of them lost her gloves and...."

"Silence!" Obsolom whipped his head toward Chatty, almost touching her head with his sharp, curved beak. "Unlike my weak predecessor, I do not need to listen or give counsel to rats." The white crest feathers on Obsolom's head bristled as he then aimed his penetrating gaze toward Skamp.

Skamp moved in front of Chatty, putting himself between her and Obsolom. The pinch of fear had erupted into a clenching panic in his chest as his pulse raced. The squirrel clung to the tiny remnant of his courage to speak. "Obs, er, Leader, what we heard is news of extreme danger for some of your birds. We felt it was our duty to inform you; as Leader, you would know what to do."

"I will grant you thirty seconds, but I will feed you both to Crete if she does not stop the incessant twitching of her tail." Obsolom pointed his wing at Chatty. Crete licked his beak.

Skamp put his trembling paws on Chatty to calm her. Then, as quickly as he could, he told Obsolom about the decree from the humans' Ayechoe-aye.

Obsolom's talons contracted tightly into fists, digging deep into the branch as Skamp's voice rose in pitch nearing the end of his story. "This is babbling! For what reason would I believe you wretched creatures who exist to gossip?"

Chatty buried herself into Skamp's chest, wrapping her tail over her face.

Skamp opened his dry mouth to speak, but no words came out.

Obsolom took a half-step toward the squirrels. "You squirrels are steeped in folly! Only a fool would incline his ear to you. Leave and bury this fabricated story along with your insect-ridden acorns. If I hear that you have spread this tale, the council will silence you!"

Terrified, Skamp and Chatty backed away step by step, keeping the two birds in view. Once far enough away, they turned around and jumped onto another tree, skittering back the way they had come.

Crete watched the squirrels leap through the trees. "You do know that the action of the humans will soon support their story. I assume you have a strong reason to have dismissed their report?"

"You should know that I must be the one to give my version of the humans' edict and not have their minds swayed by senseless rats."

Crete moved closer to Obsolom. "Was there anyone else you have failed to mention who witnessed the humans discussing this?"

"The new crow family. The wife was in their nest and may have listened and likely told her husband. I know how to deal with him."

CHAPTER 6

Chatty and Skamp crashed through the trees toward their home, knocking off leaves and dead twigs in their haste to distance themselves from Obsolom and Crete. Suddenly, Chatty stopped on a large oak branch, causing Skamp to collide with her and nearly knock both of them off the tree.

"Skamp! I don't understand why Obsolom treated us like that. And he called us rats; I don't think that is nice. Why was he so mean and scary?"

Skamp's heart was still racing from the encounter and hurried exit. Adding to that was a light-headed hopelessness. The protectors had not believed the squirrels. "Let's just get home where it's safe. You heard Obsolom; some protective leader he is."

"Is there anyone else on the council we can go to? Should we start a protest?" Chatty caught her tail, which was beginning to twitch, and held it tightly in her paws.

"Chatty, if we go to anyone else, Obsolom will find out about it and come after us, not just you and me—our kids, relatives, neighbors. Ospreys are not fond of squirrel meat, but the Great Blues will eat anything that breathes and can fit in their beaks. If Crete is allowed to target us..."

Skamp took Chatty's paws, releasing her self-willed tail, and looked into her eyes. Lines of anguish creased his brow. "I just want us to be safe."

"Skamper," the endearing nickname was reserved for Chatty's use only, "I know. Me too. But I don't think we are safe. What if they want to get rid of the squirrels next? We can't just sit on our tails and pretend we didn't hear what we heard. What is the Great One always saying?"

"I know, I know. You remind me all the time: be strong and courageous." Skamp marveled at Chatty's resolve for protection and justice. Despite her nervousness, in some ways, she was stronger than he was. Her bravery and the words of the Great One fanned a slight spark of hope. "We can go to Oz."

Chatty's tail started swishing again, and her voice rose in pitch. "Oz? Obsolom's younger brother? Wouldn't he immediately go straight to Obsolom? Why Oz? You don't know him."

"I just have a sense he will help us. He listens and talks to everyone with respect at the council meetings. And all the birds, it doesn't matter to him if they are pure fish eaters or not."

"But Oz is so meek and quiet." Chatty twitched her whiskers. "And he flies crooked."

"Last season, he encouraged the turtles to ask for help when they couldn't find egress points because the canals were getting low. Same thing with my Uncle Scurry. A year ago, when it seemed the Great Blues were targeting the squirrels, Oz spoke up for him at the council."

Chatty was fumbling around, trying to get her tail under control. "Well, why wasn't Oz considered for leader last month when Leader Otto went to fly with his fathers?"

"I don't know. When Otto was leader, Oz encouraged other council members to listen to all animals. Otto had always said that the Great One had commanded the ospreys and council to be protectors, and never limited who they should protect."

Chatty finally captured her tail again. "But Oz hasn't done much lately."

"I think he will listen to us, Chatty."

"If you are sure, and I mean really sure, like as sure as acorns in the fall, then OK. I'm just glad ospreys only eat fish."

Skamp hugged Chatty close and smiled at her. "Still, his wife is pregnant and probably always hungry, so let's not look appetizing."

CHAPTER 7

The sun had climbed higher in the sky and had diced the clouds into a few small puffballs by the time Oz returned to the nest.

"Preya, I told you, no more nest building! This nest has gotten too big, and you should not be carrying anything now. You are almost ready to start laying eggs." Oz had landed on the side of the nest and was trying to scowl at Preya. It was hard to be upset with her. They were both looking forward to finally having a family to raise, but she was anxious and exhausted as she approached her time. Oz did not want anything to hinder this clutch.

"What makes you think I was nest building?" Preya looked down, avoiding Oz's gaze, and rocked from foot to foot.

"Because I see another layer of twigs on the south side. And, what is that purple stuff?"

Oz tramped over to inspect the purple stuff tucked into some crevices. As he poked a wad with his beak, it stretched against his beak but returned to the same place as he pulled his beak back. He poked another section, pushing hard against it.

Boing! Thwap!

Suddenly, some purple stuff broke off and slapped against Oz's face, sending him sprawling back on his tail. The strange-smelling material had tightly bound itself around his beak. Shaking his head hard, he tried to get rid of the purple bands. Finally, he bent his head down, used his talons to pry the stuff loose, and flung it away from the nest.

Oz inspected the purple stuff that remained in the nest more closely. He had never seen anything like this growing in the neighborhood; it must have belonged to a human. Great. Not only had Preya not followed his advice, but she had also stolen from a human. Oz eyed Preya quizzically.

Preya kept her gaze lowered and tried hard to stifle a laugh. "I had just gone for a short flight to stretch my wings when I saw these purple objects below. You know how I love purple. So, I went to inspect and knew I had to have them for the nest."

"Preya," Oz felt his resolve to remain angry faltering, "what about the palm fibers I brought you yesterday?" Oz thought of the fifty trips he had made to get just the right kind of fibers in the quantity Preya had asked for, which, apparently, she had plucked out and replaced with the stretchy purple objects.

"I'm sorry, Oz," Preya started to cry. It did not take much lately to bring on a torrent of tears. "I just want everything perfect this time."

"I know." He maneuvered around her giant belly and rubbed his head against her cheek, wishing he could do more to comfort her. "This time will be different. You'll see."

Oz stroked Preya's head with his wing. "I think it's time for Aunt Huldah to stay with you when I am not here."

Preya opened her beak to protest, but Oz shook his head and held her close.

"Everything will be fine, and in a few weeks, you will

have your wings full taking care of babies." Oz hoped that would be true. This was their third attempt at raising chicks.

Oz was a year older than Preya. They wed at the beginning of the nesting season and were ecstatic when they realized the Great One was blessing them so soon with children. The nest they now had was built that year. He remembered finding the most suitable Norfolk pine with a tri-branched top located far enough away from the noisy humans but only a quick flight to their favorite fishing spots. The pine stood taller than the surrounding trees, giving the blissful couple a panoramic view of the forest and a glimpse of the sparkling bay to the south. Planning the nest and working with Preya to construct it was hard labor, but they both enjoyed seeing their new home take shape.

It was still more than a week before it was time for Preya to start laying the eggs when she suddenly collapsed in the nest with severe pain in her belly. Oz flew off to get Aunt Huldah, and when they returned, two tiny cracked and oozing eggs lay beside Preya. Oz remembered feeling like the breath had been knocked out of him. Preya sobbed, blaming herself for cracking them when she attempted to lay on them. Huldah had seen this before when eggs were laid prematurely. These eggs were always small, and the shells paper-thin and translucent. They would not have hatched even if they had not cracked. Huldah tried to comfort them both, but it would take several months for Preya and Oz to heal enough from their grief to gain a semblance of normalcy.

And they did. Preya helped her sister-in-law, Obsolom's wife Priscilla, raise her brood of three. Oz got more involved in the council, serving on several committees, and was being considered for leadership positions. As the next nesting season approached, they enlarged their nest. Preya laid one perfect egg, and after forty days, Oscar peeped his way out of his shell and into the world. Oz and Preya were overjoyed at the little fluff of feathers wobbling on the nest. They took turns getting food and cleaning up the nest. Oscar was never left alone.

Until one day when Oz was needed at the council for a meeting. Oz couldn't remember now what the meeting was about, but it went on for hours. Back at the nest, Preya waited as long as she could but finally decided to make a quick run for dinner. It was the last fishing time of the day, and Oscar needed to eat. Preya said a quick prayer and flew toward the neighborhood's lakes and canals, looking for fish in the fading light.

When she returned ten minutes later with a catfish, Oscar was gone.

Stunned with fear, she searched to see if Oscar had wandered off onto a nearby branch. Instead, she saw a six-foot-long orange and brown snake with a bulge in its body slip down the trunk and disappear under the sound of dead leaves rustling on the forest floor.

Preya blamed herself for leaving the nest. Oz blamed himself for staying at the council meeting too long.

Oz then vowed never to get involved in so many committees or take a leadership position on the council. Let his brother Obsolom take over when the time comes.

Oz needed to tend to his family and not let anything get in the way. But the unwelcome question barged into Oz's mind again. Why would the Great One let these things happen? Wasn't the first command to be fruitful and multiply?

Catching a whiff of fresh fish and feeling a slight flutter behind him, Oz turned his head around to see his Aunt Huldah land on a bough. She had a fat mullet in her talons.

"Breakfast, anyone?" Aunt Huldah had helped raise Oz when his mother had been lost in the big wind. She was always looking out for her favorite nephew and wife and often seemed to know when they needed something or to talk about something important. But that should be expected; she was from a long line of prophetesses for the Great One and was the council's spiritual advisor.

"I love what you have done with the nest, Preya. Those purple accents are gorgeous!" Huldah winked at Preya, who was devouring the mullet.

"Don't encourage her! She had promised not to build anymore. Do you see how large this nest has gotten? It's not like we are having two broods at once." Oz tried to sound firm and angry.

"Preya is just doing a few final touches and livening up the nest with some much-needed color. The place would look like a drab pile of dead twigs if it were up to you. And I think you will find the nest is not too big."

Huldah hopped down onto the nest. "However, Preya, it is time for you to stay at the nest. Let me look at you." Aunt Huldah stepped over to Preya, who was still munching her breakfast, and began to examine her, beak to tail feathers.

"Your eyes are bright, that's good, but you have some

puffiness around them. How have you been sleeping?"

"Well, not so good," Preya wiped her beak with her wing. "I'm just so uncomfortable. No matter how I try to rest, something hurts. My back, my legs, my belly. I was not this miserable the other two times."

"How has your flying been?"

"Mostly good."

"You said 'mostly.' When have you had problems?" Huldah would not let Preya get away without telling her everything.

"Um, well, I had some trouble bringing back the pretty purple things today. I had to rest several times." Preya glanced at Oz and then looked down.

"Preya! You could have injured yourself or lost the eggs!" Oz flapped his wings in exasperation.

"I know! I'm sorry, Oz!" Preya set aside the remains of the fish and started to weep again. "I promise I won't leave the nest until the eggs are laid."

"Preya, stand up. Let me check your belly." Preya stood, and Huldah reached her head down to gently palpate Preya's belly with her beak. "Hmm. Ahh. Oh my. Just as I thought."

"Aunt Huldah, what's wrong?" The alarm in Oz's voice matched the fright in Preya's eyes.

"Oh, nothing is wrong. Everything looks good. Very good, in fact. Any day now. I will stay close now until all the eggs are laid."

Oz let out a sigh of relief. "Thank you, Huldah, and please pray to the Great One that everything will go well, that all the eggs survive, and we have a healthy brood to raise."

"Oz, I pray for that every day. You can, too. You do not need me to intercede for you, and the Great One desires to hear from you."

Oz turned his head away from Huldah.

Huldah moved closer to Oz. "It is time for you to unchain yourself from your past sorrows and let him back in your life."

"How can you say that, Huldah, when I have seen so much misery? Falling from the nest when I was a chick and having this life-long injury with constant pain hampering my flight, and then my mother dying soon after. That was bad enough, but I still thought the Great One looked out for us." Oz rubbed his left shoulder at the mention of his injury.

"Then, Preya and I lost both of our broods, Father dying so tragically. It is too much. When has the Great One heard my prayers?" Immediately, Oz was struck by the deep sadness in Preya's eyes and wished he could take back the words he had just spoken.

"Preya, I didn't mean it like that. You are the best thing that ever happened to me. You and our new family are precious to me. I will protect you with my life. I love you."

Preya turned to Oz with tears in her eyes. "I love you too, Oz. But Huldah is right. You need to release your hurt. For all our sakes."

Huldah stepped toward Oz and touched the tips of her wings to either side of his head. Peering fiercely into Oz's eyes, she spoke with a deep confidence. "You are needed for great purposes. The Great One has plans for you, and they are for your good. Not only yours but many peoples. But you must arm yourself with his protection. Your own strength is far too weak."

Alarmed by his aunt's actions, her words seared into his being and made his head ache. He had seen her like this before when times were pivotal or she predicted emergencies. But then, only to his father, or now, Obsolom. "Aunt Huldah, why are you getting so preachy with me? It's just me, Oz." Adding to his unease was her stare, which seemed to see his thoughts.

"You are needed now." As Huldah said these words, she looked toward an intensifying noise of crashing and chittering traveling through the branches.

CHAPTER 8

"**S**quirrels?" Oz questioned as Skamp and Chatty jumped over to a nearby tree.

Suddenly, the squirrels stopped and sat on a branch about twenty feet from the nest, looking nervously at the three ospreys watching them. Chatty held her tail as it tried to pull itself free and whispered to Skamp. "Are you sure Oz will listen? He is much smaller, yes, much smaller than Obsolom. And see, I told you, he has a droopy wing. Wow! Look at Oz's wife's belly! She must be having at least three eggs! And his aunt; I think she is the biggest osprey I have ever seen. I wonder why she is here?" Chatty's whiskers twitched, and her tail bobbed harder in her paws.

Skamp put his paw on Chatty's shoulder and, swallowing the lump in his throat, tried to calm the panic rising in him. He had expected Oz and Preya but not their strange, large aunt who was keenly eyeing him. As he looked into Huldah's eyes, though, he experienced an unexpected calm. While he knew she could lunge at him in a moment and strangle him with her talons, an assurance of safety seemed to be communicated in her gaze.

"Welcome, Skamp and Chatty. Please come closer." Huldah's voice was as soothing as a cool rain after a hot day.

"How does she know our names?" Chatty whispered

to Skamp. "I think we should stay here. Or, maybe I was wrong. Let's go." Chatty nudged Skamp and began to lose the contest with her tail as it squirmed wildly back and forth in her paws.

"You are both safe here. You come with news for us. I have been expecting you," Huldah said.

Skamp and Chatty traded suspicious glances. Yet again, Skamp felt a reassuring calm. "It's OK, Chatty."

Skamp took Chatty's paw in his, and the two squirrels crept over to the nest, keeping their eyes locked on the three raptors. The nest was large, and there was plenty of room for them to sit on the farthest edge away from the birds and be close to an exit route. They noticed Oz's wife was lying on her humongous belly, nibbling on the remains of a mullet. "I'm glad she just ate," Chatty whispered to Skamp.

"My Aunt Huldah apparently thinks you have news for us. Is that true?" Oz asked, looking down at the squirrels.

Flags of warning had popped up all over Oz's mind. One thing drilled into him all his life was to never, ever trust a squirrel. They were too unreliable. They were known for spreading stories that were exaggerated at best and untrue at worst. This was not done maliciously; they just could not keep the facts straight. They would also promise to do something and honestly believe that they would but then get distracted over finding an acorn they buried six months ago, teasing a dog they saw walking by, or chasing each other's tails, and completely forget all about what they said they were going to do. Why did his Aunt Huldah want to listen to them?

"Yes, sir, Oz. My name is Skamp, and this is my wife Chatty." Skamp stumbled over his unnecessary words, remembering Huldah had already mentioned their names.

Chatty's tail, now released, was wildly switching back and forth. "We live on the other side of the neighborhood by the canal with the large oak that has mistletoe killing it, you know the one where the humans have a speckled roof? This morning, Skamp and I and the kids, we have three: Chatarina, Skitter, and Scatter. They will soon be leaving the nest to go out on their own. It looks like Mrs. Oz is going to have a nest-full soon. How exciting! We were all having fun playing with the orange cat; he is so ..."

Skamp noticed Oz starting to roll his left shoulder and cast inquisitive looks at his aunt. Reaching over, he caught Chatty's tail and gently placed it in her hands. He couldn't do anything about her whisker twitching. "Sweetheart, let me tell them." Looking back at their hosts, he thought he saw a slight smile on Huldah's beak. Preya had moved her wing over her beak; he hoped Chatty had not offended her. Oz was still looking stern and beginning to unfold and fold his wings.

"Sorry, sir. Thank you for listening to us." Skamp then told them about the humans' Ayechoe-aye decree to capture and deport the muscovies and that the humans should destroy muscovy eggs.

As Oz listened, he felt a deep stirring in his gut. If this was true, the muscovies needed protection. "Why didn't you go to Obsolom with this? Why come to me?"

Skamp and Chatty both lowered their eyes. "We did. We just came from Obsolom and Crete at the meeting site," Skamp said.

"Crete? What was Crete doing there?" Oz could not imagine that Obsolom had given ear to the heron based on the council's past dealings with the Great Blues.

"I don't know, sir. We did not hear any of their conversation."

"Quit calling me sir. That doesn't matter; I can find that out. If you have told Obsolom, I still do not understand why you are here. Did Obsolom send you here?"

"No sir, er, Oz." Skamp's heart beat hard against his chest as he realized that now, rolling both his shoulders, Oz may not believe their report of how Obsolom treated them. And his wife was probably getting hungry again. Skamp was thinking seriously about grabbing Chatty's paw and high-tailing it out of there before they were next on the menu.

"Do not fear for your lives, brave ones. Tell us what happened when you informed Obsolom about this news." Huldah's voice and slight nod again gave Skamp the reassurance he needed. Chatty reached over and patted Skamp's shoulder with her free paw. Her tail was still clutched in her other paw but had calmed down to a slight intermittent tug.

"He said we were lying and to bury the story with our acorns and not tell anyone else," Skamp said.

"And," Chatty stood on her hind legs and faced the ospreys with her chin up and her paws on her hips, "he called us rats and that if we did tell anyone, the council would silence us. He said some other mean things, too."

"Obsolom has taken an oath to lead and protect. Are you sure this is what happened?" Even as Oz said this, the squirrels' words added to an uncomfortable feeling that sometimes nagged him about his brother.

Obsolom was dignified, controlled, and attentive before the council or flock. The people had always respected him. Oz could not pinpoint why he had a feeling of—what? Was it distrust for Obsolom? Perhaps it was because Obsolom seemed to agree too quickly when Oz stepped away from leadership positions on the council last year. Maybe it was Obsolom assuming his father's role the day he died, even before a formal vote, or convincing the council not to perform due diligence in searching for other candidates. Oz was never asked, not that he would have agreed to lead, but he was as eligible as Obsolom to be leader. Or maybe there was something buried deeper in his memory. He seemed uneasy about Obsolom's character since before he was a fledgling.

Oz caught Huldah's calm, steady gaze. Oz knew then she shared his doubts about Obsolom and that the squirrels were relaying the truth about the muscovies and Obsolom. But, if what they reported about the decree was true, why had Obsolom dismissed them? Was it because Obsolom thought squirrels could not relay truthful information? And why did all this have to happen now that Preya was so close to laying her eggs? Oz's thoughts ran back and forth in his mind. If, however, this was true, the council needed to act.

Oz looked down at Skamp and Chatty, holding their breath and tightly clamping each other's paws. "Something should be done about this."

Skamp and Chatty released their breath and hugged each other. Preya also exhaled a long sigh of relief as she smiled at Oz.

"There is a council meeting tonight to vote on who will fill the empty council seat." Oz felt a stab of grief. The seat was vacant because of his father's death. "I can bring this to their attention, but two or three witnesses are needed for the council to agree to take action. Was there anyone else there when you heard about the humans' decree?" Oz asked.

"Well, there are the two of us and our three kits. They even calmed down to listen. We all heard the humans talking about this," Chatty said.

"They are your children, so the council would not count them as witnesses, and you both are considered one witness."

"That lady's cat was there and heard," Skamp said.

"He is so much fun to play with! We didn't notice anyone else," Chatty added.

Oz scratched his crown feathers with the tip of his wing. "I'm not sure how much the council will want to hear from a cat. And I can't imagine bringing a cat to a meeting of birds. That is, if the cat could even be trusted."

Preya cleared her throat after swallowing the last bit of mullet. "Oz, from Chatty's description, this is the house where I found the lovely purple things. I know this cat. We have spoken before. I think he might help. He seems to like birds—as friends."

Oz pondered about his wife befriending a cat. He was surprised enough several weeks ago when he found her talking with a group of turtles. But a cat?

"Please, Oz," Preya urged.

"I will fly over and talk to the cat. The council may accept second-hand testimony, and it's possible that others at the meeting will have overheard human conversations about the decree."

Oz shifted toward Skamp and Chatty. "Will you come tonight and tell what you have heard?"

Skamp felt a renewed flush of fear that made his mouth dry and his knees weak as he thought about facing Obsolom again after clearly defying his order.

Huldah stepped toward the squirrels. "I will escort you to the meeting, stay by your side, and escort you safely home. I will not allow harm to come to you." The glint in her eye and the stretching of her talons on the nest cracking some of the larger sticks told them exactly what she would do to anyone if she needed to defend them.

Skamp hesitantly relaxed. "I will come. Chatty, I think staying home with the kids would be best." If something happened to him, the kids would have their mom.

CHAPTER 9

"Very good, Mary Cathryn, you found one!" Girdie patted the mallard duckling on the head and looked around to see if she could spot the duckling's family. "Now, who else can find a snail?" Girdie smiled as her brood of nine and the mallard duckling ran into the pile of decaying leaves and turned them over one by one, looking for the crustaceous treats.

Girdie settled down under the oak that grew next to the pond to watch the children and keep a lookout for Mary Cathryn's mom. The shade was welcome in the mid-day glare. She hoped Gunther would be back soon from foraging on the other side of the pond. She had promised the kids they could all go over to the lake to swim. And she wanted him here when the mallards showed up, which would be any minute now. Maybe they wouldn't be upset about Mary Cathryn playing with *our kind*. Girdie could only hope.

Girdie continued watching Mary Cathryn foraging alongside her own children, oblivious to the established social hierarchy. Why couldn't the adults look beyond physical appearances and where their ancestors were from and accept each other like these children?

"Look, Mommy, I found a snail, too!" Joey ran up to Girdie, depositing a tiny snail the size of a grapefruit seed in front of her. "I got it for you, Mommy."

Girdie gathered the yellow duckling in her wings. "Thank you, Joey. What a good forager you are!"

Joey squirmed free and hurried back to the other ducklings. Girdie thought about what Joey's adult coloring might be and when his bright yellow fluff would be replaced by muted camouflage tones. She prayed it would be sooner than later. A bright yellow duckling was an easier target for predators. Just the other day, Gunther had chased off a great blue heron twice from sneaking up on Joey.

Girdie turned her head to a rustling sound coming from behind her.

Gunther waddled over, nuzzled his head against hers, and pointed to the ducklings. "Is that little girl a mallard duckling?"

"Yes. Her name is Mary Cathryn. She heard our kids peeping when I was showing them how to find snails and came over." Girdie nuzzled back and gave Gunther a peck on his cheek below his glossy red spots. It seemed she had loved Gunther since she was an awkward fledgling with big feet and stubby wings. She was first attracted to his deep green feathers, which were so much like her own, but then even more so by how he noticed her. He never seemed to look anywhere else but at her when he was near. Girdie looked back over to the ducklings. "Do you think we should tell her to go home?"

Gunther crinkled his brow. "Maybe. Does her family know she is here?"

"I doubt it. That's what concerns me."

The muscovy parents watched as the ducklings continued to rustle through the leaves. Now and then, one would peep that they had found a snail. Mary Cathryn and Tina, one of Gunther and Girdie's smallest ducklings, seemed more interested in whispering and giggling than finding snails.

"Tina's sure found a friend," Gunther said.

Just then, they heard loud honking approaching. They looked around to see Mary Margaret, better known as the Matron of the Mallards since her husband Peter Paul had joined the council, strutting toward them across the lawn and making enough noise to wake a rock. Following her in beak-to-tailfeather formation were four ducklings. Several yards behind them were a few more mallard moms and their broods.

"I guess that answers our question." Gunther pulled Girdie close. "Kids, come here," Gunther called to the ducklings.

Mary Margaret stopped about fifteen feet from the muscovy family and glared at Girdie and Gunther. "What are you doing with my daughter?"

Gunther and Girdie held each other's wings. Girdie opened her beak to explain. "Mary Cathryn came…"

"You stay away from my family," Mary Margaret hissed. Suddenly, her beak dropped open at the sight of Mary Cathryn having hooked wings with Tina.

"Mary Cathryn, get yourself over here! You know you are not to socialize with that kind."

"But Mom, Tina and her family are going to the lake to swim, and I want to go. I like Tina, she's nice," Mary Cathryn begged.

"Get over here now!" Mary Margaret watched her precocious middle child slowly shuffle across the lawn with her head down. Mary Cathryn's four siblings never gave Mary Margaret any trouble. They came immediately when they were called. They only made friends with their kind. They never argued with her. Couldn't her daughter see that she was trying to protect her?

Safety was only had by staying close to her family and blending in. Going out on her own would only be allowed when she could fend for herself, and even then, she would not be allowed to mix with the muscovies—those oversized, ugly, foul excuses for ducks. Mary Margaret shuddered at the thought that one of her children had gotten close to a muscovy, especially that family. The lardaceous parents' iridescent green heads mocked Peter Paul's stately crown. Disgusting! Who knew what diseases, pestilence, or unacceptable behavior could be transmitted? Wasn't her daughter now showing defiance? She worried about what the other mallards were thinking seeing her daughter socializing with those muscovies. How soon would everyone in the neighborhood know? Would this embarrassment harm her husband, Peter Paul's position on the council?

"Mom, why can't I go with Tina?" Mary Cathryn complained when she finally reached her mother. "She has three sisters and five brothers. It is really easy to tell them apart because they all look different. Her brother Joey is all yellow; he is so cute! Her mom is cool, too. She showed me how to find snails and…"

"Mary Cathryn Mallard!" Mary Margaret was waving her wings wildly. She knew her voice was shrill, but she did not care. Her message must be heard. "You will not step near that family of refugee wart-heads again. Do you understand?"

Mary Cathryn slumped down and began to cry. Her sister and brothers scurried to and fro, upset by their mom's sternness and their sister's tears.

Mary Margaret held her head high and looked over to the muscovies. Girdie was looking at her. Her brood of nine was tucked under her wings, and her husband was close by her side. As their gaze met, Girdie looked down and, gently nudging her children with her wings, turned and started waddling away. Gunther took another few seconds to look into Mary Margaret's eyes before he turned to join his family.

Mary Margaret turned around and, seeing her ducklings peeping and crying at all the commotion, decided to do a roll call. Roll calls were routinely done every morning and evening. Each child would announce their name in the sequence of hatching. The ritual should reestablish order.

"Roll call!" she announced. Her five children lined up from left to right.

"Peter Alexander!"

"Peter Bartholomew!"

"Mary Cathryn!"

"Peter David!"

"Mary Elizabeth!"

CHAPTER 10

Oz arrived ten minutes early to the council meeting to speak with his brother. Obsolom, however, was a few trees over talking privately with Cronan, the crow. Oz was surprised at the number of residents who had shown up. Usually, only the seven council members and three or four others who had brought complaints or suggestions were there. But there were at least thirty attendees, and more were arriving. They all wanted to know who would fill the empty spot on the council.

Oz took his council seat next to Horatio, the owl, to wait for the other three members, one of whom was Huldah, who was to bring Skamp. "How are you, Horatio?" Oz asked.

"If you are asking about my health, the arthritis in my neck is causing me some issues; however, the condition I had last month with my eyes has cleared up, so all-in-all, I continue to exist with minor but sometimes major frailties. If you are asking about my outlook on life, well, life is for the living and that I am doing, yet my thoughts sometimes meander to my ancestors who have gone before me, and I yearn to see them. But my time is here, and here I will be until I am no longer here. You hear?"

Oz was sorry he asked. Horatio had been on the council for as long as Oz could remember. He always had wise insight into situations, but after listening to him, Oz often came away confused and not knowing what Horatio meant to say.

The broad branch below them swayed as Peter Paul, the mallard, landed. Peter Paul's bright yellow beak contrasted with his iridescent green head feathers, which were slicked back from a recent bath and oil massage, giving him a dapper look. His orange legs and feet were immaculate from a fresh pedicure. "How goes it, Oz, Horatio? Ready for the big decision tonight?"

"Yes, and it looks like many others are, too," Oz said.

"I'm rooting for Carmen, the cardinal. He would bring diversity to the council, being mainly a seed and fruit eater. And you have got to love that red." Peter Paul smoothed an errant tail feather.

Horatio stroked his chin with the tip of his wing. "Peter Paul, you are correct in that he would bring diversity, but is he as diverse as we could hope for? And what is diversity? In diet? In size? In color? Do we not all fly? Do we not all lay eggs? Do we not all serve the Great One? We must be unified in that most important aspect."

"So, what you're saying is what?" Peter Paul looked questioningly up at Horatio.

Without warning, a large bird plummeted past them in a great heap of feathers and crash-landed on a branch several feet below.

"Welcome, my dear Petunia! I see you have been improving your landing technique," Horatio said as the pelican collected herself and made her way up to the branch Peter Paul was on. Many meetings she overshot the council tree and would end up in another tree or the marsh below.

"Good evening, Horatio, Oz, Peter Paul. Lovely weather,

don't you agree?" Petunia acted oblivious to her clumsy landing skills and her rumpled feathers from the fall. She poised herself on the branch next to Peter Paul. One of her wing feathers was poking straight up, and Oz had a great urge to point it out to her before she tried to fly off, but knew from experience she would rather fly off crooked than admit anything was amiss.

A shadow glided over them, and the old snag barely moved as Obsolom alighted a few branches above the others. His feathers glistened gold from the sun slowly sinking toward the trees in the west. He held his head high, surveying the council members below him and the residents scattered in the trees and marsh below. Most of the forty-plus species of birds were represented by at least one member.

Absent were the muscovies. Being refugees from farms and not natural citizens, they weren't allowed at the meetings since Obsolom had taken office. He reasoned that since their voice did not have weight, it was more efficient to hold meetings without them present. Oz wondered why his father had never granted the muscovies citizen status. Still, it hardly mattered since Otto treated all birds equally and even extended protection to other animals when he could.

"I call this meeting to order," Obsolom declared.

"Obsolom, we are still waiting for Huldah." Oz was concerned that something had happened to deter Skamp from coming with her. "She always opens in prayer."

"Huldah knows the timing of the meeting and that we start on schedule so as not to waste anyone's time. We have five members present. We have a quorum."

From above, there was a swooshing sound and a skittering noise in the tree directly in front of the council post. "I'm here," Huldah announced as she took her place on the snag. "Please excuse my tardiness as I was chaperoning a guest to the meeting." Skamp clambered across the branch and sat panting close to Huldah.

Oz saw a flash of hatred streak through Obsolom's eyes as he aimed his gaze at both Huldah and Skamp and then shot a momentary glance at Crete in the marsh below. A cold wave of disappointment rose in Oz's consciousness. Was his brother as cruel as the squirrels had said, and was something happening with Obsolom and Crete?

Obsolom squared his shoulders. "Very well." Obsolom had no choice but to allow the squirrel's attendance since the council permitted a member to bring an outsider to state relevant business. "We will listen to the squirrel after we take care of our primary business this evening of voting for the open position in the council. As you all know, we had two..."

"Obsolom," Huldah interrupted, "shall we pray?"

Obsolom ground his beak from side to side as he nodded slightly to Huldah.

Huldah looked above the trees into the evening sky and lifted her wings. "Oh, Great One! We gather here in your name. Please give us discernment and wisdom tonight. We know it is you who ultimately appoints and removes leaders. Let your will be done according to your plan and timing. Amen."

Obsolom shifted on his perch, squared his shoulders again, and looked over the group. "As I was saying, we had two eligible candidates. My son, Othello, and Carmen, the cardinal. Both have been long-term residents and have served on several committees in the past two years."

Oz looked over at Othello, who was perched in a cypress several trees away from the council snag. He was looking down at the marsh. Othello was the natural choice for the open seat, being Obsolom's oldest son, so why wasn't he perched closer, looking proud and confident at his father?

Oz noticed Obsolom quickly glance at Othello with a creased brow. Obsolom continued. "Unfortunately, Othello has retracted his candidacy."

A soft murmuring of chirps, squawks, tweets, and clucks rose and swelled among the amassed birds. Oz turned toward Huldah, and their eyes met. Carmen was getting congratulatory wing bumps from his fellow cardinals. With Othello out of the picture he was the only candidate, he thought.

"However," Obsolom raised his voice, "we have a replacement candidate." Carmen stopped wing bumping and looked confounded. The murmurings grew louder. "You all by now have met Cronan the crow." All eyes trained on Cronan, who was perched by himself near the council snag. Unusually quiet, Cronan kept his gaze focused on Obsolom.

Oz was perplexed as he was sure the others were when their murmurings became an inharmonious cacophony. Cronan had just moved to the neighborhood. And, at past council meetings, he argued any point adding nothing of importance.

"Obsolom," Huldah's voice rose like a clear bell above the din, "we have not been apprised of Cronan's qualifications, and, as you know, there is an expectation that candidates have been residents in the neighborhood for at least a year." The assembly hushed to listen.

"Huldah speaks wisely, Obsolom. It is in the community's true interest that candidates are known and have proven themselves to serve, lead, make decisions, and protect. Leaders need the support of their constituents. Constituents need to trust their leaders," Horatio the owl added.

Obsolom kept his composure and peered down at Othello, whose shoulders were tightly hunched.

Othello refrained from looking up at Obsolom as he addressed the audience, looking at no one in particular. "I spent some time in the Palmcrest neighborhood courting my fiancé and can vouch for Cronan. He has been on the Palmcrest council for the last two years. He was well respected and only decided to leave to take advantage of our schools in Havenport for their new family." Oz could see his nephew's jaw was tensed. Othello continued. "For now, I want time to devote to my nuptials and did not think it right to short-change my attention to the council."

Oz looked directly at his nephew, trying to catch his gaze. Something did not make sense. Othello was level-headed and respected and had been looking forward to serving on the council.

Petunia, the pelican, lost her balance briefly as she shifted her weight to lean forward. Swinging her wings to regain balance, the rogue tail feather still stood askew. "Obsolom, council, why do we need a second candidate to consider since we all supported Carmen's candidacy?" The muttering crowd echoed Petunia's question. She had been on the council for three years and had always offered an objective and fair voice. Everyone respected her despite her physical imbalance at times. Pelicans were not known for their graceful moves.

Obsolom glared down at Petunia. "It is in everyone's interest to have the most qualified candidates considered; would you not agree?"

"Obsolom brings up a valid point. It is in the community's true interest for the council to evaluate all candidates that fulfill the requirements and are dedicated to serving," Horatio said.

Obsolom faced the council members. "You are all aware that we each have an equal vote. To fill the empty position, I suggest we vote now between Carmen and Cronan for our next council member."

Oz shared another glance with Huldah; this did not feel right. Oz asked himself again why a new candidate had been presented. The majority of the council members would vote for Carmen anyway.

"Does anyone have objection?" Obsolom peered below at the five council members and out at the group, glancing from bird to bird and ending with Valafar, the vulture. Only the council could vote, but anyone could object if they had further information to share.

Wafting a musty, decaying odor, Valafar drifted down a few branches to get in better view. A few flies buzzed around his head. "I have an objection to one of the candidates." All eyes turned toward Valafar. "I have witnessed Carmen violently jump and peck at his image continually for hours in a human's window." Shocked, the crowd looked from Valafar to Carmen, whispering to each other.

Oz thought he saw a slight smirk on Obsolom's beak. Carmen, however, stood looking at Valafar with his beak open and eyes wide.

"Is this true?" Obsolom veered his attention to Carmen.

"Well, yes. But it is not uncommon for cardinals to get a little overreactive in the springtime when we protect our broods." Carmen nervously fluttered his wings.

"Battling your image seems much more than a little

overreactive and does nothing to protect your brood. I question if your dedication to the community is impaired during this time, not to mention if your decision-making skills are being compromised." Obsolom stood taller. "Thank you, Valafar. We do not need a second witness since Carmen has admitted to this obscene behavior that demonstrates a mind obsessed with unfounded and uncontrolled rage." Obsolom turned his eyes toward the council members below him. "Council, it is now up to us to decide who should fill the empty council seat.

Many attendees sneered and puckered their beaks at Carmen, clearly conveying their thoughts. Oz didn't understand why such a big deal was being made of the cardinal's occasional behavior. Or why Othello had withdrawn. Or why Cronan was being considered. It all seemed to point to Obsolom orchestrating all this. But why? Unanswered questions bounced around in Oz's head and soured his stomach. Did Oz know his brother? He looked over at Huldah, who appeared to be sharing his thoughts.

"Obsolom, I advise that we postpone this vote tonight and seek the Great One's will in this matter," Huldah called out.

"Postponing this will not gain anything. As I stated earlier, we all have an equal vote. The council can each vote as they see fit. All in favor of Cronan filling the council seat, raise your wing," Obsolom announced, lifting his wing.

Horatio lifted his wing, and Peter Paul followed. Petunia glanced over toward Oz and Huldah but then looked down at her pelican patrons, who nodded at her, and she hesitantly raised her wing.

Obsolom glanced at Oz and Huldah, giving them a few

seconds to vote for Cronan. When they did not, he spat out his following words. "We already have a majority, but to fulfill council practice, all in favor of Carmen filling the council seat, raise your wing." Oz and Huldah raised their wings. "Welcome to the council, Cronan." Obsolom motioned for Cronan to come over to the council snag and take his place. The cardinal held his gaze steady and gave a nod of support toward Cronan. Shouts of praise and congratulations were heard from the audience.

CHAPTER 11

Attendees started to leave now that the council seat decision was finalized. "I know it is getting late; if you want to leave, please feel free to do so." Obsolom dropped his head down to Cronan and whispered something in his ear.

Several more groups of birds flew off, leaving only a few still interested, including the mallards, Crete, and Valafar. "Huldah has brought a guest whom we will hear from next." Obsolom looked directly at Skamp, who was tucked under Huldah's wing, shaking in fear.

"Are we really going to listen to a squirrel?" Cronan crowed but quickly decided against further objection as Huldah, Oz, Petunia, and Horatio all looked at him with varying degrees of indignation.

"Squirrel, state your business." Obsolom cast a loosely veiled gaze of wrath at Skamp.

Huldah nudged Skamp out from underneath her wing, giving him a reassuring look. "Thank you, council, for hearing me. My name is Skamp."

Controlling his shaking as much as he could, Skamp told the council of the conversation he overheard about the decree from the humans' Ayechoe-aye to capture and exile the muscovies because they thought they were ugly and they spread disease.

As Skamp spoke, the residents and council members

hushed and passed around bewildered looks. When he finished, a hum rose and turned into a heated discussion. Some were appalled and asked each other how the humans could do this. Others, mostly the mallards, asserted that it was about time the ugly muscovies were removed from the neighborhood, allowing true citizens to occupy the areas the muscovies were residing in. Still, others questioned the validity of the squirrel's story.

"I must say your news is alarming Mr. Scamp, and my deductive reasoning is seriously challenged to embrace truth in this report. We see you have come to this council with great fear, but can anyone attest to what the squirrel is saying?" Horatio asked the other council members and audience. "The testimony of two or three witnesses is needed for the council to take action."

Nods of agreement rippled through the group.

"Huldah, you have chaperoned the squirrel; what is your stake in this matter?" Petunia asked as she grabbed an upper branch to avoid falling.

Oz felt his insides squeeze and his head throb. How did he get himself into this mess? He just wanted to get back to Preya. But the muscovies could not speak for themselves. He cocked his head toward Huldah, whose calming gaze and slight nod of the head confirmed what he must do. "Council, citizens, I can address Horatio's question and provide additional testimony."

Obsolom straightened himself and peered down at Oz. This was not expected. Oz had not taken any stance of confrontation or risk for over a year. He had melted into the background, letting Obsolom or one of the other council members take the lead on everything.

Oz tried to swallow, but his throat went dry. "What Skamp has reported is true. After he told me what he heard, I flew over to the house where the humans had the conversation and verified the details with the cat that lives there." Oz omitted the part about the squirrels' encounter with Obsolom and Crete.

Oz glanced at Obsolom, who was shaking and looked like he was about to explode in rage. "A cat?! Do you expect us to consider second-hand testimony from a cat?"

The council members and scattered residents were all talking at once, with reactions ranging from surprise to disbelief to amusement.

"This is dumb," Cronan cawed. "First, we listen to a squirrel, and now we are expected to believe what Oz says a cat said the humans said their Ayechoe-aye, whatever that is, said?"

Oz felt the deep ache in his shoulder and an intense throbbing as his headache worsened. They were not taking Skamp or him seriously. Maybe he should have just ignored the squirrels' story himself. What had he gained except sneers and jeers?

"Order! Order!" Obsolom called out. "Order!" Slowly, everyone settled down and looked up at Obsolom. "I can give testimony regarding this." The group drew in a surprised breath. Obsolom locked eyes with Crete for a split second and then continued. "I, too, heard the humans' conversation."

Oz and Huldah both looked at Skamp with confused expressions. Skamp shrugged his shoulders and opened his paws with a puzzled look on his face. "We did not see Obsolom there," he whispered to Huldah. "But you ospreys fly so high, we may not have noticed him."

Huldah directed her gaze at Obsolom. "Tell us, Obsolom, what did you hear?"

"The squirrel's story is unusually accurate but deviates

in several key details that cast a very different light on the situation. There is indeed a decree from the humans' Ayechoe-aye to remove muscovies. But it is for their own good. *They* are diseased, and the humans are *rescuing* them to bring them to a refuge where they can heal and live in a protected sanctuary." Everyone started murmuring again with each other.

Horatio rose his wing. "Obsolom, you claim that the muscovies are being removed for their own good, but the squirrel and Oz claim that the humans just do not like the muscovies, and that is why they will be removed."

"What is your point, Horatio?" Obsolom looked down his beak at the owl, clicking his talons on the branch.

"This is a conundrum of immense proportions that dismays and confuses the senses, making it astronomically difficult to know what to act on. If the muscovies are ill, should we not come to their aid? If the muscovies are being removed because they are not liked, should we also not come to their aid? Yet, can we admit testimony of a squirrel and second-hand testimony of a cat, as neither of them is in our realm of protection? But to not consider their testimony in the decision-making process has the shadowing of exclusivity." Horatio looked around at the attendees and council who had varying looks of confusion on their faces.

"I'd take Obsolom's version over a squirrel's and cat's any day," Cronan said. The sounds of the audience increased as they questioned each other on what to believe.

Obsolom flexed his talons and dug into the branch he was on. "Peoples!" Obsolom cried out, "Let us not forget The Order!"

Silence blanketed the meeting. Oz watched Huldah

stare at Obsolom with creased brows. Since when had Obsolom referred to The Order? That was something Huldah did. Otto often would, but never Obsolom. The uneasy feeling swept over Oz again in sickening pulses. What was Obsolom up to?

"As you all know, and Huldah will correct me if I am wrong, written in The Order, the Great One commanded the humans to have dominion over all other living creatures." Obsolom peered at Huldah, who nodded her head slightly. "Therefore, if the humans have decreed the removal of the muscovies—for any reason—it is not our place to aid or protect these ducks. That would be akin to declaring war against the humans and, in fact, against the Great One." Exclamations of horror at any suggestion of warring against the humans or the Great One spread through the gathering.

"Obsolom, you are taking The Order out of context, just as you did in Sunday school when you were a fledgling!" Huldah admonished.

"You didn't consider my views then, but they always had as much merit as yours, Auntie," Obsolom replied with a gritted beak. "And, in this case, if I err, I would rather err in support of the humans than the muscovies." Shouts of agreement were coming from all around.

"We would be wise in any decision we make to carry out the letter of The Order to every jot and tittle no matter how grievous that might be in this situation," Horatio orated with a sweep of his wing.

Oz looked over at Huldah and perceived deep anguish. Above the shouts, he heard a distinct clucking in the marsh. Crete flew up to a branch closer to the council snag.

"Peoples, Obsolom, may I trouble you with a proposal

that will demonstrate your support of the humans and obedience to The Order?" All eyes turned, and the voices hushed to hear Crete's low rhythmic tone. The great blue was the largest bird in the audience and stood with his neck extended straight to achieve his full height. The wispy plumes on his head and body swayed mesmerizingly in the evening breeze. "We have an opportunity to assist the humans in removing the muscovies. If the muscovy duckling limit that the previous council set is lifted, the Great Blues would be honored to contribute their expertise to help support the humans' decree." Crete folded his right wing across his chest and bowed his head.

Oz couldn't believe what he was hearing. Had Crete and Obsolom prearranged this proposal before the meeting? It didn't make sense why they would do this, but the residents supported this with nods of head and clapping of wings. Was Oz crazy to want to help the muscovies? Why did the humans' decree feel so wrong?

"Crete, this is an honorable offer." Hums of support were heard across the audience as Obsolom spoke. "I move that we vote not to obstruct the humans' plans and that the muscovy duckling limit is removed."

"I'll support that," quacked Peter Paul.

"I second!" crowed Cronan.

"All in favor, raise your wing." Obsolom, Peter Paul, and Cronan immediately raised their wings. Horatio followed. Petunia looked down, shaking her head, but seeing her patrons nodding and mouthing "yes," raised hers.

"Opposed?" Huldah and Oz raised their wings in defeated opposition. "So moved. We will not obstruct the humans' plans, and the muscovy duckling limit is removed. The meeting is adjourned. Thank you all for coming."

◆ ◆ ◆

Oz hopped over to the branch where Huldah and Skamp were. The sun was dipping lower behind the trees. It would soon be dark. Skamp was shivering underneath Huldah's wing. Oz looked out at the departing birds. Obsolom had flown off as soon as he adjourned the meeting. So had Crete. And Valafar. With an awkward '*thwok*,' Petunia fell off the branch into a crooked flight, catching Oz's eye. Was that shame he saw in her expression? Horatio had already left, and Peter Paul and Cronan were finishing up an animated conversation about the ugly muscovies.

"What just happened? This went so wrong. I'm sorry." Oz reached out his wing and touched the squirrel's arm.

"I also don't understand why Othello backed out and Cronan was chosen over Carmen. None of this makes any sense to me." Anger raged in Oz's mind. "Is Obsolom right in his view that protecting the muscovies would be disobedience to the Great One?"

Huldah looked strangely at peace and looked directly into Oz's eyes. "Oz, you know the truth in your soul, and the Great One will lead you in the right path."

"Yeah, right," Oz muttered, feeling a crushing defeat.

Silence echoed. Oz noticed that Peter Paul and Cronan had left.

"Oz, it is getting late; I must escort Skamp home safely."

CHAPTER 12

Oz watched his Aunt Huldah hop and fly from branch to branch, following Skamp as he scurried toward his home. He was alone now except for the chirping crickets and singing frogs. A dimming sliver of pinkish light filtered past the soft needles of the cypress. The mud exposed by the receding tide smelled of decomposing plants, adding a dankness to the approaching night.

Oz felt a nudge burgeoning deep in his soul as he repeatedly turned the situation in his mind. Only Huldah and a couple of squirrels seemed to care about the muscovies. The council and the people thought it more important not to ruffle the feathers of the humans than to come to the muscovies' aid. It appalled Oz that so many quickly turned away from the large ducks. What if it had been the mallards, or the hawks, or any of the other birds? Oz felt his stomach roil as he thought about the vote to allow the Great Blues free reign, preying on muscovy ducklings. Instead of helping them, they all voted to make their plight worse. A righteous rage boiled and expanded in his chest. Oz lifted his beak to the night sky and spread his wings upward. "Why are you allowing this to happen? Why does everything have to be so messed up?"

The rhythmic duet of the cricket and frog continued

unabated as an owl hoo-hooed in the distance. A breeze tousled the leaves overhead and carried the scent of jasmine from a nearby vine. The full moon tossed silver bits of light onto the stage of branches and leaves, where they danced from the sway of the gentle wind. The day was ending like all other days, as if nothing was wrong. Acidic anger rose in Oz's throat. "Where are you? Answer me!" Oz shouted heavenward, standing on the tips of his talons. "Why don't you do something?"

"I did. I created you."

The soundless words from the Great One were as sharp and clear as the call of a jay and felt like a cold blade had speared through his chest, slicing to his core and puncturing the rage that had grown tight around his heart. Emptying his lungs of breath, Oz collapsed on the branch, sunk his head low, and hung his limp wings by his side. Oz felt like he had just flown a marathon. Gradually, he became aware that the cords of anguish that had been strangling him had loosened and slacked away to expose a fragile fragment of his soul.

"Oh, Great One," Oz choked out a gasp as he realized the Great One's presence.

"I am with you."

Another burst of anguish escaped Oz's beak as he looked up into the night sky.

"Forgive me." Oz breathed out the words, expecting fearful shame to envelop him. Instead, a calm warmth spread through his being, like when his mother used to take him under her wing.

Oz lifted his head as a tender seed of hope stirred within him. "Great One, you know the unfairness the muscovies are facing. Rise up for truth and justice and deliver them!"

"Lead them."

Oz rubbed his ears. He must have heard wrong; he was not a leader—he could not lead. Leading anything more than a nest-building effort with Preya was absurd.

"Great One, I'm sure you did not just tell me to lead because you, my creator, know I cannot. I am small and crippled; the people do not respect me; I need to be with Preya and..."

"Lead them."

The repeating words sent a shock down Oz's back to the tip of his tail.

Oz raised his wings skyward. "Lead who? Lead what? How? When?" Oz felt fear rise in opposition.

Drooping his head down in defeat, the seed of hopefulness froze. He could not imagine himself leading an effort to help the muscovies. The end result would be worse. "I can't lead. I don't know how to; I would just fail anyway."

"Yes, by your own efforts, you will fail."

Oz jumped up in alarm, almost falling off his perch, and whipped his head to where the voice came from. On a branch not three feet from him sat his aunt. "Aunt Huldah, how long have you been there?"

"Long enough to hear you whining and bellyaching after the Great One has clearly spoken to you."

"But it's true. I'm not a leader; I don't know how to lead."

"What do you think should be the solution, Oz?"

"I want the Great One to fix this somehow. Maybe change the humans' minds about removing the muscovies, miraculously protect them, block the herons from eating the ducklings, make Obsolom see that we must do the right thing to protect and come to the aid of the muscovies." Oz was waving his wings in agitation. "I don't know! Come down here himself or send a deliverer."

Huldah came to sit next to Oz. "What did the Great One say when you asked why he didn't do something?"

How long had Huldah been listening? "I think I heard him say, 'I did, I created you.'"

Huldah draped her wing over his back, "Oz, you have your answers. You need to put the pieces together. You know you are small, disabled, and inexperienced. That is actually a good thing."

"Huldah, how can you say that?"

"You belong to the Great One; he is all powerful and wise."

Oz looked down deeply, inhaling and exhaling. His left shoulder throbbed, and his head ached.

"So, I'm just supposed to trust that if I lead them, whatever that means, everything will work out?" Oz snorted.

"Yes."

"Well, Huldah, that is like trying to fly through a thick forest in the pitch dark." Oz tensed his wings against his back. "In a hurricane with a hood on!"

"Yes. As long as you rely on your strength and understanding. If you trust the Great One with all your heart and acknowledge him, he will clear your path and give you the wisdom and courage to do his will."

"I hear what you are saying, and I know I am supposed to believe that, but I've tried that before, and it doesn't work."

"Oz, you, or I do not know why things sometimes turn out very differently than we had expected or hoped, but that is what faith is, believing that the Great One does have things in his control and he does have you in his care under the shadow of his wings."

"Huldah, I need to get back to Preya. It's late."

Huldah touched her wing to Oz's shoulder. "Don't turn your back on the Great One, Oz."

"I'm not!"

"Talk to the Great One. Don't let fear get in your way."

CHAPTER 13

Oz pushed off the branch, stiff from the several hours he had been sitting there. Flying high above the leafy canopy in the moonlight, he looked up at the moon. So bright, so far away. He wished he could fly up to it, away from this nagging at his soul.

Oz startled to find that Obsolom was there with Preya as his nest came into view. What was his brother doing there at this time of night? In some animated conversation, he could hear his wife laughing and his brother's deep voice.

Oz landed on the nest and faced his brother. "Hello, Obsolom. Preya, what's so funny?" Preya was holding her swollen belly as she laughed. It bothered him that she enjoyed his brother's company so much.

"Obsolom was telling me funny stories from when you grew up." She started giggling again and put her wing over her beak.

"Yes! I was telling her about when you entered the fishing contest with the other newly fledged that year."

"Not that story." Oz glared at his brother, who ignored him and continued his tale.

"All the others had already caught two or three fish, but you hadn't caught any!"

"That is not funny." Oz dreaded where this was going.

"Oh! But it is!" Obsolom turned toward Preya. "Oz stole

a net of fish out of a human's boat!"

"Really? My Oz did that?" Preya started to laugh again but quickly stopped when she saw the hurt look on Oz's face.

"Yes, and the fisherman reached up and..."

Oz rolled his shoulder. Obsolom was talking and laughing so loud that a nearby family of mourning doves started cooing in protest for him to be quiet.

"And tried to grab the net, but he fell out of the boat!"

More laughter from Obsolom. Preya looked over to Oz and shifted uncomfortably.

"But here is the best part! He brought the net back with the fish, and the other judges and I disqualified him for stealing!" Obsolom pointed at Oz and laughed. "All that valiant effort, and you failed!"

Oz clamped his beak shut and stared at his brother.

"Isn't it funny that Oz thought he could bend the rules like that?" Obsolom asked Preya as he wiped tears of laughter from his eyes. "And, do you want to know what happened to the net? We made Oz bring it back to the human!" Obsolom started laughing again. "You should have seen the look on his face when we told him to do that!"

Preya glanced at Oz and looked down.

The sting that Oz had felt back then from being laughed at and publicly shamed flooded over him as if the event had just happened. He looked over at his brother, who stood towering, his broad white chest gleaming in the moonlight. His long pinions fell over the edge of the nest in elegant drapes. "Obsolom, I am sure you did not visit to tell stories from my childhood."

"No, my little brother. I came to talk to you." Obsolom turned to Preya. "If you would excuse us, lovely lady, I will borrow your husband for just a few minutes." Lowering his voice, he growled in Oz's ear. "This won't take long."

The brothers flew a few trees over and settled on a thick oak branch. "What do you want, Obsolom?"

"I know how you feel about the muscovies and the council's decisions tonight." It was hard to believe they were brothers. Obsolom stood tall and proud, poised, and perfect in appearance. Oz was two-thirds his size and in a persistent crooked hunch from his shoulder disability.

Oz tilted his head sideways and looked up at Obsolom. "I did not try and hide my convictions, and I'm sure everyone knows how I feel." Oz felt a tingle of warning and knew his brother was up to something.

"It is not right that we, as brothers, do not show a unified front to the people."

Oz smirked. "What does it matter? They only listen to you anyway."

"Oh, that is true. But I would like your support. As brothers."

"Obsolom, you know I think we should protect the muscovies."

"And that is still in the realm of possibilities." Obsolom cocked his head.

"What do you mean? You didn't indicate that at all tonight."

"My dear brother, the people can only hear so much at once. They are like dogs. You give them too much to think about at once, and they just run around yapping their heads off."

Oz wasn't sure that was a fair analogy. "So, what are you saying?"

"Give me some time to observe what the humans are doing, and let's discuss this again in a week or so."

"A week is a long time. Many muscovies could be exiled by then."

Obsolom motioned back to where Oz's nest was. "Your beautiful wife is going to start laying her eggs very soon. I'm sure you do not want to be fettered with other concerns."

Obsolom reached down with his sharp beak to remove a speck of dirt off his left forefront talon. "And I'm sure you do not want to leave the eggs alone when Preya needs to fish or stretch her wings. She is the better fisher."

Oz felt the obvious barb, truthful as it was. He thought about what the Great One had said to him. Did he hear the Great One? Or was it Oz's aspiration to finally do something grand? Oz felt a deep sadness at that thought.

"I know when Priscilla and I have our clutches, one of us is always with the eggs. Bad things can happen to eggs left alone." Obsolom looked squarely at Oz.

Oz's thoughts were tangling like a discarded fishing line. Waiting a few more days to do anything, if he was going to do anything, surely would not hurt. They could see if there was a threat. Perhaps they had heard wrong anyway. Maybe the squirrels had gotten their story mixed up, and it really was for the muscovy's good and that they were being rescued, not exiled. The prudent choice would be to wait instead of flying into action and doing something prematurely.

"When will you have another council meeting to discuss your observations?" Oz hoped that by then, Preya would have laid her eggs and that he would find out that all was well with the muscovy ducks.

Obsolom smiled. "I will keep you informed." Obsolom tread closer, squeezing his wing around Oz's left shoulder. "Brothers support each other."

Oz clinched his beak to keep from reacting to the pain. He wasn't sure his brother cared about Oz's support, but for now, being with Preya was what was necessary.

"I'll check in with you in a few days. Let us know when Preya starts laying her eggs." Obsolom took a leap that left the thick branch bouncing and flew off into the night.

CHAPTER 14

Oz paced from one side of the nest to the other. Preya was pretending to sleep but had one eye open, watching Oz. He hadn't slept all night but kept up his pacing, pausing now and then, as he was now, to stare into the night. The eastern horizon now hinted of indigo.

"Oz, why don't you try and get some rest?" Preya yawned and stretched her wings.

"You should be resting. I'm fine." Oz resumed pacing and staring. He was here, with Preya, where he should be. This jumbled-up feeling did not make sense.

Oz stood there for a few more minutes listening to his neighbors making morning sounds as the sky bedecked with wispy orange strips. Oz loved the mornings, the freshness of a new day, watching the sky paint itself moment by moment with ever-changing arrays of purples, oranges, pinks, and blues. A mockingbird twittered in a neighboring pine. Finches nearby awoke to their brood of hungry, peeping chicks. A small animal skittered in the leaves on the ground below. Probably a squirrel.

Oz thought about how sincere Skamp and Chatty had been as they relayed their story yesterday. And how brave Skamp was to come to the council. Huldah had seemed to know about the squirrels before they came to the nest, and she was not surprised at what had happened at the council. What else did she know that he did not? Oz wondered what her reaction would be when he told her that Obsolom was considering protecting the muscovies.

Oz had felt so sure he understood what the Great One was telling him. But now, it almost seemed like a dream. Obsolom was the leader and knew what he was doing. Oz could rest in that. So, why wasn't he able to?

Oz paced back and forth again across the nest. The constricting feeling of agitation grew more intense moment by moment as the morning brightened. Oz knew what he had to do. He could trust only one person to give him honest advice. "Preya, I have to find Huldah." Oz looked back at his wife, who nodded her head.

CHAPTER 15

Oz flew across the neighborhood and surrounding areas until he spotted his aunt perched on a cypress branch overlooking a marsh. "Huldah!" Oz called from above. The sun was now entirely over the horizon. Huldah watched as Oz descended and settled on the branch next to her.

"I need to talk to you." Oz kept his head down, avoiding Huldah's eyes. For some undefinable reason, he felt dirty, like he hadn't preened in a week.

"What happened since I spoke with you last night?" Huldah took her wing and lifted Oz's chin so she could look into his eyes.

"Obsolom was at the nest when I returned," Oz said, still averting her gaze.

"I'm not surprised. I figured he would try to demean and discourage you."

"He said he is open to protecting the muscovies." Oz looked briefly at Huldah and then away again.

"And you believe him?" Huldah's voice was resolute.

"He said he is going to observe what the humans do. We will talk again in a few days if the muscovies need protection."

"And I suppose he mentioned something like brothers should stick together?" Huldah leaned forward toward Oz. "Didn't he?"

"Huldah, he is the leader. What if he is right about the humans wanting to protect the muscovies? Shouldn't I trust him to lead?" Oz held up both his wings in question.

"OK, Oz. I will tell you what your dilemma is because you are struggling to see it."

"Please do!" Oz wasn't sure he wanted to hear what Huldah had to say.

"You are conflicted, wondering if you should trust what the Great One told you or your brother."

"Why can't I do both? Why can't I wait a few days to see what Obsolom comes up with?"

"Because you know you are at least procrastinating and more likely disobeying what the Great One told you to do."

"Huldah, all my so-called valiant efforts fail! People laugh at me! I'm crippled! And I need to be with Preya. We are just talking a few days."

"Oz, I'm not the one you are arguing with. And you are only arguing because you already know what to do."

"I just want to be with Preya. Isn't there someone else who can lead a protection effort? What about you, Huldah?" Oz looked directly at Huldah for the first time.

"I'm not who the Great One told to do this."

Oz looked away.

Huldah put her wing on Oz's shoulder. "Oz, look to the Great One first for direction and trust what he says. Even if it is like trying to fly through a thick forest in the pitch dark."

Oz's shoulders drooped, and his head hung low.

"Don't you see Oz? If you trust the Great One, he will guide you to succeed in *his* plans. If you try on your own and rely on your efforts—or anybody else's—that is when you will ultimately fail."

"What about being with Preya? I want to be there for her as she lays her eggs. And help protect them."

"Don't you think the Great One knows that and is big enough to protect Preya and the eggs?"

The seed of hope Oz had felt last night stirred again. He did not feel brave, but he knew he only had one choice.

Oz spoke hesitantly. "OK, Huldah, I'll attempt to fly in the forest in the pitch dark."

"You need to pray. Talk to the Great One. Seek his will and his guidance. And, when you doubt—because you will—call out to him. Remember the word the seer wrote long ago in The Order: "Those that call upon the Great One will renew their strength; they will mount up with wings of eagles.""

The morning sounds of bird trills and calls continued in the background. Oz shut his eyes. Prayer had not been part of his life for a while. How did he start now? How was this all going to come together? As he looked down at the marsh below, he saw through the brush a giant turtle near the edge of the marsh with a distinctive orange spot on the corner of its shell munching on some leaves. He wished his life could be simple like that turtle's, and all he had to worry about was munching leaves.

"Huldah, can you tell Skamp and Chatty to meet me later this morning at the peninsula that juts out into the lake?"

"I can."

Oz turned to Huldah in exasperation. "I can't do this alone with just a couple of squirrels! How do I get any others to help? It's not like I can make an announcement. Obsolom would stop any efforts before I even get started."

"Oz, what did we just talk about? You are not alone. The Great One is with you and will lead and guide you, but you must trust him and be strong and courageous. And I certainly will be a part of this." Huldah tilted her head to the side and put her wing tip to her chin. "There is someone I know who I think will want to help. I'll talk to him."

Oz watched Huldah fly off. He felt like he was teetering on the edge of a cliff. "Great One, the muscovies need protection. They are just as much your creation as any of us are, and you love them the same. This is your rescue campaign, not mine, but I need your eagle's wings." As he prayed, a peaceful assurance settled over his troubled soul. The peaks of anxiety and crevices of fear were not as acute. He had no idea how this would unfold, but he kept repeating the Great One's words: *I am with you.*

CHAPTER 16

"Anton, wake up." Tilly nudged the snoring anhinga again with her snout as she tried not to fall back into the lake. It had taken her over an hour to swim through the marsh, plod over the road to the lake, swim across to where the anhinga nested on the far side, and drag her twenty-pound form up the steep muddy embankment. She had already slid back into the water twice and was annoyed that her splashing and grunting had not aroused the sleeping bird.

"Anton!" Tilly shouted as loud as a turtle could. Digging her front and back claws into the mud to brace herself, she poked Anton's side hard with her head.

"To the canons! Batten down the hatches!" Anton extended his long, skinny neck, sputtering, squawking, and batting his wings.

"Anton, it's me, Tilly. Wake up!"

"Tilly?" Still batting his wings, Anton looked around with darting eyes, finally focusing on Tilly. "Why are you here? Are we under attack?" The morning sun highlighted the white feathers scattered amongst the black ones on his head.

"No, no, no, we are not under attack. I'm sorry I startled you, but it is important." Tilly wallowed her shell into the soft mud to help keep from sliding back into the water.

Anton yawned. "And I was having such an enjoyable dream that I was in the Navy Special Forces scoping around enemy territory gathering intelligence."

"You weren't at the council meeting last night," Tilly said, repositioning her claws for better traction.

"Those meetings are more pomp and fluff than action. Give me the good old days when Otto was the leader, and we carried out protection deployments. That Obsolom thinks he is a royal peacock!"

"Well, you missed some happenings," Tilly told Anton about Skamp coming to the meeting and what had been heard about the muscovies being exiled.

"Who do I see to enlist? I will need to brush up on my protection procedures."

"There is no protection effort sanctioned. Obsolom and Crete convinced the council that protecting the muscovies would go against the humans and The Order."

"Horsefeathers!" Anton held his head high. "Protecting each other is never against The Order! Everyone knows that!"

"Not according to Obsolom. And most everyone agreed with him."

"And what does that snake of a bird Crete have to do with all this? Birds of a feather flock together!"

"But here is the real reason I came to talk to you. I heard Oz talking to Huldah this morning. He is going to run a secret protection campaign to help the muscovies and is looking for volunteers."

Anton rubbed his gray chin with the tip of his wing. "A secret protection campaign. Hmmmm. And against Obsolom's ruling?"

"Oh yes. Oz heard the Great One telling him to do this."

"It is hard for me to picture Oz leading something as important and dangerous as a protection campaign. He is compassionate but does not have marine instincts, nor is he experienced in military tactics." Anton bowed his head and laid his wing tip over his heart. "He will need my assistance to keep an even keel."

"I thought you would want to help. So do I. Oz is having a meeting later this morning at the peninsula in the lake. The two squirrels will be there, too."

"Squirrels. Interesting. I suppose they can be trained in some stealth reconnaissance maneuvers. They won't be of any use in the water. I will have to strategize about this." Anton again scratched his chin with his wing. "I will most definitely be there to offer my skills. It is always wise to be on the side where the Great One is."

CHAPTER 17

"Carly, I just fed you. Are you still hungry? Caitlin! Stop pecking at your brother's head; you wouldn't like that if he did that to you!" Just as Caitlin tried to get one more peck in, Cara put her wing between Caitlin and Corey. "I said stop it, Caitlin! That's it! No dessert bugs for you!" Cara's frustration grew as she thought about Cronan not being there to help her this morning. The sun had risen above the horizon over an hour ago. A southerly breeze rocked the palm where her nest was tucked into the topmost fronds. The news he had from the council last night was strange enough, and now he was a full-fledged member of the respected leaders. Why he had to be gone since daybreak for these all-of-a-sudden significant responsibilities, she did not know. He promised to be back by mid-morning to relieve her and bring some fresh nest material.

Even more shocking was the council's decision not to protect the muscovies. Cara looked down to where she had seen the humans talking yesterday and remembered the conversation. She was devastated about the fate of the unwanted ducks. She knew about being unwanted. Humans often labeled crows a noisy nuisance and thought they were unattractive. Several times, Cara had seen humans covering their ears from her calls. Cronan, however, did not want to hear her opinion about the muscovies. He kept telling her that Obsolom was the wise leader, that the council had agreed, and therefore, it must be the best decision.

From the corner of her eye, Cara saw one of the neighborhood squirrels bounding up her palm, carrying something. As it got closer, she recognized Chatty. Chatty had introduced herself when the crows first moved in and had brought Cara some sprigs of Spanish moss to line the nest.

"Hi, Cara!" Chatty called out as she neared the nest. "How are you and the babies doing? Look at them; they have grown since I last saw them! Now, what are their names? Carey and Courtland and Corney? Aren't they adorable? You must have your wings full! My three nestlings are almost ready to leave! They grow up so fast! Oh, here, I brought you some fresh pine needles for the nest. I imagine you need to change bedding daily." Chatty dumped the pile of pine needles onto the nest and began tossing soiled bedding over the side.

"Hi Chatty, it's good to see you, thank you. Yes, they keep me busy. Their names are Carly, ..."

"Where is Cronan?" Chatty interrupted, standing up on her hind legs to look around and twitching her tail back and forth.

A look of anguish swept through Cara's eyes. "Apparently, now that he is on the council, he has critical matters to attend to."

Chatty sat down on the broad base of the frond near the nest and settled her tail. She reached out with her paw and gently touched Cara's shoulder. "Cara, what's wrong?"

"I don't know what has gotten into Cronan. I know he wants to be accepted and respected, and I think it is great that he is on the council. Cronan really can have some excellent ideas. But it just seems he is leaving me to take care of the kids all by myself so he can be chummy-chummy with his new friends."

Chatty moved closer to hug Cara.

Cara leaned into Chatty. "And I am so upset about the muscovies and the council's decision not to protect them and to let the herons have their fill of their ducklings! It is awful!" Cara covered her face with her wings. "And I can't do anything about it!"

"Yes, you can." Chatty picked up Caitlin, still restless, and rocked her in her arms. The other two were having trouble keeping their eyes open. Chatty lowered her voice to a whisper. "When is Cronan coming home?"

"Well, he should be home any moment. At least, he said he would be back mid-morning."

"How would you like to help the muscovies on a secret mission?" Chatty's voice was squeaking higher. It was hard to contain her excitement. Her whiskers twitched, and her tail began to jiggle.

"A secret mission? To help the muscovies? Chatty, what are you talking about?" Cara looked around to make sure they were not being overheard.

Chatty whispered about the secret protection campaign that Oz was leading and how he needed volunteers. "The Great One told Oz to do this. Oz is having a volunteer meeting at the peninsula. Why don't you come?"

"What can I do for the campaign? I'm nest-bound. The only thing I do all day besides taking care of the kids is watch what is going on."

Chatty's voice raised a pitch. "Watching is something, yes, it is! And moral support and prayer; that is something too."

"But I can't leave the kids until Cronan returns, and what do I tell him?"

"You can tell him the truth. The truth is always the best thing. And this is the truth; I was going to ask if you wanted me to show you where I got that soft Spanish moss because I was sure you could use a fresh batch. And I was right! You do need a fresh batch!" Chatty chittered as she started throwing soiled moss over the side of the nest with one arm while holding onto Caitlin with the other. "And it so happens this moss is located on the peninsula where the meeting is." Chatty winked at Cara. She could no longer control her tail, switching up and down.

A crow called from the north. "Is that Cronan? Isn't it just like the Great One to get Cronan back in time? What do you think, Cara; will you help?"

At that moment, Cronan swooped down and landed on the nest.

"What's she doing here?" Cronan glowered at Cara. "I don't want vermin near the kids." Cronan pulled Caitlin off Chatty's lap and corralled his daughter close to him.

Chatty lowered her head and tried to control her tail, which was now flipping wildly back and forth. "Cara, I've got to skedaddle anyway. If you want that Spanish moss meet me at the peninsula. If you can." Chatty glanced briefly at Cronan, who looked away.

Cara watched as Chatty clambered to the middle of the palm frond, jumped to the pool cage below, and skittered up over the roof, disappearing over the peak. "Cronan, you were rude to my guest. She was kind enough to bring fresh pine needles. Which is a good thing because I see you did not."

"I'm sorry, I forgot," Cronan crowed, throwing his wings in the air. "I'm on the council now and have important things to do."

"Your family is important too! The kids are hungry, and so am I."

"If you noticed, I brought this back for our lunch. Give me a break." Cronan scowled and shoved some sort of food closer to Cara with his beak.

Cara inspected what Cronan had brought. It smelled like burnt fat and starch. It was golden brown and about the size of a large twig. It had crinkled ridges. There was some thick, red, sticky goo on one end. She bit off a small morsel. The outside was salty and crisp, and the inside was a white, grainy substance. The red goo had a tangy taste.

"The kids need more than fatty carbs. I need to stretch my wings, and I do need to get more of that moss." Cara's voice cracked as she tried to contain her feeling of abandonment. The three chicks started peeping softly, sensing their mom's distress.

"Alright, I am sorry." Cronan's voice softened as he reached out to Cara. "It just feels good to be included in the decision-making and be part of the council." Cronan drew Cara close to him in his wings. "You go to the peninsula with that ver... *squirrel* and get us some nice moss. I will take care of the kids."

Twenty-five feet below Cara's nest, Sophie was watering her plants on the Lanai. "Jeffrey, have you called Jared yet?" Sophie called into the living room.

"Calling him now. I texted him yesterday but did not hear back."

"The HOA president should be more responsive."

"I'm sure he is getting lots of calls about this and... Hello, Jared? This is Jeffrey." Jeffrey sat down on the couch. "Yes, the muscovy decision, that's why I'm calling."

Jeffrey held the phone away from his ear; Sophie couldn't make out the words but could hear Jared's agitated voice from the lanai.

"I know people have complained about the ducks, but...." Jeffrey paused as Jared interrupted. "Jared, this ..."

Jeffrey stood up and started pacing. One hand held the phone to his ear, and the other motioned in the air as he spoke. "Jared, could you please just listen to me for a moment? By the number of calls you are getting, it seems the decision should have been vetted with the whole community before the HOA voted on this." Jeffrey yanked the phone away from his ear.

"Jared, calm down. I know it's too late for that." Jeffrey put the phone back to his ear. "Uh huh.... Right, I'll tell her... Yeah, you too, bye."

"Well?" Sophie stood in front of Jeffrey with her hands on her hips.

"Several residents have been calling him. He is angry with who he calls 'the muscovy lovers' because they never voiced an opinion..."

"How could they? They were never asked!" Sophie exclaimed.

"That is when I said they should have vetted the situation with the whole association. Anyway, the board is going to meet to discuss this and decide what to do, if anything."

Sophie crossed her arms. "If anything? Reverse the decision until they hear everyone's view! When are they meeting?"

"Next week. They have already signed a contract with the capture and release company. They are supposed to start right away."

CHAPTER 18

Oz flew over the red, brown, and gray tiled roofs toward the lake, where the mid-morning sun glinted off the water's surface. He hated leaving Preya. She had not slept well last night, primarily due to his restlessness. But something was different today; she seemed achier and had no appetite. At least Huldah was with her and would get him if needed. He hoped again he was doing the right thing. Trust. Trust the Great One, he repeated again and again to himself.

The lake was on the southeast side of the neighborhood. All the canals in Havenport merged at the lake like spokes to the hub of a wheel. Between the canals were fingers of land with houses on either side and a street in the middle that connected to the main road lacing through the community. A small peninsula jutted into the lake on the far east side. Several large oaks shaded some picnic tables. Long tendrils of Spanish moss clung to the branches and flittered slightly west in the breeze.

"The moss on this tree is the softest. How much can you carry? Skamp and I can take some back, too." Chatty skittered through the oak, yanking clumps of moss with her paws, biting them loose from the branch. Cara came behind her, testing the softness and pushing the rejects with her beak to the ground. Skamp followed, gathering the moss Cara had approved.

"Hey! Watch where you're tossing that!"

The three looked down to see a giant turtle with a pile of Spanish moss over its shell. Chatty climbed down the trunk a few feet, swishing her tail back and forth, and held onto the bark with her four paws facing head down. "Sorry! Hi Tilly! Did you come to help Oz, too? Isn't this exciting? How did you find out? Oh! Anton! You came too!" The anhinga was sitting on top of the picnic table with his wings outstretched to dry them.

"What do you think Oz will do to protect the muscovies? Where is he? Huldah said he would be here. Maybe Mrs. Oz is laying an egg?" Chatty ran back up the oak and resumed collecting moss.

A slight flutter caused everyone to look over to a neighboring tree. Giuseppe the gull was sitting on a branch partially camouflaged by some leaves. "Shush already. You guys gotta keep the racket down. Obsolom; he may have spies listening."

"Giuseppe?" Skamp bounded to the end of the branch toward the tree the gull was in.

"Yeah, that's me."

As Oz neared the peninsula, he heard chittering. The squirrels, at least, were there. But who belonged to these other voices? Oz landed on one of the oak's lower branches where the squirrels were. He was surprised to see Anton and Giuseppe. Oz's hope buoyed.

"Oz!" Chatty squeaked. "We were just wondering where you were. I thought you would be here sooner."

Just then, Cara flit down a few branches. Oz startled at the sight of her, and a feeling of dread peaked in his chest.

If she was here, was Cronan nearby?

Chatty saw Oz looking at Cara with a skeptical gaze. "This is Cara. She has the nest in the palm over the humans…"

"Yes, I know Cara." Oz inhaled slowly. He might as well face his fears upfront. "Cara. I have to ask, why are you here, and where is Cronan?"

"He is back at the nest with the kids," Cara said, "I want to help."

Sensing Oz's concerns, Skamp jumped to a branch closer to Oz. "Cronan doesn't know anything. He thinks she is getting moss."

Oz's shoulders unhunched slightly.

Oz was trying to trust that the Great One could do amazing things when it seemed hopeless. Still, as he surveyed the small group, he was having difficulty imagining they could do much and wondering how long before Cronan found out about Cara's involvement. Oz didn't even know where to start or what to say. Struggling to feel brave, he sat up straight while he turned and nodded toward each bird and squirrel. "Thank you all for being here."

"Uh, hello! Notice the turtle!"

Oz looked down and recognized the turtle he had seen earlier this morning crawling out from underneath a pile of Spanish moss.

"That's Tilly. Doesn't she have a pretty shell?" Chatty climbed a few feet down the tree, twitching her whiskers.

"I'm sorry, Tilly. I didn't see you."

"Hrmph," muttered Tilly.

Oz wanted to feel encouraged by another volunteer, but he wondered how much help a turtle could be. She couldn't fly nor move quickly like the squirrels.

Oz swallowed and addressed the group again. "Thank you all for joining me in helping the muscovies. I'm sure you realize that you are going against the direction of the council and, in your case, Cara, also your husband."

"No one should be allowed to snatch babies or mothers or fathers or destroy eggs. I can't just sit in my nest and do nothing. If Cronan finds out, he will be mad at me, but he'll get over it. He's more noise than anything else."

Giuseppe flew over and landed on the picnic table next to Anton. "If that guy Cronan finds out, we're done."

"Well, he won't find out from me!" Cara scowled at Giuseppe.

Oz saw in Cara a determined strength and passion to stand up against this injustice, but he questioned in his mind how she could support the campaign along with her parenting duties. Oz also knew there was a real danger of Cronan finding out about their activities because of Cara's involvement. But she was here willing to help.

"Everyone, the first thing we need to do is trust the Great One in this. And we need to trust each other." Oz looked around at each of his volunteers, ending with Giuseppe.

"Yeah, trust," Giuseppe smirked.

"Giuseppe, how have you been?" Oz had not seen the gull for several months. He had lost weight and was hunched over in a slump.

"I'm fine. The family is fine. Maria still loves me. She's a saint, but being back home, well, Oz, it's not great. My children have grown up without me. They don't come over. Even my godchildren. They don't want to be seen with me." Giuseppe kept his gaze down.

"I'm sorry to hear that." Oz remembered the council

meeting late last summer when the gull had been convicted of stealing fish several times from ospreys as they carried their catch to their nests. If the osprey, or any other fishing bird, accidentally dropped a fish, it was fair game for the gulls. But Giuseppe had been seen darting and swooping at the osprey causing them to drop their dinner. Many gulls were suspected of doing the same thing, and it was rumored they even had organized clans that made detailed plans for raids, which they carried out as a mob. But Giuseppe was the one who got caught. The sentence given was four months of excommunication.

Oz knew the gulls treasured their large extended families and community. Any excommunication was a harsh sentence. His children at that time were just about to fledge, and his daughter from his brood a year ago was having an elaborate wedding soon with flocks of relatives from the old country flying in. Giuseppe had to miss all that.

"Giuseppe, forgive me, I have to ask, are you up to working with me on this campaign?" Oz saw the depth of painful brokenness in Giuseppe's eyes as he looked up at Oz. He hoped Giuseppe would be more of a help than a hindrance. But what could a depressed gull do?

"Oz, my family, they treat me like a bad omen. I'm not welcome at the squawk-fests us gulls have at the lake every day. When Maria and I showed up last week, all my goombahs flew off. They don't trust me. They think I'll rat on them." Giuseppe turned his head away. "Huldah—she came over this morning and told us what you're doing. Well, we want to help. Both my Maria and me."

"Thank you, Giuseppe." Oz turned his attention to Anton and tried to remember how old he was. The anhinga was already ancient when Oz was a hatchling.

Oz hadn't seen Anton for several months, and since then, Anton's wing feathers had thinned even more, and his once glossy black-green head and back had dulled and were now peppered with specks of white. "Anton, it's good to see you."

CHAPTER 19

"**C**aptain Anton and Seaman Tilly reporting for duty, sir!" Anton marched forward a few steps on the picnic table and whipped his right wing up, tipping his forehead. Tilly rolled her eyes.

Oz repressed a chuckle at the old bird's salute and calling himself a captain. "Thank you, Anton and Tilly, your help is appreciated." Oz felt a reactionary urge to salute back but kept his wing in check.

Oz looked over the small group. What could a few birds, a turtle, and a couple of squirrels do to help the muscovies? The Great One would have to come through.

The group sat and waited for Oz to speak. Oz's left shoulder ached. It always did when he was tense. Oz had no experience leading and had never been involved in a significant protection campaign. He tried to calm himself by breathing thoroughly and slowly.

"Anton, you have many years of experience working on protection campaigns with my father and his father before him. How do you suggest we proceed?"

Anton saluted again and stood at attention. "Sir! Seaman Tilly and I would be honored to serve as the USU."

"What's the USU?" Tilly asked.

"The Underwater Surveillance Unit, which, if you had studied the manual I gave you, Seaman, you would know."

Tilly rolled her eyes again.

Anton continued. "We will perform underwater reconnaissance and report to you on the enemy's position and activities when they are on or near the water."

"That is a valuable service, Anton and Tilly," Oz said.

Anton remained standing at attention in front of Oz, apparently waiting for further orders. "Um, at ease, er, or dismissed," it occurred to Oz to finally say.

Chatty bounded over to Oz and stood on her hind legs. "We can do all sorts of things, too!" Chatty's voice began to rise in pitch as she rattled off suggestion after suggestion. "We can spy, we can bring you news, we can warn the muscovies if we think we see danger, we can…"

"Shush! Stop being a scooch! You're making too much noise!" Giuseppe lifted his wings toward Chatty.

Skamp jumped over to Chatty, took her flopping tail, and handed it to her. "Oz, we will do whatever we can."

"That is all I can ask or expect. Thank you."

Cara flit down a branch. "I can keep watch from my nest. But what would I do if I saw something? I can't call out without Cronan or a neighbor knowing what I'm doing."

Anton raised his wing. "Airman Cara has brought up a critical point. We will have to devise a secret communication code for this operation."

"Oh, brother." Tilly wagged her head.

"Na, the old bird's got a point. I like it," Giuseppe said.

Oz smiled. Maybe the group could work together.

Giuseppe continued. "Oz, my Maria wants to help, too. After Huldah left, Maria and I scoped out the area and found a nice, quiet spot near you to move to. Preya, she's just about ready to lay her eggs, yes? With you running the campaign, my Maria thought she could be there for

Preya. Sei una famiglia, you're family now; we take care of each other, you know? Maria can come find you if Preya needs you."

Oz felt like a weight the size of a cypress had been lifted off his wings. Aunt Huldah would help with the brood, but she was also needed for the campaign. Having an experienced mother like Maria help Preya was a precious gift. Oz was not sure what being considered family meant to Giuseppe.

"Thank you, Giuseppe. You don't know how much that means to me."

"Fuhgeddaboudit. That's what families do. And I can use my, er, *planning* skills when we need to take care of business. Capeesh?"

"What planning skills?" Then it dawned on Oz what Giuseppe meant. So, the stories were true about the raids. "Got it, I know."

Oz could not deny that this was a useful skill, but the thought of doing something illegal left him with a sour taste in his beak.

As if reading his mind, Giuseppe said, "Hey, what's wrong with using my skills for good now? I'm no criminal; I did my time."

Oz questioned his own motives for the umpteenth time. Was he doing the right thing, going against the council's decree and the humans' decision? Was this worth putting Preya, his soon-to-arrive chicks, Huldah, himself, and now these volunteers in danger? The still, small voice reverberated firmly again in his mind; *lead them.*

Oz noticed the sun was directly overhead. He should be getting back home to check on Preya.

Just then, a rustling noise sounded in the oak above

them. Oz looked up and could only see the dense weave of leaves and branches. Maybe it was just the wind.

"Who's up there?" Giuseppe called.

Another small rustle. Silence.

"Quark!"

Something cried out, and the ground shook as it fell right in front of Tilly, who quickly retracted her head, tail, and four legs into her shell. A cloud of dirt and dried leaves formed as whoever had fallen kicked and struggled, trying to recover. Giuseppe and Anton readied themselves to attack if needed.

Oz sailed to the ground. "Petunia?"

The pelican smoothed her feathers and shuffled over to Oz. She held her head high and acted like her entry had been the most ordinary way, her dusty and ruffled appearance a figment of everyone's imagination. Several dried oak leaves stuck to her head, forming a tiny lopsided hat.

"Petunia, are you OK?" Oz asked.

"What's she doing here? How long you been up there spying on us?" Giuseppe shot an accusing look at the pelican.

"I am perfectly fine." Petunia ignored Giuseppe and spat out a few specks of dirt. One of the leaves from her hat slid down her face onto the ground. "What you and your group of riff-raff are calling a campaign is the most ridiculous thing I have ever heard." Petunia stuck her beak up in disdain.

Chatty stood on her hind legs and pointed at herself with her thumb. "We're not riff-raff! We are brave citizens who care about what happens to others, unlike some people we know."

Petunia stayed her attention on Oz. "You have a

slithering anhinga, two useless squirrels, a young crow mother, who, may I add, is married to one of your stark opponents, a reluctant turtle, and a criminal gull." Petunia paused as she stared directly at Giuseppe and then turned back to Oz. "And you! With your wall-flower style of assertiveness! I've asked myself several times this past year why you remain on the council, even with your family ties."

"Oz, you want me to whack her?" Giuseppe stalked closer to Petunia. "Snitch! She's the one who ratted on me!"

"Criminals should expect to pay for their crimes!" Petunia huffed.

Oz spread his wings. "Everybody, settle down!" Was this campaign going to work? Giuseppe sat down but kept a stern look on his face.

Oz continued. "Petunia, why are you here? Are you here representing the council?" If the council had sent Petunia to gather evidence against Oz, he and his volunteers were already in trouble.

Petunia shook her head, dislodging the remaining leaves. "No. I am not here on behalf of the council."

"Yeah, right. She's a spy!" Giuseppe called out.

"Then, why are you here?" Oz repeated his question.

Petunia sighed in frustration. "That's a great question, Oz, and I'm not sure I know the answer. I am concerned that the decision to support the humans will undermine our core mission of protection."

Oz saw Petunia grappling with herself and remembered her hesitancy during the vote. "So why did you vote to support the humans' decree against the muscovies?"

"Yeah, this has got to be good," Giuseppe snorted.

"You must know what it is to represent others' interests on the council, don't you? You saw how my patrons wanted me to vote." The pelican hung her head. "There was no time for me to discuss this with them so they could maybe see the ramifications."

"Petunia, if you had stood up for your concerns..."

"I know Oz!" Petunia stomped her foot. "I tried to make it right. I spoke to Obsolom privately after the council meeting. I asked that the decision be reviewed in one week as we observe the humans' actions."

Oz remembered his conversation last night with his brother. Maybe he *was* going to observe and possibly reconsider.

Petunia continued. "I also questioned why lifting the limit of muscovy ducklings for the Great Blues was even part of the decision. He had the audacity to tell me my socialist views are of no consequence; the council had made their decision, which I had supported."

Oz felt a sinking feeling in his gut; Obsolom was *not* going to reconsider.

Anton saluted Oz again. "Sir! Perhaps we need to stage a coup to restore justice. We will need to muster air, ground, and marine troops."

Oz rolled his shoulder. "We're not going to stage a coup!"

"I don't believe that pelican!" Giuseppe squawked.

"I can't believe you all are comfortable working with this convicted gull." Stumbling on a small rock, Petunia stepped closer to Oz. "I'm swimming in murky waters with Obsolom, but I can be your eyes and ears on the council. Everyone knows you believe the muscovies should be protected, but nobody thinks you will do anything about it. They don't know how I really feel."

"Yeah, and how's that?" Giuseppe glared at Petunia, who avoided his gaze.

"I believe her." Oz looked around. "I've worked with Petunia for several years. Her intentions have always been honorable. She is taking a big risk keeping her alliance with us secret."

Giuseppe pointed his wing at Petunia. "Lady, you're gonna have to prove yourself to me. I'll be watching you."

CHAPTER 20

Suddenly, Oz looked up toward a piercing call overhead. Hearing Huldah's voice sent a slice of anxiousness through him. Had something happened to Preya? Huldah was flying 100 feet high, diving almost to the treetops, calling at the top of her lungs, and swooping heavenward again. Then Oz realized Huldah's call was not one of alarm! She was singing for joy! A wave of relief swept over him.

"Preya must have laid her first egg! I'm a father!" Oz raised his wings and jumped up to a higher branch.

Chatty hugged Skamp, and Cara crowed. Tilly poked her head out of her shell long enough to smile at Oz.

"You better go. The muscovies are deserving as anyone of our protection, even if the people and the council do not see that, yet. I will do what I can; that is until Obsolom finds out." Petunia looked from Oz to Giuseppe.

Despite Giuseppe's distrust in her, Oz knew Petunia would be a faithful partner.

"Thank you, everyone!" Oz called out as he launched into the air and flew as fast as possible.

As Oz neared the nest, he saw Huldah had returned and was sitting on the nest near Preya. Preya was panting and had one wing holding her still large belly but had an expression of pure delight in her eyes. Peeking out under her downy belly feathers was the rounded shape of an egg.

"Preya! Are you OK?" Oz landed lightly on the nest, reaching out his wings to his wife.

"Everything is fine." Preya smiled at Oz. "See?" Preya stood up slowly, wobbling as she put her weight on her legs.

"Let me help you." Oz quickly supported Preya and helped her move a few steps so Oz could see the egg. The tawny-colored egg was the size of a large chicken egg splashed with red, brown, and gray blotches. It was the most beautiful thing Oz had ever seen. "I'm so sorry. I should have been here." Oz had a sinking feeling that maybe this campaign idea was wrong, and he should've been here with Preya.

"Oz, it's alright. You are here now, and we have a beautiful egg." Preya moved to lower herself carefully on the egg. "And by the way, I'm feeling, there are two more to come."

Oz faced Huldah. "Really? *Two* more?"

Huldah nodded. "That is what I think. The eggs will come two to three days apart, giving you more opportunities to be here. Preya is fine, and the egg is healthy."

"Thank you, Great One." Oz's soul was overwhelmed with thankfulness. Suddenly, he leaped heavenwards with strong wing beats, quickly climbing on the updrafts into the clear afternoon sky. The air grew cooler as he reached a height of 400 feet. Oz sang an exuberant song as he swooped down, climbed back into the sky, glided around a complete circle, and repeated his dance.

CHAPTER 21

Oz flew over the neighborhood on the lookout for any sign that the humans had started to exile the muscovies. He didn't like leaving Preya again. At least Maria was there with her and the newly laid egg from yesterday. As he passed over the boulevard leading into the neighborhood, he noticed a human couple running along the sidewalk.

The female human wore a white top that exposed her belly. Something glittered from her navel. She had white legs and bright white shoes. Her long brown hair was pulled back and tied with a bright pink ribbon and bounced from shoulder to shoulder as she pranced down the sidewalk. Oz was amazed at her eyelashes. He had never seen a human with eyelashes that long. Or lips that were the same bright color pink as the ribbon in her hair. Or blue eyelids. Her ears had large gold rings dangling from them. Oz thought that if he could find something like those rings, Preya would like it in the nest.

A head taller than her, the male wore a tight black shirt with no sleeves. He had on shiny black shorts and black shoes. A dark band of glass covered his eyes, and black marble-like things protruded from his ears.

Suddenly, the woman stopped and screamed out. Oz landed in a tree nearby to observe.

"Douglas! Stop!" She stomped over to the grass and

scuffed her shoes, one of them now stained a brownish green. "This is disgusting!"

The male kept running. The woman picked up a stick and threw it, smacking her mate in the back. "Douglas! Take out those stupid earbuds!"

Taking out the earbuds, the man turned and slowly walked back to her. Oz noticed he was being careful where he stepped. A female muscovy waddled by and headed for a line of bushes that edged the park. A few mallard moms and their ducklings were sitting at the base of a nearby oak. Oz felt a twinge of caution and took a closer look. Yes, as he suspected, Mary Margaret was among the group.

"Eww, this is so gross. I just bought these cute shoes, and now they're ruined." The woman kept trying to wipe off the bird droppings on the grass but only succeeded in grinding the mess further into her shoe.

"Yeah, it stinks too." The male pinched his nose with his fingers and remained about ten feet away.

"Those disgusting muscovies. I'm glad the HOA is getting rid of them." The woman picked up a small stick and tried to dig out some of the mess that had oozed up into the grooves of her shoe. As she furiously dug, the stick broke, and her hand jammed into the sticky shoe. "Yuck!" The woman flung the stick behind her.

Giving up her efforts, she stomped back to her mate and stepped into another pile of droppings. At least now her shoes matched, Oz thought.

"Did you see where that muscovy went?" The woman had her hands on her hips. Her hair flung left to right as her head darted from side to side, looking for the muscovy.

"It went over there." The male pointed to the line of bushes. "Why?"

"Was that a female?" The woman crossed her arms and jutted out her chin.

"How am I supposed to know?" The man followed the woman as she marched over to where he had pointed.

As they got close to the bushes, they were met by a male muscovy. Oz now recognized the pair. Klara and Klaus had just celebrated their third wedding anniversary. Klaus didn't like the humans approaching so close. He spiked his crown feathers in warning, hissed, and strutted in front of his nest that was hidden deep in the underbrush where Klara had gone to sit on their eggs. Oz hopped down a few branches so he could get a better view. He saw that Mary Margaret and the other mallards were watching the scene.

"There is a nest in there," the woman announced, stepping closer to the nest the male muscovy was guarding.

"How do you know?" The man kept a distance away. Oz was puzzled that he was letting his female get so close to a protective father muscovy. Didn't he know muscovies sometimes attacked humans who got too close to their nest?

"That is what it said on the internet. The male will guard the nest when the female is on the eggs or away from the nest." The woman crossed her arms again.

"So what?" The man shrugged his shoulders. "Come on, let's go. We're supposed to be at the club for brunch in half an hour, and you need to get cleaned up."

"Not until we addle the eggs." The woman took another step toward the nest. Klaus hissed louder, marching back and forth and jutting his head forward and back.

"What are you talking about?" The man stayed back.

"It's easy. I watched a couple YouTubes."

"What is adding eggs? What do you add to them?" The man was stepping back. Oz hoped they would both go and leave the muscovies alone, but a disturbing feeling tightened his chest. And, with Mary Margaret there, Oz could not interfere. He could not risk her reporting him to the council.

The woman turned back to the man. "Add-*LING*. You shake the eggs, and they won't hatch."

"Why would you want to do that? Come on, Deborah, let's go."

"No. The HOA told us we should do this. It's a community service." The woman turned away from the man and closed her eyes. That is a strange shade of blue on her lids, Oz thought; her lids even sparkled.

Klaus was still strutting back and forth and hissing. Oz could hear Klara chirruping from the nest.

The man looked warily at the woman and the muscovy. Oz wondered who he was more afraid of. "How are we supposed to get to the nest with that duck guarding it? He could scratch my eyes out."

"You will distract the male, and I'll scare off the female, reach in, and addle the eggs."

"You're nuts. I'm not getting near him. He could kill me." The man started walking away.

"Douglas!" The woman took a few steps toward the man, reaching out to him. "Do this for me, will you?" The woman batted her eyelashes a few times. "Pleeeeeeeease?"

The man stopped and turned toward her. "I don't want to get scratched up by a bird."

"You won't. Just run at him shouting and act bigger and braver than him, and he will fly away. That's what the

YouTube video showed." The woman reached down her shirt and pulled out the small, shiny black rectangle all humans carried. "Do you want to watch the YouTube?"

Oz heard the man sigh. He trudged back to the woman with his head down. "No. But if that bird starts attacking me, I'm out of here. You're on your own."

The woman jumped up and down and clapped her hands together. "First, you run at the male shouting and waving your arms as wide as you can."

The man looked around. There were no other humans in sight. "I hope none of our friends see this. You better appreciate this, Deborah."

"Oh! I do!" The woman made a kissy face at the man. "On the count of three. Ready?"

"As ready as I'm going to be. Let's get this over before anyone shows up."

The woman braced herself. "One, two, three!"

The man ran toward Klaus, waving his arms and making all sorts of loud noises. Startled at the unexpected show of dominance, the male muscovy ran away from the nest with the man close behind. The woman then darted toward the bushes and, kneeling, crawled forward on her hands and knees. Oz's alarm rose as he heard her shouting and saw the bush shaking. Klara flapped out of the bushes and ran a few feet away, honking in distress. The bush kept moving. All Oz could see was the woman's white rump and soiled shoes sticking out of the bush.

Klaus abruptly stopped a few hundred feet away and turned toward the man, hissing, honking, and beating his wings in warning. Jumping up into the air, the muscovy flew at the man, who screamed, turned around, and ran. He dashed past the woman who was trying to extricate herself from the dense woody bush. As she attempted to pull out her head, the bright pink ribbon caught in the bushes. Yelping, she wrenched her head out, leaving the ribbon wrapped tight in the branches with a tangled hunk of her hair. She jumped up, wiping her muddy hands on her white leggings, adding several more splotches of grass and dirt. Oz noticed the long eyelashes from her left eye were now stuck on the side of her nose.

Klaus then focused on the woman and ran at her, hissing and honking. Screeching, she ran after the man.

Oz watched the human couple run back the way they had come. Klaus and Klara were now back in front of their nest, softly pecking at each other to make sure they were both alright. Klara went back into the bushes, and Klaus took up his protective post again. Oz hoped the humans had not damaged the eggs. The feeling of dread in his chest remained.

"Mom, what were those people doing?" Mary Cathryn asked.

All the mallards were twittering, asking each other the same question.

"I don't know. This is none of your concern, Mary Cathryn." Mary Margaret turned to walk toward the pond, followed by her five ducklings. The other mallards followed her lead.

But Mary Margaret did know. Peter Paul had told her about the humans' high-counsel's edict to shake muscovy eggs. She shrugged off an involuntary shudder that left her feeling cold and empty. This was as it should be; she told herself.

CHAPTER 22

The sun glided along its path over the retention pond that edged the pickleball courts and dog park. It had been broiling for a full hour, and the pickleball players had left. The early dog walkers were gone, and the late-morning walkers had not arrived. Gunther and Girdie waddled between the pickleball courts and dog park with their nine ducklings plucking bugs from the air and rooting out grubs with their rounded bills. From across the street, they could hear the squeaky swing set and human children's laughter.

"Tina, Sammy, come on now, stay close." Girdie looked back at her two smallest ducklings, who trailed behind the family about six feet. If they could survive the next couple of weeks and put on a few ounces, they would be fine. But for now, they were easy prey for herons and other predators.

"Don't worry about them; they will be fine. I won't let anything happen to them." Gunther stroked Girdie's head with his beak, gently outlining the red skin around her eyes.

Girdie nuzzled back. "I worry about Joey, too."

Just then, the bright yellow duckling ran up to Girdie and Gunther. "Can Tina and I go over and play with Mary Cathryn?" Joey pointed across the retention pond where a group of female mallards with their broods of ducklings meandered toward them, quacking and cackling with each other, ignoring the muscovy family. Their conversation could be clearly heard.

"My husband, Peter Paul, the esteemed Director of Waterways, said everybody supported the vote." Mary Margaret stood erect and addressed her followers. Everybody already knew Peter Paul's position on the council, but Mary Margaret liked to remind them.

The mallard moms all talked at once. Some argued how they would divide the nesting areas that the muscovies would vacate. Others squabbled about the possibility of orphaned muscovy ducklings and how they would deal with the problem if it arose. Still, others debated that the Great Blues enjoyed eating mallard ducklings as much as muscovy ducklings and questioned how the council was going to protect the mallard ducklings.

No one noticed the van pulling into the empty parking lot adjacent to the pickleball courts.

The mallards continued quacking. Each had an opinion and expected to be heard. Mary Margaret's five ducklings were peeping and darting back and forth with all the spirited debate. There was only one thing to do to reestablish order for her brood.

"Roll call!" Mary Margaret shouted, taking a few steps away from the group. Her five children lined up in order behind each other.

"Peter Alexander!"

"Peter Bartholomew!"

"Mary Cath—Mom!" Mary Cathryn chirped, "Look!"

"Mary Cathryn, I have just about had it with you. You know you are not to interrupt during roll call."

"No, Mom! Look over at Tina's family!" Mary Cathryn pointed over to the muscovy family.

Turning back around, it took a few seconds for Mary Margaret to make any sense of what she saw. A man about as wide as he was tall, wearing a khaki-colored shirt with wide sweat bands under his arms and across his chest, was chasing after Girdie's family while carrying a long pole with a large net at the end. His tangled orange beard bounced side to side across his tattooed arms as he wheezed across the grass. Running towards the pond, Girdie was in front of her brood, and Gunther was in the rear closest to the man.

In his prime at thirty-three inches long and weighing about fifteen pounds, Gunther suddenly turned around, hissing and raising his wings, intent on protecting his family from the chaser. Girdie was getting close to the pond, and Mary Margaret could hear her calling her children to run as fast as they could. The ducklings tried their hardest, but their teeny legs could not keep up with Girdie. Tina and Sammy were lagging even further behind. The man was now about twenty feet away. Gunther rushed toward the man, hissing louder and stretching his wings to the entire six-foot span.

The man brought his pole up in the air and quickly brought it down around Gunther, pinning him to the ground, leaving one wing protruding from under the metal rim of the net. Gunther struggled to free himself, which only resulted in him pulling his wing out of joint and getting more tangled. The man deftly secured the net so Gunther could not escape and pulled a smaller net out of his pocket. Girdie had reached the pond with all but the two straggling ducklings and was now ten feet out into the water. Still calling the two to urge them on, she watched as they neared the pond edge—the net cast in front and over the ducklings as they jumped into the water.

"Mommy!" called Tina. "Daddy, help!"

Girdie started swimming toward her captured children. When her other ducklings followed her, she realized that if she went back to help, she and the other ducklings would also be caught. She swam back and forth, honking, and could only watch helplessly as Gunther struggled and her two smallest babies were trapped, peeping and squirming and calling out to her.

"You be next." The man pointed a fat, grimy finger at Girdie as she chirped and honked unceasingly from the center of the pond.

"I love you, Tina and Sammy, don't be afraid! Gunther, can you hear me? Great One! Please help us!"

Mary Margaret had gathered her ducklings close under her wings and watched the scene in shock.

Mary Cathryn poked her head out from under Mary Margaret's wing to see what was happening. "Mom, what's happening to Tina and Sammy and their daddy?"

Mary Margaret had no good answers. She had never seen anything like this. Maybe once in a while, a human child or dog chases the mallards or muscovies for fun, but never something like what she just witnessed. Although, wasn't it for the best? Indeed, they were finally bringing the muscovies back to the farms they had escaped from generations ago. Back to where they belonged. And hadn't Peter Paul said it was for their good? Besides, they should have done this long ago and rid the neighborhood of the unwelcome, dirty immigrants.

The group of mallards had become silent and continued watching. Girdie was still crying out from the pond. The man took the net with the peeping ducklings and trudged back up the bank to retrieve the net that held

Gunther, who was still struggling and hissing. Walking to the road, he opened the back door of the dented work van, which may have been white if it had ever been washed but now appeared a dingy greige. The sound of hissing, peeping, and the sour smell of fear wafted out. The man tossed the two nets atop a pile of similar squirming nets.

"Six adults and thirteen ducklings. Not bad for a morning. Now, to find a place to dump them." The man slammed the back door and walked to the front of the van. He pulled out a crumpled foil pouch from his muddy pants pocket. Shaking out a small pile of brown flakes, he wadded it between his fingers and shoved it in the back of his mouth between his teeth and cheek. He climbed into the van and threw the empty pouch to the ground a few feet away from a trash can.

The woman stood across the street in front of the playground with her two small children clinging to her legs. Having seen the whole incident, she continued watching as the vehicle started with a coughing rumble and shot black soot from the tailpipe. The wheels spun, and road grit spat as the van sped out of the parking lot and down the road. The woman pulled out her cell phone and made a call.

CHAPTER 23

"Reposition and periscope up," Anton commanded from where he and Tilly were stationed behind a thick cluster of water iris. They had heard a commotion of ducks from across the pond and had come over to investigate.

"What do you mean 'periscope up?'" Tilly asked.

"It means to look around, sailor. You need to brush up on your terms!"

"Aye, aye, captain." Tilly dove and swam in front of the water iris to the surface, revealing only her snout and eyes.

"Report findings, sailor."

"I see a man chasing a family of muscovies. The mother, I think it's Girdie Green, has led her ducklings into the pond. Oh no!" Tilly gasped.

"Roger that, report!" Anton peeked out between the stalks of water iris.

"Who's Roger? Anton, you have to see this yourself. I think that man got two of the ducklings. And their father Gunther is in some sort of a trap."

Anton swam over to where Tilly was stationed. In dismay, they watched as the man took the netted muscovies to his van and drove away. Girdie was still honking, and her remaining ducklings swam nervously around her, peeping. On the shore, they noticed Mary Margaret and her ducklings had also witnessed the scene.

"Periscope down! Retreat!" Anton and Tilly dove beneath the water's surface and swam back across the pond. They could not risk Mary Margaret seeing them and telling Peter Paul, who would undoubtedly alert the council. The campaign must be kept secret.

As the morning wore on, puffy clouds grew and shrunk intermittently as they played hide-and-seek with the sun. At her nest, Cara's eyes grew heavy as she finally was able to rest after several hectic hours of feeding and cleaning. Carly and Caitlin had fallen asleep, and Corey was playing quietly with an inchworm that was measuring the nest's perimeter. Corey had not yet grasped that worms were food, not toys.

Suddenly, from the yard below, Cara heard a man's voice and a pair of muscovies chirping and hissing. Looking down, she saw Hannah and Herbert, a pair of black and white muscovies, being chased in and out of some bushes by a short, fat man carrying what looked like a large spider web. The couple emerged from the bushes near a clearing, hoping to fly away, but the man dropped the web over them. Their running forward caused the web to wrap around them.

"Got you!" The man grabbed the web with the two struggling ducks and walked away toward the front of the house.

"Uh oh! Uh oh!" Cara's voice rang out. One, two, three, she counted to herself, pacing her calls. "Uh oh, uh oh!" She waited ten more seconds. "Uh oh! Uh oh!" Cara called out again. One, two, three. "Uh oh, uh oh!"

Cara hoped Chatty and Skamp would remember the secret code that Anton had devised.

CHAPTER 24

Oz trod back and forth across the branch. Where were his volunteers? They were supposed to meet at the peninsula sharply at noon. Oz checked the position of the sun. It was at least five minutes past noon. Great, he thought. A sinking feeling coursed through him.

"Oz, you are making me dizzy. Stop pacing," Huldah said from her perch a few branches over.

"The volunteers must have decided to back out. Of course. Why would they want to go against the council and risk getting caught?" Oz continued pacing. "The meeting I had with them was a delusion. They have all come to their senses."

"You are the one being delusional. Have some faith in these folks. And the Great One."

"Even if they still think capturing the muscovies is wrong, they have probably decided I will not be able to do anything anyway. We will just make fools of ourselves. This campaign was a bad idea."

"If I recall correctly, this was the Great One's idea. He does not have bad ideas."

"Well then, where are the volunteers?" Oz craned his neck upward. From the east, he saw a gull approaching. Giuseppe. Thank the Great One for Giuseppe, at least.

Within seconds, Giuseppe had landed on a branch near

Oz. "Sorry I'm late. I had to get my Maria situated. Your Preya, she is looking very happy. She had to show us the egg again. Molto bello!"

"Thank you again, Giuseppe. I appreciate Maria being with Preya."

"On my way over, I saw those two squirrels; they're on their way. And I saw Anton and Tilly. They're swimming over from the pond."

Oz felt a flush of embarrassment as Huldah tapped her talons and gave him an 'I told you so' expression.

"And I've been here since 11:55."

Oz jumped at a loud squawk from several feet above, closely followed by a crashing clonk, landing the pelican on a branch just above Oz. "Petunia, I didn't know you were here." Oz inwardly cringed, realizing Petunia had heard him complaining.

"No, you did not." Petunia preened a few ruffled feathers. "I cannot stay long. I will be missed, and people will question where I have been. Can we get this meeting going?"

Giuseppe frowned at Petunia, who sneered back at him. Oz asked himself if the two would ever get along.

"We're here! We're here!" Skamp and Chatty bounded out of the underbrush and clambered up the tree. They stopped on the branch near Huldah, panting to catch their breath. Chatty grabbed her tail and sat on it.

"We have news from Cara. That's why we're late. She called out right as we were leaving, you know, the secret code Anton taught us, so I had to go over and talk to her. And her kids were awake, and they were hungry and making noise and..."

"Chatty, calm down. Let Oz get the meeting going." Scamp put his paws on Chatty's shoulders.

"Alright, already." Chatty switched her whiskers side to side. "I just think everyone wants to know what Cara said." Chatty's tail twitched underneath her.

"They do; let's just wait our turn."

"Ahoy, mateys!" Anton called as he swam ashore and hopped over to the base of the tree. Behind him, Tilly pulled herself out of the water and made her way over.

"Let's get started. Huldah, could you pray?" As Huldah prayed, Oz felt relief swell through him. His small band of volunteers had not deserted him. He was sorry he had doubted. "Chatty and Scamp, what did Cara tell you?"

Chatty jumped up, releasing her tail, which swished in a wide circle behind her. "Cara wanted to come, but she can't because Cronan is busy with the council and always comes back late, so she has to take care of the kids all by herself and…"

Scamp laid his paw gently on her arm. "Sweetheart, tell them what Cara saw."

"Cara saw a man take Hannah and Herbert away, you know, the muscovy couple who just got married last week. They are such a sweet couple and had a really nice wedding, and we got to watch from the oak that grows above…"

Oz's shoulder began to ache. "Chatty, I'm sorry to interrupt you. Did Cara say anything else about the man or what she saw?" Oz was trying hard to contain his aggravation at Chatty's rambling. He hoped no one had heard the edge he felt in his voice. Another reason he was not hatched to be a leader.

"She said he was fat and used a big spider web to get them."

"A spider web? That is ridiculous," Petunia harrumphed and clucked her tongue.

Chatty put her hands on her hips. "I'm just telling you what Cara told me."

"Alright already. Can we get on with this?" Giuseppe raised his wings.

Oz tried to relax his tensed and aching shoulder.

"I think what Cara observed was a capturing device called a net, which, if Cara had not seen one before, a spider web is a good description."

"Thank you, Anton." Chatty shot a glance back at Petunia and imitated her harrumphing sound.

"That is what we saw too. It looked like a fisherman's net," Tilly said.

"Anton, Tilly, tell us what you saw," Oz said.

"Well, as you know, we were on USU duty..."

"And what, again, does USU stand for?" Petunia asked, arching an eyebrow.

"I remember!" Chatty chittered, jumping up and down. "It means 'Under the Otter Sure as a Veil Unit.' "

"Na, that don't sound right. It means 'Under Surface Unlimited,' " Giuseppe said.

Oz rubbed his head, which was starting to throb.

Anton held out his wings and extended his long neck. "It means 'Underwater Surveillance Unit,' of course. Didn't any of you read the Manual of Military Terms I gave you yesterday?"

"I read some until I fell asleep," Tilly said, raising her front foot.

"As I was reporting, we were on USU duty when we responded to distress signals at the pond. Seaman Tilly and I observed a man, likely the same man Cara saw, give chase and capture two Green family ducklings along with their father. He used netting to detain and remove the muscovies."

"This is awful; I can't believe this is happening." Chatty buried her eyes in her paws. "That sweet family broken apart. Which of the children were captured? Was one of them Joey, the bright yellow one?"

"No, not Joey. I think Tina and Sammy," Tilly said.

"So, it has started." Oz flew back up to the branch he had been sitting on. He closed his eyes and sighed. Somewhere in the back of his mind, he had hoped the news about the Ayechoe-aye was not real and that there was no decree to capture and exile the muscovies. But now he had two reports confirming the hideous plan was being executed.

"Anton, Tilly, what about Girdie and the other ducklings?" Huldah asked.

"After the man left, Girdie kept swimming around the pond and honking till her voice was hoarse. The kids were peeping non-stop; I'm sure they do not understand what happened." Tilly retreated slightly into her shell.

"Those poor bambinos. How could they know?" Giuseppe said.

Everyone was silent for a few moments, trying to absorb the tragedies.

"Have you seen anything yourselves, Giuseppe or Petunia?" Oz asked.

"My Maria, she visited our son. He don't want me to come over." Giuseppe wiped his wing across his eyes.

Petunia interrupted. "I can certainly understand not everyone is comfortable being around criminals."

"Get off your high perch, lady; I paid for my crime. I'm not doing that anymore. You're the one that voted to not protect the muscovies," Giuseppe shot back.

"Giuseppe, Petunia, can you please work with me together on this?" Oz pleaded.

Giuseppe sighed. "There are rumors at the squawk fest about a man with a net chasing muscovies. Some say he just chases; others say he captures them. A few saw him take the nets with muscovies away in a big vehicle. But me? Nah, I've not seen anything."

"I cannot say for sure," Petunia said, "but on one of my flights this morning over the neighborhood, I did see a man carrying something struggling in what could have been a net to a large dirty vehicle."

"Does anyone know where the man is taking the muscovies?" Oz asked. Murmurs of 'no' and shaking heads gave him his answer. "Maybe that is something we should find out."

"And, if we know, what could we do?" Petunia questioned as she teetered on her branch.

"I don't know yet. Just seems we should know." Oz felt a hopeless thought threaten to suffocate him. What could he do about any of this? Oz hung his head and wished he could just go back to only being concerned about being a good husband and father.

"Oz, whadayagunnado? You want me to, you know, have a persuasive talk with the guy?" Giuseppe gestured his open wings toward Oz.

"I didn't sign up to be a criminal," Petunia huffed. "I'm still on the council, remember?"

"Petunia, is what is happening to the muscovies right?" Huldah looked directly into Petunia's eyes. "Do you want this to continue?"

"Don't get your tailfeathers in a bunch, Huldah," Petunia squawked. "I told you already that I want to help the muscovies, but if you want me to appear to agree with the council's decision and not attract attention to this effort, I must be discreet. That should be obvious to you all."

"It is," Oz said. "Your position on the council is valuable."

Waving her wings in frustration, Petunia continued. "Do you think pretending to support Obsolom is easy? And quit sneering at me, Giuseppe!"

To Oz, leadership seemed more like refereeing a bunch of argumentative fledglings than guiding wise and civil adults. He now understood what his father meant when he said that leading the council and people was sometimes like trying to herd catfish. They just wanted to dart around on their own.

"At least the humans are not hurting the eggs. I can't imagine anyone being so cruel to do that. And the moms…" Chatty quieted suddenly as Oz raised his wing. "What, Oz?"

"Yesterday, I saw a human reaching into Klaus and Klara's nest." The callousness of the act still wrenched his insides.

Silence again enveloped the group. All they could do was look at each other in bewilderment.

Anton then stood straight and saluted Oz. "Sir! May I make a suggestion?"

"Please do, Anton."

"Along with the USU, ASU, and GSU that are already deployed, we raise the level of involvement to ResOps."

Everyone looked at each other with shrugs.

Tilly sighed. "The turtle can decipher; it's in the manual. Anton means we should start rescue operations along with water, air, and ground surveillance."

A twinge of anticipation spread through the small group. As the seconds ticked slowly by, it seemed to Oz that everyone was holding their breath, waiting for him to speak, to either agree to engage in rescue operations or advise against. Oz felt like he was standing on the edge of an abyss with his wings tied behind his back and a gale-force wind pressing him forward. He looked down and noticed his talons had pierced into the hard oak branch, and his toe knuckles were white from clamping so hard.

Oz felt the Great One's presence. *I will never leave you or forsake you. Be strong and courageous.* A calm assurance rose within his soul.

"We must start rescuing the muscovies."

A unanimous cheer erupted from the group.

"Bada bing! We've got some planning to do!" Giuseppe whistled. Just then, a gull's cry was heard above. "That's my Maria."

"Preya!" Oz leaped off the branch and was soon soaring toward his nest. Huldah followed closely.

Reaching the nest in record time, Oz plopped down, sending bits of palm fluff and leaves spurting into the air. There, he found Preya resting peacefully. Huldah lighted softly on a branch near the nest. Maria had already returned and was standing on the side of the nest next to Preya.

"She's sleeping," Maria whispered.

"What's the matter?" Oz tiptoed over to Preya, who opened her eyes slightly and smiled at him.

"We have another egg, see?" Preya shifted slightly to the right to reveal another perfect egg next to the first one.

With the feeling of elation, Oz also experienced a pang of guilt. "But I wasn't here again for you. I'm so sorry." Oz nuzzled his head against Preya's.

"Oz, us women have been laying eggs all by ourselves for millennia."

Preya's words helped, but Oz thought again about how the protection campaign was keeping him away from Preya. "Do you still think there will be another egg?" Oz looked from Preya to Huldah.

"Oh yes, I know for sure." Preya laid her wing over her belly.

CHAPTER 25

Oz flew high over the canals the next day, searching for the man. Stacks of clouds climbed toward the sun in the day's rising heat. There would be a thunderstorm later. Oz just hoped he could locate the man before the deluge started.

Rounding the bend of the long canal into the lake, Oz spied some activity and heard hissing from a male muscovy below. There was the man. It had to be him. He looked exactly as Chatty and the others had described him. His orange beard bounced around his head as he chased the muscovy through a backyard. A little too late, the muscovy attempted to fly away; the man expertly swung the pole net down on top of the bird, encapsulating the mesh around him.

"Fweep, fweep, ker-cheep!" Oz called to his campaign volunteers from above, diving and rising in a figure-eight pattern repeatedly. "Fweep, fweep, ker-cheep!"

Oz dove directly toward the man and, with the speed and force of a cannonball, flew directly at the man's head with his talons outstretched.

"Fweeeeeeeep!" Oz screamed out as he drew close, seconds away from his target.

"What the..." The man looked up and, seeing the osprey zeroing in on him with his wings outstretched and sharp talons aimed at his face, dropped the net and dove for cover behind a garden wall.

Perfect. Oz had hoped that would happen. He didn't want to hurt a human. Oz quickly adjusted his angle toward the net that was around the muscovy. Oz grabbed the net and worked it off the struggling duck he now recognized.

"Quick, Rolf! Fly away!" Oz called as he tightened his talons around the net. Rolf did not pause and took off over the canal. Oz sprang into the air, dangling the net and pole beneath him, then dropped them into the canal. As it splashed and sunk, Oz felt an exhilarating warmth of victory flow through him. He had saved a muscovy. Oz rose again and repeated his figure-eight calling routine, trying to ignore his aching shoulder. The others would know he had located the man.

Oz kept watching from his aerial view. The man had climbed back over the garden wall, shaking his fists and yelling at Oz. He then went to retrieve his net with the captured muscovy. Running, he searched under bushes and around trees; he had no clue what had happened to his prisoner.

"Blasted duck!" The whole neighborhood probably heard that, Oz thought.

The man finally gave up his search and stomped back toward the street to his van and yanked the side door open. Unmoved by the stink and sound of fear from half a dozen netted muscovies, he reached in and grabbed another pole net. He did not see the two squirrels jump into the van just before he slammed the door shut.

"I can't believe we really did it! We did it, Skamp! We

jumped into the van!"

"Chatty, quick! We have to get to work."

Skamp and Chatty climbed over the piles of netting interspersed with ant-infested fast-food wrappers, empty tobacco pouches, and paper cups with tobacco spittle molding in the bottom. Reaching the six muscovies, they chewed away at each net until the muscovy could escape. Soon, the muscovies were flapping their wings and honking, looking for a way out of the van. They jumped into the front seat and poked at the closed windows with their beaks, colliding with each other and shaking the van in their clamber to get out.

Skamp tried to get their attention. "Shhhhh! Listen, everyone, you have to be quiet!"

Skamp and Chatty finally settled down the muscovies and shared the plan in squeaky whispers.

The man crossed the street and went behind another house. There was no use going back to where he had just been. That netted muscovy would have scared off any others. He laughed to himself. *That stupid duck will die trying to get out of my net.*

Creeping along the side of the canal, the man spied two male muscovies and one female splashing around on the other side of a dock. They could not see the man. Perfect. *I can get at least two of them with one swipe,* the man thought.

"Fweep, fweep, ker-cheep!" Oz cried out, seeing the man approaching the three muscovies.

Petunia heard Oz's call and saw his figure-eight message. She was stationed on a boat lift across the canal.

Oz held his breath as the man approached with the stealth of an alligator toward the ducks. Petunia's timing would need to be perfect. The man trod closer. Still, the muscovies were oblivious, enjoying their playful bath. The man was now less than ten feet away and was easing his net into position. The knot in Oz's stomach tightened as the man drew his net high. Three more steps. Two.

Kersplash!

Oz watched as a seven-foot plume of water shot up from the canal, drenching the man, knocking him off balance in his lunge for the muscovies, and causing him to fall into the canal. He splashed around to grab and hang onto the seawall. The muscovies had flown off. He watched his hat slowly sink several feet from him. Petunia bobbed up and down near the man on the waves her cannonball plunge had created. Was that a smile on her beak?

Hanging onto the seawall, the man looked around and, seeing Petunia, shouted a curse. Petunia looked directly at him and, with a long squawk, flew away.

After several attempts, the man finally dragged himself onto a nearby kayak dock. Trailing puddles of water, he sloshed over to where he had dropped his net under a cypress. Looking across the canal, he saw Petunia up on the boat lift. She held her head high, looking directly down at him.

"You stinkin' pelican." The man cursed again. "I can get rid of pelicans if I need to." Oz heard Petunia honk at the man.

"Fweep, fweep, fweep!"

"And you too, you scrawny fish hawk!" The man pointed up at Oz with his net.

As the man turned to head back to his van. Oz

saw movement about twenty feet away on the seawall. Unaware of the previous events or the dangers around him, a male muscovy was waddling along the seawall toward the man.

"Fweep, fweep, ker-cheep!" Oz tried to warn from above, but the muscovy was preoccupied with getting to where he was going or did not recognize the call. He kept heading toward the man. Humans were generally not feared and might give out a free meal. The muscovy also knew he could get away soon enough. All he needed was about five feet to escape.

Oz saw that the man, half concealed by the cypress, had also noticed the muscovy approaching. He slowly raised his seven-foot pole and simply stood still, letting the muscovy plod toward him. This looked too horrifyingly easy. And there was no way Oz or Petunia could do anything about this; they were too far away. With one quick swoosh, the duck was bagged.

"No mite-infested bird is going to stop me!" The man secured the net and trekked up through the yard, careful to stay under the protection of trees in case the osprey tried to attack again. He was not going to let this duck get away. Reaching the street, he ran to where his van was parked and grabbed the handle to jerk open the back doors. He had already removed the net from the pole to throw the struggling bird in the back along with the others he had caught that morning.

Just as the trapper opened the door, a crow flew close overhead and let the previous day's digested waste plop directly on his hatless forehead with the precision of an Air Force bomber. The man swiped at his eyes with the back of his hand.

At that exact moment, the door burst toward him,

knocking him to the ground behind the van and causing him to drop the net. Out from the van shot the six angry muscovies. Some flew out wildly, sending shreds of netting and trash from the van all around. The rest landed directly on the man, scraping his arms and ripping his shirt with their claws in their clamber to escape. Two squirrels had also leaped from the van, over the man, and to the net, quickly severing several strands with their sharp teeth before they bounded up a nearby tree. The muscovy kicked the net loose and flew away just as the stunned man rolled over to grab the net.

Oz watched from above. This could not have gone better! Eleven muscovies saved! And the campaign was just starting.

CHAPTER 26

Oz awoke startled to hear Preya moaning. She had moved herself to the far side of the nest and was crouched down, holding her belly.

"Preya, what's wrong?" Oz jumped over to her and laid his wing on her shoulder.

"I think another egg is coming." Preya let out a loud groan, holding her eyes shut, gritting her beak together, and clenching her belly.

"What can I do? Should I go get Huldah?" Oz had started pacing back and forth in front of Preya.

Preya panted as she recovered from the contraction. "I'm fine."

"Are you sure? You don't look good. Can I rub your neck or shoulders? Should I lay on the other eggs?" Oz hopped over to the two eggs. The moonlight reflected off them, making them seem to glow with hope.

"Oz, just calm down. This is normal."

A muffled shriek escaped Preya's beak. Oz hurried over to her, folding and unfolding his wings. His body wrenched with anxious pangs. "Preya, what can I do?"

"Nothing. Go sit on the other side of the nest." Preya's voice shrilled in the night breeze. She took one more deep breath and held it; clamping her eyes shut, she braced herself with her wings against the side of the nest and pushed with the contraction of her belly. And then, she collapsed. Her head hung low, and her eyes were closed as she panted softly. Her wings lay limp against her sides, resting on the nest.

Oz rushed to her side. "Preya! Tell me you're alright." Her breathing had calmed, but she just lay there blinking her eyes. Oz's thoughts conflicted between staying with Preya and flying to get Huldah. He was sure there was something very wrong with Preya. He hovered close and held her wing, stroking her beautiful white crown.

After what seemed like hours to Oz but was, in fact, hardly five minutes, Preya stirred and reached her wing out to Oz and slowly stood up, tottering on her feet. Carefully, she stepped to the side. There, where Preya had been sitting, was another egg. This one was noticeably larger than the first two. "No wonder this one gave me so much pain," Preya said with a smile in her voice. "Oh, Oz, isn't it amazing?"

"Chireeeep!" Oz called out into the night. They had been trying to have a family for two years and now had three beautiful eggs.

"Do you think this one is a boy or a girl? I can't believe we are going to have three chicks soon! The Great One is so good to us!" Oz gyrated around the nest in an excited dance, pumping his wings up and down. "Have you thought of any more names? I know we have considered Olaf and Oliver and Owen for boys and Prasha, Primrose, and Prudence for girls, but I don't know if I like Olaf or Prudence. And I suppose we won't know until they hatch. They may just pick out their own names."

"Oz, you are being so silly!" Preya's look of love toward Oz warmed him to the tip of his talons. "And I think we need one more name on the lists."

Oz was now walking around the perimeter of the nest

with his wings against his back. "So that we have a backup? Good idea. How about, um…"

"No, Oz, I still have an egg to lay. We are going to have four eggs."

"Four eggs? Four? Well, that does happen, but two or three are the normal clutch. Are you sure?"

Preya chuckled softly. "I think I know what an egg feels like in my belly, and another egg is growing."

"Maybe you just have indigestion?"

"I don't have indigestion!" Preya was laughing out loud now as she watched the expression on Oz's face turn from disbelief to surprise to elation and then to sober realization.

"I'm going to have four kids to raise at once?"

"*We* are going to have four kids to raise at once. Oh, Oz, you are being silly. If the Great One gives us four children, don't you think he will give us the ability and means to bring them up?"

Oz's expression relaxed to a tentative trust. "Yes, if there is anything I have been learning the last few days, the Great One helps me get through all kinds of situations."

"We just need to keep remembering that. Now help me roll this beautiful large egg to the others so I can keep them warm together." As they gently rolled the egg, Preya noticed Oz looking at her with the softest look of endearment. His eyes were moist, and his beak curved in a crooked little smile.

"I love you too, Oz," Preya said as she nuzzled her head against his chest. "Go on now; I need new bedding, and I am as hungry as a robin after a day of migration."

CHAPTER 27

Girdie swam along the side of the canal with her remaining seven ducklings. She knew she could not stay in the canal forever; she would have to bring her family up to the lawns to forage for insects. They could get some nourishment from the spiders and bugs that lived on the pilings and underside of docks, but that would not be enough to sustain them. But getting out of the canal meant being on land where that man was. As she had watched from the canals and lakes the past few days since he took Gunther, Tina, and Sammy, the man seemed to appear out of nowhere. Just this morning, she witnessed him chasing and capturing the Brown family: Bertha, Brun, and all their ducklings.

"Mommy, I'm scared," Joey said as he paddled closer to Girdie.

"I know, baby, just stay close to me."

Girdie worried most for Joey. His bright yellow feathers made him an easy target, even at night. She prayed his plumage would change quickly to the muted tones of his siblings.

Girdie heard a boat engine sputtering slowly toward them from down the canal. As it came into view, she saw it was a small row boat with a small motor on the back. Fear impaled her as she recognized the man in the boat. It was the same man that had taken away her family, friends, and relatives. He was looking directly at her with a downturned mouth and a dark gleam in his eyes. The pole with the net on the end was lying across the boat in easy reach.

"Kids! Quick! Under the dock! Get against the canal wall!"

The ducklings obeyed and peeped wildly, scrunching together alongside the wall. This particular dock had been built many years ago and badly needed repair. Many of the boards were missing, and others were splintered and rotted. The dock covered about six feet of the wall and jutted into the canal about four feet. Two dirty and moldy kayaks lay upside down on top of the dock. While the ducklings were relatively safe and out of reach of the trapper, Girdie's size made it almost impossible to get under the dock. As she struggled to get her form under the crossbeams of the dock, she felt the metal hoop of the pole net smash against her back.

Pain rushed through her body and down her left wing as she paddled to the other side of the dock, trying to find a bigger opening. Close behind her, the boat maneuvered, and out of the corner of her eye, she saw the man get in position to swipe at her again with the net. Girdie realized her efforts to get under the dock were futile. Her ducklings were frantically peeping, but she could not get to them. "Stay where you are. I will come back for you."

She took the only action that made sense to her. If she could not get to safety under the dock, she could at least distract the man away from her ducklings. Swimming around toward the man and his boat, she pulled herself out of the water, flying directly for the man's head while trying to ignore the pain in her left wing. As she came near him, the trapper made a pass at her with his net and just caught the tips of her tail feathers as she made a sharp right turn, flying out toward the middle of the canal where, honking loudly, she plunked in the water about twenty feet from the boat.

The man, exclaiming angry words, reached around to the motor, gunned the engine, and steered toward Girdie. Girdie waited till the last moment and lifted again, intending to fly again at the trapper's head and lure him further away from her children. As she rushed toward him, she banked again to the right, but her wounded wing would not extend its full length to give her the turning momentum she needed. The man reached toward Girdie with the net, and while she could turn away some, he delivered another hard blow to the same wing. Searing pain shot up and down Girdie's wing, forcing her to fall into the water where all she could do was paddle. Her wing hung loosely at her side as she dragged it through the water. At least she could still lead the man away from her family. Even if he captured her, the kids could still be safe.

But the man did not follow Girdie. "I'll come back for you, lame duck." The man snarled as he pointed his muddy finger at Girdie and turned the boat back toward the dock where the ducklings were.

As he neared the dock, he heard the ducklings peeping underneath it. "Shut up brats." The ducklings huddled together at the midpoint of the dock against the canal. "You no match for me."

As Girdie watched from the middle of the canal, the man tied his boat up to the dock and hefted himself onto it. Climbing around the kayaks and carefully avoiding loose and missing planks, he went over to the left side of the dock. Taking something out of a pocket from his trousers, he unfurled a net. Attached to either end of the net were ropes, which he tied to the front and back of the dock at the corner posts near the planks. He then let the net into the water, effectively blocking off the left side of the dock. He pulled two more nets out of his pocket and did the same to the back of the dock and most of the right side of the dock, leaving only a small opening.

All during this work, Girdie watched as the ducklings peeped louder. She could tell by their crying that they were swimming under the dock, not staying together by the canal wall. Just then, she saw Joey jump up on the dock through a hole left by a missing plank. The man was on his stomach, securing the ropes under the dock, and had not seen Joey.

"Run Joey!" Girdie honked in desperate tones. Joey turned toward her and, for a moment, looked like he was going to come to her. Girdie knew she could not protect him with her injured wing. "No, Joey! Run away!"

Joey turned toward the lawn at the edge of the dock and was just about to hop off the dock when the trapper noticed the escaping quarry. Rolling onto his side, he reached toward Joey but caught the edge of his sleeve on a rusty nail protruding from where a missing plank had been. As he cried out in agony, a red streak quickly formed on his arm. "You blasted varmint!" Joey had now reached a row of thick hedges, where he dove into their protective covering.

While the trapper turned his attention back to the remaining ducklings, Girdie saw a greater danger swoop down onto the lawn near the bushes where Joey was crouched and frantically peeping. Crete, the great blue heron, had witnessed the scene from a perch in the oak above and hoped for an easy meal if the ducklings started scattering. Joey was an easy target. Even in the gloom of the underbrush, Crete could see the bright yellow duckling shaking in fear.

"Come out, little duckling; your destiny is mine." Crete's mesmerizing voice slithered through the bushes, and Joey's peeping calmed. "Come to me. Come to me." The enormous bird repeated his chant while stepping closer, one small silent step after another, and keeping his eyes locked on his prey. All he needed was to get two feet from Joey with a clear enough opening in the bushes. Girdie watched in desperation as the heron drew back his neck and thrust his four-inch bill into the bushes. One loud, anguished peep was all Girdie heard. Crete pulled back his head and flew away as downy yellow feathers drifted slowly to the ground.

"Joey!" Girdie cried out with calls of despair.

"Mommy! Mommy!" She heard her other six children calling her in their panic. They were desperate to be with her, and to her terror, she saw them emerging from the small opening the trapper had left and were heading out into the canal to get to her. No sooner had the ducklings swam out than the trapper scooped them out in one sweep of the net. All six ducklings squirmed and peeped in a pile at the bottom of the net.

"Got you! Can't escape from me!" The trapper grinned, exposing his brown teeth, and spat a phlegmy wad of tobacco juice onto the dock. Climbing into the boat with the net, the trapper untied the boat and started up the smoking engine. "Coming for you, lame mama! You can be with your stinkin' brats again!" Steering the boat out in the canal, he looked to see where Girdie was. She could not fly or go far with an injured wing. But she was nowhere to be seen.

"Blast it!" The trapper swore and yelled, gunning the engine to move the boat back and forth across the canal. He drove slowly by docks and boat lifts to see if she was hiding around them. He peered into yards. He poked his head through the railings of gazebos. "That duck ain't seen the last of me," the trapper growled as he turned his boat around. "Tomorrow is another day." As he sped out of the canal toward the lake, a cloud of black soot trailed from the boat, and the 'No Wake Zone' buoy bounced wildly up and down.

CHAPTER 28

"**Q**uiet!" Mary Margaret commanded her ducklings as they peeped with fearful excitement. "Get back under the bushes farther." Mary Margaret had heard Girdie calling and had watched the man trying to capture what was left of the muscovy's family. Joey had escaped and was running up toward the bushes where she and her five ducklings were.

"Joey, come in here!" Mary Catherine peeped.

"Get back and be quiet!" Mary Margaret shoved her daughter further back and watched Joey run into the bushes, still calling out to Girdie. And then, the heron plucked Joey out. With a swoosh of large wings, he was gone.

After a tearful roll call, her ducklings nestled close to Mary Margaret. "Children, what you just saw will not be the last time you see something like that. You need to be wary of the Great Blues, but the muscovies are sanctioned for the herons. Stay away from the muscovies. Mary Catherine—do you understand me?"

Hrack, hrack, hrack! Hrack, hrack, hrack!

Shannon looked up from her backyard flower bed, where she had been weeding, and saw a green muscovy standing on one of the pilings by their dock. "Mrs. Green!" Muscovies came in a wide range of colors and combinations of plumage. Some were mottled black and white, some were primarily black with a white chest or a white wing stripe, some were mostly brown, and still others, like this pair she had named Mr. and Mrs. Green, had iridescent green heads and wing pinions. There were unlimited combinations. They were all different.

Hrack, hrack, hrack! Hrack, hrack, hrack!

It was unusual for the muscovy to be making so much noise; Shannon had half expected the noise to be coming from one of the mallards who always had to make themselves known. Where was Mr. Green and the ducklings? Mrs. Green must be calling to them to come to her.

The pair had been coming to Shannon's morning feeding for several years. Three weeks ago, they had proudly paraded their new brood of sixteen ducklings, keeping them a safe distance away but showing them off nonetheless.

As usual, the number of ducklings had dwindled over the past two weeks, and a few days ago, Shannon had counted only nine. It was always sad for Shannon. She would wonder what the fate of the missing ducklings had been. It could be anything from falling prey to a great blue heron or coyote getting trapped in the canal and drowning to just being too weak to live.

And now there was the new danger of being captured by the trapper.

Hrack, hrack, hrack! Hrack, hrack, hrack! Hrack, hrack, hrack!

Mrs. Green's cries were getting louder and seemed to be full of grief. "Oh, Mrs. Green!" Shannon dropped her tools, stood up, and ran down to the canal's edge where the piling stood.

Hrack, hrack, hrack! Hrack, hrack, hrack!

Shannon felt sad as she realized Mrs. Green was calling to Mr. Green and her ducklings, hoping they would come to her but sensing they could not. The trapper must have taken them. That was the only explanation.

"Oh, Mrs. Green, I'm so sorry!" Shannon's eyes stung. She wished she could somehow comfort the bereaved duck. She couldn't imagine what it must be like to lose your husband and your children like that. Even more horrific, Shannon realized that Mrs. Green had probably witnessed it all. Trapping was the only thing that made sense to have taken her family away from her so suddenly.

Mrs. Green attempted to fly over to Shannon but fell awkwardly on the dock. Shannon could see her left wing had a deep gash and was bleeding. Mrs. Green chirruped softly as she waddled around Shannon's feet, dragging her injured wing. Exhausted, she plopped in front of Shannon and laid her head on Shannon's foot.

Shannon's tears slid down her cheek as she bent down and reached out her hand to Mrs. Green. Surprised that the muscovy did not pull away or object, she gently touched her head and stroked the green feathers with her finger. None of the ducks had allowed Shannon to get that close and certainly not touch them. Mrs. Green relaxed her shoulders and breathed out a long sigh.

Shannon's compassion for the bird caused a rising heat of anger at the HOA's decision to depopulate the muscovies. It was cruel to remove the muscovies from their home and to break up families. The trapper probably hurt Mrs. Green. This had to stop. It couldn't go on.

Shannon carefully stepped away and hurried to get her veterinary supplies to clean and bandage Mrs. Green's injury. Returning to the backyard minutes later, Mrs. Green was gone. Shannon sat and wept as she pulled out her phone to text Jared about what she had seen. As president, he needed to know that muscovies were being injured because of the HOA's decision.

CHAPTER 29

Intense conversation and blaring emergency alarms filled Sophie's ears as she headed out the screen door to the gazebo on the dock. She carried two plates of sandwiches.

"Jeffrey, are you and that anhinga watching *The Hunt for Red October* again?" Sophie walked over to Jeffrey, careful to step around a sleeping Duke, their eleven-year-old golden retriever. She placed the plates on the bar and sat on the barstool next to her husband. "And put out that smelly pipe, please, while we eat."

Jeffrey tamped out the pipe in the ashtray and paused the movie. "Yep, he's my movie buddy. That bird showed up as soon as I put in the DVD. He takes his usual spot on that piling and spreads his wings to dry."

"I always know when you're watching submarine movies. I can see him from the kitchen window."

"Yeah, he likes submarine movies. He will watch the whole thing with me. Sometimes he stays for an Air Force or battleship movie, but he'll take off if it's a Western."

Without raising his head, Duke thumped his tail up and down on the wooden floor planks.

Jeffrey took off his Navy cap, setting it beside himself on the bar. The ceiling fan above gently wafted down and cooled his nappy head. "And the craziest thing is that he seems to understand what is happening. He makes that funny gurgling noise whenever there is a good action scene."

"Well, I think he is an old Navy veteran like you, Jeffrey. Looks like he is graying around the temples, too."

"Graying? I'm long past graying," Jeffrey chuckled as he looked in the mirror over the bar. His thick black hair had turned white years ago and was barbered in a short military cut against his dark skin. He still maintained a trimmed beard and mustache, even though Sophie would prefer he shave them off.

Just then, a sputtering engine propelled a small boat through the canal, sending waves against the sea wall and leaving a gasoline-smelling cloud of soot. A gruff-looking man with a long red beard piloted the boat toward the lake.

Duke barked, jumped up, and ran over to the canal side of the gazebo, putting his front paws up on the railing. Jeffrey quickly followed and cupped his hands around his mouth to form a megaphone. "Slow down! This is a no-wake zone!"

The man turned to Jeffrey, sneered, and spat into the canal. Without slowing down, he sped forward while grabbing a net containing several squirming muscovy ducklings, held it high above his head, and threw it back into the boat's hull.

"That must be the trapper the HOA hired to remove muscovies." Jeffrey strolled back to his stool, scratching his head. Duke remained at the railing and whined.

"Well, I don't like him, and I don't think your anhinga friend does either!"

Anton stood on the piling, squawking and jutting his head out toward the retreating boat. He hoped his call would alert some of the volunteers; maybe they could save the ducklings.

Sophie stood up and watched the boat as it turned into the lake. "Those poor baby ducks! I hate to think what may have happened to their parents. Does the HOA know what an awful man he is? He looks malicious to me."

"He didn't slow down at all when I called to him."

Sophie sat down and crossed her legs. The sandwich remained untouched in front of her. "I know the newsletter said he was taking them to a reserve, but in what condition? Did you see him throw the net full of baby ducks back into the boat?"

"I did." Jeffrey picked up his sandwich and took a small bite. "I'll email Jared about what we saw."

Sophie pointed over to the piling where the anhinga stood and squawked. "Jeffrey, look at that large turtle with the orange mark over by the anhinga. What is it doing?"

"You know, I see that turtle around often when the anhinga is here. It looks like it is trying to get the anhinga's attention." Duke, still at the railing, watched also, his ears perked and tail wagging.

Four feet below Anton's perch, Tilly bobbed up and down in the water and swam back and forth, trying to get the anhinga's attention. "Anton! We must find Girdie and help her; she's been hurt!"

"Lead the way, Seaman!"

Jeffrey and Sophie watched as the anhinga bent his head toward the turtle and let out a loud *hronk*. The turtle disappeared under the water, and the bird took off, flying down the canal in the direction the boat had come from.

CHAPTER 30

Othello circled high above and watched below as the trapper pulled alongside a dock with peeping muscovy ducklings hiding beneath. A growing sense of disgust drew bile up into his throat. He had endured the embarrassment at the council meeting of "stepping down" from his nomination to be on the council. Othello, better than others, understood his father's shrouded intentions. He had been willing to support him, in the beginning anyway. When Obsolom first took the respected position of leader, he had assured the community that he would carry on the pillars of community protection and fairness to all the animals. However, as the days passed, Othello noticed his father's initial public facade chipping away.

Growing up, Othello had seen the darker side of his father. Once, when his mother, Priscilla, had returned empty-taloned to the nest after an unsuccessful fishing spree, Obsolom had exploded with rage and called her useless. Another time Othello came home with a black eye from a young osprey with whom he had gotten into an argument. When he told his father he did not fight back, Obsolom struck Othello across the cheek with his wing, calling him weak and an embarrassment. But profuse apologies had been made, and these family matters had been kept private. Other incidences had happened over the years, but Obsolom was always regretful and would do whatever he could to smooth things over. Othello loved and respected his father despite the occasional burst of anger. There was nothing he would not do for Obsolom—including stepping away from being on the council. Maybe another opportunity will present itself in the future. Or maybe, Othello did not want to be a part of what he saw happening on the council.

Just then, Othello heard wild hronking below from the muscovy mom. One of the ducklings, a bright yellow one, had somehow gotten out of the water and was running up the lawn. As he ran into the bushes, Othello saw a movement in the tree above, and then he saw Crete dive down after the duckling. Othello knew Crete had already reached his allowance of muscovy ducklings for the season, but with the council's decision to allow the Great Blues unlimited ducklings, he could legally hunt again. A fresh heatwave of nausea flowed through Othello as Crete's head disappeared into the bushes and reappeared with a struggling yellow duckling in his bill.

As the heron flew above the lake, Othello's attention was caught by movement below. He watched in disbelief as a gull shot up from the water and rammed into Crete with a full-body blow. Even though the gull was only a quarter of the size of Crete, the jolt was enough to make Crete drop the duckling. Othello had never seen anything like this. Gulls ate fish, not muscovy ducklings.

Even stranger, the gull then looked directly up at Othello and gave a call of alarm. Without thinking, Othello hugged his wings close to his body and dove straight toward the falling duckling with his talons outstretched. The yellow ball was peeping frantically, and as Othello neared him, he could see his eyes growing wider as the duckling saw he was going from the heron's mouth into an osprey's talons.

Othello reached the duckling just as he was about to crash into the water and, as gently as an osprey can, wrapped his talons around the duckling, creating a cage. Back up into the clouds, Othello soared. And then it hit him; what was he going to do now? The duckling was deathly still in Othello's talons; he hoped he had not killed it. Othello looked below. Both Crete and the gull were gone.

Othello flew back and forth as conflicting thoughts raced through his mind. If the duckling had died, he needed to drop it somewhere. He would certainly not eat it; the thought of eating fowl was foul. Only if he were starving would a proper osprey stoop to that. If it was still alive, could he return it to his mother? Othello saw she was injured. She could not care for the duckling, and the trapper would get it. And isn't that what the council had sanctioned?

Hot anger erupted in Othello. The muscovies had as much right to live here as anyone, no matter what his father believed or the council had agreed on.

The duckling stirred in Othello's talons. "Hang on, little one." Othello peered at the duckling, who was now shaking uncontrollably. I must seem like a monster to him, Othello thought.

Othello banked to the left and headed toward a grove of trees. A visit to Uncle Oz and Aunt Huldah was in order.

CHAPTER 31

"Yes, Oz, Preya is fine. And yes, there is another egg developing."

"You are sure about that, Huldah? It couldn't just be indigestion?"

"Oz, will you stop it?"

"Who, or what is that?" Preya was looking above and behind Oz and Huldah toward the lake.

Oz turned his head. "It looks like Othello, but what is that yellow thing he is clutching?"

Within seconds, Othello had reached the nest and, hovering close above it, gently opened his talons to release the yellow fluff of feathers. Othello then lighted on a branch close to the nest.

The duckling dropped the few inches into the soft nest and lay still. Othello slightly waved his wing and put on an exaggerated smile. "Hi, Uncle Oz!"

Oz studied the yellow lump. He could see the duckling's chest rising and falling rapidly and heard his tiny heart thumping as he glanced from osprey to osprey, blinking his eyes and shaking. "Othello, why did you bring this muscovy duckling here? This is my family's nest; it is an osprey nest."

"I didn't know what else to do." Othello then told everything he had seen and how he could not leave the duckling to die. "My father is wrong. I know that now."

Oz approached Othello. "But why bring it here? What am I supposed to do with it?"

The yellow duckling peeped slightly and moved his legs and wings. Preya leaned closer. "He is saying something about seeing a big eagle."

Othello stood a bit taller. "The little fellow probably thought I was an eagle." Preya and Huldah caught each other's eyes.

Othello continued, "Uncle Oz, your secret campaign is not as secret as you think."

Oz turned his head back to Huldah. "Is this true?"

"I know that there are many eyes and ears in our community. You knew we would not be able to hide behind the screen of secrecy forever."

"Uncle Oz, before seeing what I saw today, I was ready to tell Dad all I knew about your campaign and then help him put a stop to it—but seeing that brave gull attack Crete sparked my courage to finally see what I need to do. I'm ready to help you in the campaign. You have my support."

The duckling continued to peep softly and struggled to stand. In all the commotion, his right leg had been broken near the ankle, and his foot was bent awkwardly underneath him.

"Oh! Aunt Huldah! Can you do something for his leg?" Moved by compassion, Preya carefully stepped over to the duckling and ushered him with her bill back to where her three eggs were. She tucked him under her wing, where he immediately fell asleep, his breathing calming to a rhythmic cadence.

"Preya, don't do that; the eggs might get contaminated!" Oz jumped over to Preya, ready to take the yellow intruder somewhere away from his family nest.

"Oz, I can't believe you are acting like this. You are supposed to protect the muscovies." Preya held her wing close to the duckling.

"Protecting them is one thing. The Great One has asked me to do that, and I'm all in. They should be protected. But I don't think that means I have to live with them." Oz had started hopping around the nest and flinging out his wings.

Preya stuck out her beak. "*Them* is this poor orphan who just watched his mother be brutally wounded and his siblings snatched away. And then he almost got eaten by Crete! I'm not letting you take him away."

Oz had never seen Preya so fiercely defy him. He sat abruptly down and looked directly at her. "You cannot keep the muscovy duckling. What and how are you going to feed it? They eat bugs and snails, not fish!"

"I'm sure *you* can catch a few bugs and snails for him." Preya leveled her stare directly into Oz's eyes.

"What? Not only do I have to live with it, but I have to feed it? No!" Oz wrapped his wings across his chest and scowled down at Preya. The duckling awoke and was now peeping under Preya's wing.

Preya nuzzled her beak on the yellow lump. "*It* has a name. This is Joey."

Oz felt a teeny pinch of remorse at his behavior. This must be the same Joey they discussed at the volunteer meeting the other day.

Huldah tried unsuccessfully to stifle a chuckle. "Oz, just give up. You and Othello go and get some bugs and snails. Figure out a long-term solution. Right now, Preya is doing what she is meant to do. Be a protective mother."

"I can't believe this! My whole family is against me!"

Oz stomped around the nest with his wings up in the air. "Fine! Othello and I will try and get some gross bugs and slimy snails. But if that yellow thing dies before I get back, make sure you thoroughly clean the nest."

Preya watched Oz and Othello fly off and land in a clearing several hundred yards from their nesting tree. Even at that distance, she could hear Oz and Othello sputtering at each other and complaining as they pecked around the ground for bugs and snails.

"I never thought I would see ospreys trying to act like ducks!" Huldah laughed and pointed at the pair.

"Aunt Huldah, I don't understand Oz. Why is he so against Joey being here?" Preya pecked a gentle kiss on Joey's head. "I can't let Oz take him away and dump him somewhere."

Joey ventured out from underneath Preya's wing and hobbled out in front of her, dragging his useless right foot. "Where is my mama?"

"Oh, sweetie, I don't know. But we will do all we can to find her and get you back to her." Preya gathered the duckling back close to her.

"Will that mean osprey eat me?" Joey looked into her eyes.

"Absolutely not, you are safe here. Aunt Huldah and I will not let anything bad happen to you." Tears slipped down Preya's face. She stroked the tiny yellow head with her beak and preened his downy feathers.

CHAPTER 32

Obsolom watched as Crete descended on a branch near him, shaking the snag as he landed.

"What news do you come with? I perceive it cannot be good based on the ugly scowl on your face."

"Treason!"

"Keep your voice low. Explain yourself." Obsolom stood tall and glowered at Crete.

"Treason from your own family."

"Are you referring to the mockery of a protection campaign that Oz thinks he can organize and lead? I have no concerns about that. It is destined to fail. At the most, all they will do is observe as the neighborhood is rid of the muscovies." Obsolom reached back and smoothed his long, silky tail feathers. "Their failure will set my brother up as a laughingstock for generations. My reign will be embraced all the more by the people."

"Do you know that their efforts have escalated from mere observance to protecting and defending the muscovies?"

"What nonsense is this?" Obsolom whipped his head back around to look Crete in the eyes.

"And that Othello, your son, has joined their efforts?" Crete raised his beak and tilted his head sideways to peer at Obsolom.

Obsolom leaped over and shoved his beak into Crete's face. "Tell me exactly what you know."

"That gull convict and Othello worked together to save one of the muscovy ducklings."

"Ska-reeeeek! That is ludicrous!" Obsolom held his belly as he laughed in hracking squawks. "Othello would never do anything against my wishes." Obsolom's tone turned ominous. "Not if he knows what is good for him."

Crete hissed. "You would be wise to take me seriously."

"Crete, my fine-feathered friend. Tell me what happened. And do not consider lying or leaving out any details."

"I had caught one of the muscovy ducklings as it tried to escape the trapper and was bringing it back to my nest where I could enjoy my lunch when, out of nowhere, that huge gull who had been convicted of knocking fish out of an osprey's talons rammed into me. My grasp loosened on the duckling, which I should have just eaten when I caught it, and it fell toward the lake. Then, like a lightning bolt from heaven, Othello, your son, swooped down, caught the duckling, and flew off with it."

"So, let me get this straight," Obsolom again laughed in hracking squawks. "A gull made you lose your dinner, and Othello got the dinner instead?"

Crete uncoiled his S-shaped neck toward Obsolom. "You know as well as I do that osprey—especially your family—do not eat fowl."

"Do you *know* that Othello did not eat the duckling? If not, what did he do with it?"

"I thought it more important to chase after the gull and bring him into custody to have him expelled from the community forever. Or be executed."

"And where is the gull?" Obsolom tapped his talon on

the branch, waiting for an answer. "Obviously, you do not know. The gull also escaped from you."

"Obsolom, I am warning you. Do not take this lightly, and do not demean me. Having me as an ally has many benefits for you. Having me as an enemy will drag you off your lofty self-fabricated throne and ruin your aspirations."

Obsolom drilled his gaze into Crete. "As I stated before, my esteemed stature in this community has more to do with my efforts and supreme leadership than anything you have done or can do for me."

Obsolom leaped up to a branch higher than Crete. "You can already see that under my rule, our community has united for the greater good of supporting the humans in their effort to remove the muscovies. Therefore, what you reported about the gull and Othello warrants further investigation. Any act against my ruling threatens the harmony and safety of all our residents. I will question Othello myself. I will know if what he tells me is true; he never could deceive me."

CHAPTER 33

Oz pecked furiously at the ground, sending up spurts of dirt and pine needles, looking for grubs and large insects for Joey. That muscovy duckling had a voracious appetite. Oz sputtered out a mouthful of dust and chastised himself again for agreeing to let that duckling stay with them yesterday. Ospreys do not raise muscovy ducklings and certainly don't peck at the ground for bugs.

Oz glanced up at the sun and realized that if he didn't find some bugs soon, he would be late for the volunteer meeting, which would not help the fragile alliance. Giuseppe distrusted Petunia, and Anton was driving everyone up the wall with his military jargon. Chatty often took over the conversation with senseless chitter, and Oz was weary of Petunia's superior attitude, especially toward Giuseppe. The worst thing was that Oz was not a leader like his father or brother. No, he could not be late and give the volunteers any reason not to trust him.

Knowing he couldn't go back to the nest empty-beaked, Oz gave up on the patch of ground that was now dotted with numerous large borings. Leaping into the air, he soon soared fifty feet above the ground. His bum shoulder ached as he sped over the conservation area, and the manicured park came into view. Below, several female mallards and their ducklings were foraging for food.

Circling high above, he kept his eyes on the mallards to see how they got bugs. It looked easy enough; they simply walked around, grabbed the bugs from the air, or pecked them off the ground with their round bills. Maybe he had just been looking in the wrong place.

The mallards waddled to the pond, and Oz dove to where they had been. Landing softly on the grass, he looked around, hoping he had not been seen. He could pretend he had dropped a fish and was looking for it if asked. Oz imitated the way the mallards had been getting food. He jutted his sharp, curved beak back and forth into the air as he walked along. No bugs. He pecked in the exact same spots the mallards had. No bugs. He tried scraping the ground with his talons, making a few deep gashes. No bugs. Maybe he had to scare the bugs out of the ground. He jumped up and down from foot to foot, extending his wings to their five-foot span. No bugs. Oz looked up at the position of the sun again. Maybe he had to make noise.

Leaping up and letting out a screech, Oz felt a hot wave of cringing embarrassment. The mother mallards and ducklings had gathered nearby, watching his antics. One of them politely had her wing tip over her bill as she tried to muffle a mirthful honk.

"What are you laughing at? I dropped my mullet." Oz grasped at the hope that the ducks might believe him. But their growing laughter told him otherwise. Oz noticed Mary Margaret in the group, looking at him with a doubtful expression.

"Oz, really, what are you doing?" The polite mallard asked. However, her politeness soon evaporated as she no longer tried to hide her laughter. "It looks to me like you are trying to get bugs."

Oz looked up at the sun again, realizing there was no way, at this rate, he could both get more bugs and get to the meeting on time. He was also struggling with what to tell the mallards. They could not know he was harboring a condemned muscovy duckling, even if Joey was kind of cute.

"Is Preya having strange egg-laying cravings?" Another mallard asked.

"Uh, yes! That's it!" Oz felt a wave of relief. "Egg-laying cravings! She keeps asking for bugs." Well, Oz thought, it was true she was asking for bugs. "And, as you can see, I can't seem to get any." Oz spread out his wings, tips up, and shrugged his shoulders. Maybe this would work out if they had pity on him or at least on Preya.

"Well, you are not a duck." Mary Margaret strutted up to Oz. "Of course, you can't get bugs." Mary Margaret peered intently at Oz. "I have never heard of an osprey craving bugs."

Oz had to think fast. "Uh, well, neither have I, but she's been wanting a bunch of them every day." Appeal to their motherly nature, Oz told himself. "And now we are finally going to have some chicks of our own, like you all have your precious babies." Oz reached out his wings to the mallard ducklings peeping around their moms.

Soft 'awwws' and clucking spread through the group. A few of the moms nuzzled their children.

"If I could just bring her back a bunch of bugs right now, she would be so happy." Oz looked down and pretended to be sad. "Have you heard we have three eggs, and she's going to have another?"

Happy clucks and excited gasps were exchanged between the moms.

"Good grief," Mary Margaret clucked, "just ask if you want us to get some bugs for you. Preya is a good girl."

"Oh, would you, please?" Oz smiled at Mary Margaret, clasping his wingtips together under his chin.

"Ladies, let's get Preya some bugs."

With that, a hefty pile of bugs accumulated in a few minutes in front of Oz. Even some of the ducklings helped, running back and forth, catching small bugs, and peeping at Oz as they added to the mound. Mary Margaret brought over a large sea-grape leaf, which they used to scoop up the bugs and then fold around them, forming a pouch.

"Thank you, ladies. Preya and I are in your debt." Oz bowed to them and, clutching the pouch of bugs with his talons, took off toward home.

"If Preya wants more bugs, come back and see us," Mary Margaret called after Oz.

CHAPTER 34

"Cara, I'm glad you could make it." Oz smiled as Cara lighted on a branch near him next to Giuseppe.

"Yes, I am getting more of that special Spanish moss." Cara winked at Chatty, who happily chittered at her and swished her tail back and forth.

"That was some accurate aim you had the other day," Oz complimented.

Cara blushed. "I did what I could."

"That man was so angry. Skamp and I scolded him from where we had climbed in the tree. He jumped up and down and picked up that awful pole and threw it back down again and again. He shouted some nasty-sounding words, so Skamp put his paws over my ears, but I heard them anyway."

"You and Skamp were very brave, Chatty," Huldah said. "I am so proud of you both."

"Me too," said Tilly, "I don't think I could have done anything like that."

Chatty held her tail firmly, trying to control its jerking, and twitched her whiskers. "Skamp almost got his tail shut in the door, and it was scary in that van. I almost had a panic attack when that man slammed the door. It was hot in there and smelled awful. The poor muscovies were crying and calling out. The worst thing was all this moldy food and bugs crawling all over and ...."

Oz tightened his jaw. "Chatty, sorry, but we need to get the meeting going. Cara needs to return to her nest soon, and I have to figure out how to feed that muscovy duckling this afternoon."

"Sir! Please repeat!" Anton looked up at Oz from a lower branch and saluted him.

"What muscovy duckling?" Petunia scrutinized Oz from a branch a few feet up in the tree where she was trying to keep her balance.

At that moment an approaching flutter announced Othello as he landed on a branch near the group. Gasps were uttered, and Petunia almost fell off her perch. Chatty ducked behind Skamp, and Tilly scrunched into her shell. The group eyeballed Oz with open mouths. They had been found out.

"I can tell you about the duckling."

"Othello, state your business. Why are you here?" Petunia was the most at risk for wrathful vengeance if she was found out. Seeing Obsolom's son at their 'secret' meeting meant their efforts had been noticed somehow.

"I think I know why he's here," Giuseppe said with a sly grin on his beak.

Othello then related all the events of the day before, including the part where he witnessed the trapper trying to get Girdie and her ducklings.

"Seaman Tilly alerted me, but by the time we arrived at the penetration point, the mother muscovy had gone into hiding, and the enemy had escaped down the canal with the POWs," Anton said.

"And what are POWs?" Petunia asked with an impatient tone. "Oh, forget it. Just continue."

"The prisoners of war. The captured ducklings," Tilly

explained.

Othello continued relating how one of the ducklings had gotten away.

"Yeah, but that poor yellow ducky never had a chance," Giuseppe added.

Othello then told about Crete snatching the duckling and flying away. "And, as you know, the council just voted to remove the muscovy duckling limit from the Great Blues." Othello looked directly at Petunia.

"Get on with your report," Petunia uttered between her clenched beak.

Oz noticed a deep sorrow pass through her eyes. Would the others ever forgive her for not speaking up at the council meeting? Could she forgive herself?

"Then, an amazing thing happened," Othello turned to face Giuseppe with a smile. "Have you told them about this?"

"I was going to, but no, you go ahead. I wanna hear how you tell the story."

"Giuseppe attacked Crete."

"You attacked Crete? Crete, the great blue heron?" Anton saluted Giuseppe. "Well done, Airman! You deserve a medal of honor!"

"I just flew into him. Used my skills, capeesh? He can't do anything to me. I'll always be a criminal to him." Giuseppe shot a glance at Petunia.

"Giuseppe crashed into Crete so hard that Crete dropped the duckling," Othello continued.

"Oh, that poor baby, what happened to him?" Chatty held her tail up to her mouth in suspense.

"Yeah, what did happen to the yellow ducky? That is, between when Crete dropped him and Oz somehow got him. I took off to distract that cocky overgrown boombot," Giuseppe said.

"When you called out to me, I dove and caught him. Joey revived…"

"Is this the same Joey we saw the other day?" Tilly extended her head fully out of her shell.

"Yes, Joey revived, but I didn't know what to do. His mother was injured, so I brought him to Oz and Preya. I knew Oz and Huldah were sympathetic to the muscovies' plight. I was also fairly certain there was a 'secret' protection campaign. I could not leave him alone somewhere."

Huldah nodded to Othello. "The lawful thing would have been to bring the prey back to Crete. But Othello has now risked his standing with the community, not to mention his father, Obsolom, for Joey. Thank you, Othello."

Oz then had to spend several minutes answering questions about Joey, talking about his injured foot and how he was feeding the duckling. To Oz's chagrin, the entire group chuckled at him.

"If anyone wants to help feed that hungry little thing, please step up." Oz looked back at Othello. "Have you spoken to your father since this happened? I'm sure Crete high-winged it to the council tree to tell Obsolom."

Othello's expression turned serious. "My father questioned me about my actions. He, too, knows that you are leading a protection campaign."

Oz felt a rush of light-headedness. "How much does he know?"

"He knows that you, Huldah, Giuseppe, and the squirrels are at least doing observation. Based on Crete's report, he suspects others are involved and that you are doing more than just observing."

Petunia almost fell off her branch. "Does Obsolom have any idea of my involvement?"

"And what about Seaman Tilly and I?" Asked Anton.

"He did not mention anyone else. But I have learned never to assume I know all my father's thoughts or intentions."

"What did you tell him about Joey?" Oz feared for the life of the yellow duckling. What if Obsolom now knew about Joey being with Oz and had ordered someone over to the nest to take him? And would Preya get hurt trying to protect Joey? Would the eggs be safe?

"I told him I had seen the crime the gull had committed and was thinking about returning the duckling to Crete, but the duckling came loose of my talons and fell into a thicket."

"And he believed you? You don't lie so well," Giuseppe observed.

"Well, I tried to convince myself it wasn't so much of a lie so I could appear truthful. I *did* see the crime. I *did* think that returning the duckling to Crete was expected. And the duckling *did* drop into a thicket... of Oz's nest."

Far across the neighborhood, high in the council snag, Crete hunched his shoulders and craned his neck toward Obsolom. "And you believe him?"

"He thinks I do." Obsolom's expression turned dark. "No one tries to deceive me without consequences. No one."

"What do you intend to do?"

"It is to our advantage that he thinks I believe him."

Crete pulled his head close to his chest. "And are you

confident of the loyalty of the other council members? Cronan's and Peter Paul's homage to you is obvious. What about Horatio and Petunia?"

"The old owl confuses himself to the point where he is immobilized. He is not a concern. I have my plans for how to test Petunia's allegiance. She will wish she had never been hatched if I find her lacking." Obsolom straightened himself and stood tall. "She and the others will be watched. At all costs, I will crush rebellion to preserve unity and security. Summon the vultures."

CHAPTER 35

"What's wrong with him, Huldah?" Oz jumped nervously around the nest as Huldah examined Joey. Preya was laying on her eggs, which now included a fourth one, laid early this morning. That was when she noticed Joey in a feverish lump, breathing irregular shallow breaths. Oz had awoken to her cries, and his delight at the arrival of the last egg quickly transformed into alarm, seeing the muscovy duckling in dire condition. Oz had been worrying about Joey for a few days; his broken leg had not healed and was now oozing yellow pus that had a putrid smell. Oz had immediately flown to get Huldah; she always knew what to do.

Huldah was now examining Joey. "He has the death infection in his leg."

Preya shifted on her eggs. "Aunt Huldah, what can we do for him? He has been through so much."

"There is only one remedy. The leg must be removed, or he will die. I anticipated this might happen."

Oz took in a sharp breath of air, and a deep pang of anguish rolled through him. "Remove his leg?" Oz thought of his own life-long injury to his shoulder that he had to endure and learn to live with, the things he could not do, being left out of games and activities, and being looked down on as a cripple. It was one thing to have a bad shoulder, but to lose a leg?

"Yes."

Before Oz knew what was happening, Huldah darted toward Joey, severed the bad leg above the knee joint with her sharp beak, and flung the dead limb over the nest. Joey peeped once but hardly moved at the operation.

Preya gasped, "Joey!"

"Leave him be. I will be right back." Huldah sprang up into the air and disappeared into the woods.

As the minutes passed, Oz's anxiousness intensified. Where was Huldah? She said she would be right back. He looked over at Joey. His leg stub was bleeding fresh red droplets from where the bone had been nipped off. His breathing was still shallow, and he was peeping weakly.

"You are going to be alright," Oz whispered, hoping that was true. Joey tried to focus on Oz and peeped again. Oz shifted toward Preya, "What's he saying about a big eagle?"

Just then, Huldah dropped into the nest with a beak full of Spanish moss covered with a gooey amber substance. Oz recognized from the smell that it was pine sap.

Huldah worked the pine sap into the Spanish moss with her beak until it was a sticky mess, which she molded around Joey's leg stump.

"What is that for, Aunt Huldah?" Preya watched intently. She had never seen Aunt Huldah use this remedy before.

"Preya, this is something you need to learn if you are ever going to take over for me one day."

Oz and Preya gave each other questioning glances.

Huldah kept molding the wad around Joey's leg, pressing it firmly in place with her beak as it started to harden. "The pine sap will seal off the wound, keep it from swelling, and help prevent infection. The Spanish moss keeps it in place."

"How long does it stay on?" Preya asked.

"I will need to change the dressing daily. Soon, the stump should develop a soft scab; we then have to keep it clean."

Joey lay still. Maybe, too still. "Will he make it through?" Preya asked, her eyes telling of her great love and concern for the adopted duckling.

"He is a survivor. Look what he has made it through already. But he was close to death and has a distance to go. For now, keep Joey quiet and fed," Huldah said.

"The mallard moms are happy to help. But now that Preya has had her fourth egg, I can't say she has egg-laying cravings." Everyone knew that ospreys have, at most, four eggs each season.

"I'm sure you will think of something, Oz. You always do." Huldah winked at Oz.

Huldah's attention shifted to Preya. "How are you? And, let me take a look at the new egg."

Preya tried to stand but quickly lost her balance and, with a pained expression and slight gasp, fell onto her side, clutching her belly with her wing.

"Preya! What's wrong?" Oz jumped over to Preya and cradled her head with his wing.

"I'm just physically worn out and worried about Joey." Preya winced and held her belly tighter. "Or maybe my belly is just not used to being empty of eggs." Preya smiled weakly.

Huldah cast a glance heavy with doubt to Oz.

"Let me take a look at you, Preya," Huldah said calmly.

Oz sat back with a fresh spurt of worry. "Oh, Great

One," he prayed, "Please help Preya."

Huldah felt Preya's brow with the back of her wing and then gently prodded her belly. "I think she just needs rest. Laying four eggs in six days has been a lot for her body to handle. Preya, when and what did you last eat?"

"Yesterday morning. Oz brought me a catfish. I was not that hungry but did eat some of it."

"Are you hungry now?"

"A bit, but mostly, I'm just tired."

"Oz, go and get some fish, and let Preya rest as much as possible." Huldah turned her gaze to Preya. "No flying yet." Huldah's voice was stern, but her wings on Preya's back gave a gentle, loving squeeze.

"I'll stay here with her after I get some food. The campaign will have to go on without me. Preya is more important."

Joey peeped softly and looked at Oz.

"No, Oz," Preya implored. "Maria is very capable of watching me and Joey. She has been for the last several days. You have to continue leading the campaign." Shifting her gaze toward Joey, Preya's eyes brimmed full of tears. "You just have to."

CHAPTER 36

Oz perched in the boughs of a Norfolk pine, looking down at several muscovies in the canal. Two males splashed enthusiastically, trying to impress a group of females who were acting unimpressed.

Petunia had reported that the man was in his boat and headed this way. Oz hoped everyone was in position according to the plan Anton and Giuseppe had devised and briefed them on this morning. Oz's concentration bounced back and forth from the scene below him to Preya and Joey back at the nest. Oz prayed that Huldah was right about Preya and Joey; all they needed was rest and time to heal. Oz had insisted that Huldah stay with Preya.

Oz looked up toward the east and saw Othello circling one hundred feet up, weaving in and out of the clouds that had been building. He could just make out the form of Giuseppe tucked in amongst the fronds of a tall palm across the canal. Cara should be next to him. Oz heard Chatty chittering from a branch near the bottom of the Norfolk pine. Oz hoped Skamp would keep her calm until it was time to act. Oz could not see Anton or Tilly. They were to be stationed under one of the nearby docks.

Oz turned toward the distinctive sound of Petunia's call coming from several hundred feet up the canal and soon heard the sputtering sound of a boat approaching. Out of the corner of his eye, he noticed a few vultures circling several streets away; they must have found some carrion.

The limb beside Oz suddenly dropped. Petunia's weight bowed the limb down and almost made it snap off. Squawking loudly, she waved her wings to get her balance as the limb bounced back up.

"Petunia – shhhhh!" If the man knew they were there, they would lose the element of surprise. Oz wanted to save the muscovies and thought that if they could make the man go away, the problem would be solved, and the muscovies would be safe.

"I'm sorry, Oz," Petunia whispered.

Oz noticed a heaviness in Petunia's voice as she kept his gaze for several moments before looking down at the canal.

As the small boat puttered slowly up the canal, the man turned his head from side to side. Seeing the group of muscovies fifty feet ahead, he cut the engine down to a slow idle speed. The man picked up his pole net, carefully stood, and, balancing himself, silently maneuvered ever closer to the group. The muscovies kept up their courting games, oblivious to the danger approaching. The man was now only fifteen feet away from his quarry. Oz saw Tilly and Anton under the water approach the side of the boat from behind. Perfect. Everyone was in position.

Oz sprang up into the air, rising to Othello in a matter of seconds. "Fweep fweeeeeeeeeeeeeep!" Oz called out. "You ready for this, Nephew?"

Hearing the call of the osprey, the man looked up abruptly, causing him to shift his bulk and almost lose his balance as the boat swayed from side to side. Steadying himself, he turned back to the muscovies still splashing around. The man drifted closer when, suddenly, a thud on the side of the boat spun it off course. The man dropped his net and fell back into the boat. Out of the corner of his eye, he thought he saw a giant turtle and an anhinga swimming away.

According to plan, Chatty and Skamp ran down the tree and over to the group of muscovies.

"Hurry, fly away; that man is trying to capture you!" Chatty chittered to the female muscovies as loud as she could. The male muscovies were still engrossed in their masculinity contest and were oblivious to Chatty's warning. One of the females finally heard her and saw the man sitting back up in the boat with his net and steering toward them. Alerting the other females, the female muscovies began to flap their wings in their attempt to fly away. By that time, the man was only five feet away and, with a swift scoop of the net, caught one of the females.

"Ha!" The man shouted triumphantly, twisting the net closed, tossing it into the boat's hull, and grabbing another net. But before he could get the second net in position, a cacophony of fweeps, uh-ohs, squawks, and honks approached from every direction. Swooping down so close he could feel the bat of wings were two ospreys, a gull, a pelican, and a crow. The birds then took turns swooping at the man. The male muscovies, finally attuned to what was happening, had flown off.

The pole net clattered to the boat floor as the man raised his hands over his head to protect himself, flinging his arms around to ward off his attackers.

Oz and Othello flew up, and seeing the struggling netted muscovy in the boat, they nodded to each other.

The muscovy was too large to pick up in the net, but maybe they could at least loosen or damage it.

They flew higher up into the thickening clouds to gain the most significant diving force. Reaching their zenith, they gracefully turned back to the earth, aiming toward the boat with talons out and wings spread wide. Suddenly, Oz saw a group of birds fast approaching from the west, and then, the unmistakable screech of his brother almost made Oz's heart stop. With Obsolom were Crete, Peter Paul, Cronan, Valafar, and several other vultures. Before Oz could change course, Obsolom careened into his weak shoulder. The force of the blow and searing pain sent Oz into a catastrophic descent and cast him onto a lawn, where he tumbled head over tail before coming to a hard stop against a fence post. Dazed and hurting, he looked around, trying to get his bearings.

Oz watched the man in the boat head further down the canal, seemingly unphased by his encounter with the birds. Oz could hear the struggling muscovy honking from the net that still imprisoned her. Failure speared at his gut and worsened as he saw his brother sauntering toward him, chuckling in mocking tones. Behind Obsolom, Crete tightly held one of Othello's wings behind his back. Oz could see the white of Othello's eyes as he struggled to free himself from Crete's crushing grip. Anton, Tilly, and Giuseppe were pinned on a nearby dock in the clutches of the vultures. Peter Paul and Valafar stood guard above them on a railing. In a nearby pine, Cronan was cawing at Cara in harsh tones. Cara flew away, presumably toward their nest, and Cronan joined guard duty. Oz could not see or hear Chatty or Skamp. Petunia was perched on one of the pilings by herself. She did not look at Oz. Another jab of failure knifed through Oz.

Obsolom sneered down at Oz, his head blotting out the sun. His long, silky plumes gleamed like silver in the sunlight. "My dear little brother." Crete and the guards echoed Obsolom's snickers. "Have you failed so soon in your *secret* campaign?"

Oz dropped his head to his chest. He felt utterly empty.

Obsolom hissed and spat at Oz. "You are deluded if you ever thought you would succeed. And a fool!" Obsolom whipped his head around and turned to Othello, pointing his wing at his son. "And this one is a traitor!"

"Are you calling anyone who stands up for what is right a traitor?" Othello cringed as Crete twisted his grip.

Strutting over to Othello, Obsolom struck out his massive wing, lashing his son across the face, sending blood spurting from his beak. Othello stared directly into Obsolom's eyes as his father towered over him.

"I am giving you a choice, but only because you are of my own feathers and talons. Depart for good, or stay, and I will rip you open wing to wing."

Oz felt a cold sweat overtake him; he knew his brother would make good on the threat. With a forceful shove, Crete released his grip, and Othello fell to the ground. Othello stood slowly rubbing the wing Crete had pinned. It did not appear broken, but Oz knew from Othello's wincing it was painful.

Othello walked a few steps and tentatively moved his wings. He jumped up and flew east, away from Havenport and the approaching thunderstorm. Oz felt hope draining from him as he disappeared behind the treetops.

"Coward." Obsolom watched Othello fly away and turned back to Oz.

"Your campaign was bound to fail. The human decree stands. Cease before something worse happens to you or one of your pathetic followers." Obsolom paused to bend further toward Oz. "Or your family." Obsolom's look of enmity and threatening words knifed through Oz.

Obsolom sprang into flight with Crete, Peter Paul, Cronan, and the vultures close behind. With a pang of realized betrayal, Oz watched as Petunia lifted off to join them.

"Petunia!" Oz called after her. A slight half-beat of her wing was the only indication that she might have heard him. She did not look back.

CHAPTER 37

Oz shook his head, trying to get rid of the dizziness and overwhelming sense of defeat. Slowly, he rose; his old shoulder injury inflamed with fresh pain. Giuseppe had flown over. Oz noticed a puncture wound in his chest. Anton was beside him, seemingly unharmed, and Tilly was plodding toward them. Her beautiful shell was marred with a network of deep scratches.

"Giuseppe, are you alright?" Oz asked.

"Not a problem. I've had worse."

"What about you, sir? Should I call the medics?" Anton stepped toward Oz, who was still unsteady on his feet.

"I'm fine," Oz said with more confidence than he felt. "Tilly, your shell took a beating."

"And I thank the Great One for my shell. I would have been vulture meat without it."

"Has anyone seen Skamp or Chatty?" Oz looked around and up into the nearby tree where they had been, not expecting to see them.

"I observed them deserting their post as soon as Obsolom and his regiment appeared. They headed west. I lost sight of them when they retreated under that fence and into those bushes." Anton pointed behind Oz into the next yard.

Oz's head pounded from the fall, and his heart felt like

it was breaking.

"Petunia went against us. She ratted on us to Obsolom. I knew we couldn't trust her." Giuseppe shook his wings in agitation. "What was that screech when she landed next to you, Oz?"

"She had lost her balance."

"I'm bettin' that screech was the sign for Obsolom and his gang to attack."

Oz hung his head. Why had he not seen her deception? Was he that gullible?

"Want me to take care of the problem?"

"No, Giuseppe." Oz was angry at the suggestion and angry at himself for not knowing his volunteers.

"Well, whadayagunnado?" Giuseppe shook his wings harder and leaped up and down.

"I don't know, Giuseppe. I need to think, and we need to discuss this." Oz felt a heat of demoralizing frustration rising to blur his mind.

"Basta! Enough! Tell you what. When you figure it out, let me know. I'm a gull of action. I'm not going to lie down and take this."

Oz's beak dropped as Giuseppe flew off.

"Sir! Ready for orders!" Anton stood up rigidly and saluted.

Tilly rolled her eyes at Anton and turned her attention to Oz. "Whatever you want us to do, we are here for you, Oz."

"Well, that's the problem! I don't know what to do! Or even if I should do anything!" Oz's agitation set his tone on edge, and the flapping of his wings sent Tilly halfway into her shell.

"Are you disbanding the unit, sir?"

"I DON'T KNOW ANTON!" Oz jumped up and down

and flung his wings even more vigorously. Anton and Tilly took a step back.

"Just leave me alone."

Anton and Tilly eyed each other and turned back to Oz.

"Go away and leave me alone," Oz said through his tightly shut beak. "NOW!"

At Oz's final shriek, Anton flew off, and Tilly plodded back to the canal as fast as a turtle could plod.

Now, completely abandoned and alone, Oz heard his pounding heart gushing blood through his veins. He tried to calm his breathing. He had to get out of there. Go somewhere far away from all this. Let someone else care about the muscovies. Or not. He was done playing the rescuer, the fool, the loser.

Oz attempted to launch himself off the ground and crumpled in a cry of pain. Grabbing his shoulder with his other wing, he winced as he massaged it.

Oz looked up at the sky. The cumulous clouds forming all day overhead were now billowing to 30,000 feet and still growing, interspersed with waning patches of blue sky. Off to the southwest, the sky was a charcoal-gray color. The clouds slanted down to touch the earth. It was raining hard there. A streak of lightning branched across the sky. The wind picked up and shifted. Oz could smell the approaching rain. He had to get back to Preya.

Oz gave one more deep massage to his wing and, with all his strength, leaped into the air. He concentrated on working his wings with enough force to give him the lift he needed instead of the paralyzing pain that threatened to cast him back to the ground—flap, flap, flap. Up Oz went at a crooked angle, narrowly missing the peak of a roof. Flap, flap, flap. Oz flew higher, almost reaching the darkening clouds. He needed the updrafts to ease his flight so he could make it home. In the distance, he could see the grove where his nest was. He would be home in under a minute.

Crash!

The blinding streak of lightning and the deafening crack of thunder exploded around Oz, sending him into a tailspin. As Oz plummeted, he tried to right himself and stretch out his wings to gain control, but his wounded shoulder had used up any reserve of strength, and the wing hung uselessly at his side, strained by the wind streaming by in his fall. The good wing's action did nothing but spiral Oz crazily down.

With a sickening thud, Oz slammed into a large patch of tall grass growing at the edge of a half-filled retention pond just as another bolt of lightning struck close, shuddering the ground from the subsonic boom of thunder. Now black as a raven, the sky burst down rain in torrential sheets.

Oz lay motionless with his head facing down in the hammock of grass that held him just above the water.

The storm deposited its pent-up water in a relentless rage. Water from the neighborhood roofs collected in gutters, spilled down drainpipes, streamed across lawns, and gushed into the streets. Waves of water contested with each other, and cement furrows along each side of the roads ushered the surge of churning waterfalls into the storm sewers. From there, millions of gallons of water flushed through the winding tunnels under the roads and parks to finally erupt into the retention ponds where water levels quickly rose, submerging anything within its boundaries.

The rain sloshed over and around Oz and felt rather soothing as he slipped into unconsciousness.

CHAPTER 38

"**C**ome on, Duke, hurry it up." Jeffrey wished he had taken Duke for his walk when Sophie had suggested and not procrastinated. The wind from the southwest was picking up, and the storm was about to break. The time between the lightning and the rumbling thunder in the distance was shortening. They were on the park side of the retention pond, about a half-mile from their home. If Duke finished his business quickly, they might be spared a drenching.

Duke led Jeffrey further around the pond. A streak of lightning cracked across the sky. The wind picked up and shifted, almost knocking Jeffrey's navy cap off before he could catch hold of it. The patches of blue sky had disappeared behind the swirling clouds as they melded into each other and became a thick, smokey mass. The thunder's mere grumbling had turned into a boastful furor that now almost immediately followed the lightning streaks.

"Duke, do your business."

Duke sniffed at a patch of ground with some interest while Jeffrey readied a plastic bag. Some residents did not think they needed to clean up so close to the pond, but Jeffrey felt rules were in place to be followed. Besides, he sure didn't want to step in anything unpleasant any more than anyone else. The streetlamps bordering the park flicked on as the sky blackened.

Crash!

Jeffrey instinctively raised his hands to cover his head, dropping Duke's leash. Duke yelped and bolted away towards the backside of the pond. Jeffrey ran after him as the rain pelted down.

"Duke!" The rain soaked through Jeffrey's T-shirt and shorts in seconds. His sneakers sloshed and slipped across the grass. Up ahead, Jeffrey spotted Duke in a lightning strobe; his head poked into a section of tall grass at the water's edge.

"Duke!"

With a wild frenzy of barking, Duke ran back to Jeffrey. But before Jeffrey could grab the leash, Duke broke away, bounding back to where he had been by the pond. He stood, looking in and barking, looking back to Jeffrey, and barking again.

Splashing through the water-logged turf, Jeffrey ran over to where Duke was to see what had Duke's attention. A dead osprey was lying on its side in a tangle of grass just above the swelling pond.

"Ah, poor thing." Jeffrey squatted on the muddy bank and reached out his hand to stroke the majestic bird's head. Duke was still barking behind him.

"Duke, we can't do anything for him." Another flash of lightning and clap of thunder made the ground quake.

"Come on, let's go home." Jeffrey reached out to Duke to get the leash, but Duke pulled away and waded into the pond closer to the bird, barking furiously as the rain increased.

"Alright, we'll at least take him home and give him a proper burial." Jeffrey waded into the pond and lifted the bird. Holding the cold osprey close to his chest, he wrapped the bottom of his T-shirt around his limp body. Duke panted and wagged his tail, water streaming from his soggy coat.

"Good boy, Duke. Good boy."

"Jeffrey, what are you doing out there?" Sophie yelled out from the open sliding glass door, trying to be heard above the downpour. Jeffrey and Duke had come back from the walk, and instead of entering through the garage as usual, they had come to the back of the house and entered through the screened door to the pool cage.

Sophie came out onto the covered lanai and stood behind the curtain of rain falling off the roof onto the pool deck. "Why is your shirt off? What do you have in your arms?"

Duke and Jeffrey ran onto the lanai. Large puddles formed at their feet. "It's an osprey. I thought it was dead, but it stirred in my arms on the way back. Now I feel shallow breathing."

Sophie smiled and gently squeezed Jeffrey's arm. "I'll call Shannon. Honestly, Jeffrey, how do you always find abandoned and injured animals?"

"Duke found this one." Jeffrey patted Duke's head who looked up into his eyes, panting with his tongue out and wagging his tail through the puddles of water.

CHAPTER 39

The sound of crickets and night-croaking frogs was familiar. But the muffled human voices were not. The smells were not familiar either. Along with the humans, a dog and a cat were close. The cat's scent nudged at some recluse memory. An unnatural light intruded into Oz's consciousness. He tried to open his eyes and only managed to allow a slit of light in. Where was he? His head felt like a rock was weighing it down. Oz attempted to push himself up, but his whole body was bound with something. Oz forced his eyes open and coaxed his head around to see where he was.

A nest-like container not much larger than himself surrounded him. He was lying on a purple cloth. Preya likes purple. Where was Preya? Anxiety seared through him. As Oz tried to jump up to fly, the wrapping around his body kept him immobilized. His injured wing, along with his head, throbbed with pain. Oz uttered a weak cry as he realized a human had captured him.

Oz turned to the sound of a dog whining. On the other side of a glass wall was a large golden-haired dog panting and looking at Oz. The dog barked once, and a man with white hair framing his dark face came to the glass wall and pushed it aside. The man followed as the dog ran out toward Oz.

Oz first thought that the dog would eat him, but the

dog just panted, wagged his tail, and looked from Oz to the man. A fat orange cat with only one ear followed the man. Oz knew that cat from …. where?

The man crouched down next to the nest. "Hey, you're awake. How are you?" The man's voice was calm. "I thought you were a goner."

Oz struggled to move, but all he could do was squirm around a bit.

"Easy. You need to rest."

Oz struggled harder and uttered another weak cry. He had to get out of there.

The man picked up a small brown bottle from a table next to him and, inserting a slender tube, reached into the nest. Oz's eyes grew wide, but there was nothing he could do. With one hand, the man firmly but gently held Oz's head still and, with the other, stuck the end of the tube into his beak and down into his throat. Oz tried to bite down and pull away, but he could not. A cool liquid glided into his mouth and seeped down his throat. The man removed the tube and held Oz's beak shut for a few seconds. A bitter taste spread through his mouth, but with his beak held shut, he was forced to swallow the nasty stuff.

The man sat on a nearby chair and studied Oz. His eyes were full of concern. The dog sat next to the man, putting his head on his lap but keeping his eyes on Oz. The cat had gone off somewhere.

Oz's anxious thoughts began to fade, and the pain subsided. Oz felt like he was being lifted off the ground and floating, like flying without moving his wings. The light grew dim, and the chant of the crickets and frogs droned out all thoughts. The chant was the only thing Oz was aware of until it, too, dropped from Oz's consciousness.

As Jeffrey watched the osprey relax, his cell phone began chiming, *God Bless America*.

"Hey, Shannon." Jeffrey stroked Duke's head. "Yes, he woke up, and I gave him more medicine. He's asleep again…. Uh-huh…. So, you still think his shoulder was just dislocated and will be OK?" Duke looked up into Jeffrey's eyes and thumped his tail on the ground. "I'll be home all day tomorrow so I can make sure he stays calm. What time are you coming over to check on him? … And you will unwrap him? … Do you need me to pick up a cage? … Sounds good, see you then."

Jeffrey ended the call and leaned forward to better view the osprey in the box. He hoped the bird would make a full recovery. Shannon had found that along with the dislocation, it appeared the osprey had an old injury in the same shoulder that had never healed properly. It had probably been painful for the osprey over the years. She had injected a mild analgesic, which would help temporarily, but that would wear off. Jeffrey marveled at the way animals seemed to make do and survive with injuries that would cause most humans to wallow in puddles of despair.

Jeffrey stood up and scratched Duke's head again. "Come on, buddy. It's time to turn in."

CHAPTER 40

"I was right. I told you what I heard Duke announcing to the whole neighborhood, but you did not want to believe me; no, you did not. There he is, lying in that square thing over there." Chatty pointed to where Oz was lying in the box on the lanai. She and Skamp were on top of the pool cage. Her tail banged against the screen as it flipped wildly in all directions.

"Are you sure that's him? What is that white thing around him?"

"I don't know. Maybe he is cold and needs a blanket. I'm sure it's Oz, I think. He is not moving much. I hope he is alright. Oz, can you hear us? It is me, Chatty. OZ!" Chatty chittered louder and louder, trying to get his attention.

"Dad! Mom!" Duke barked from inside the house. "Let me out!"

"Duke, what is all the barking about?" Sophie opened the sliding glass door for Duke, who bounded out and stood next to Oz's box, barking up at two noisy squirrels.

"Silly squirrels. I think they like teasing you, Duke." Sophie returned to the house, leaving the glass door open so Duke could go in and out.

"Chatty, Skamp! I think he is going to get better!" Duke barked out.

"Maybe, maybe not." Copper the cat had ambled out

and laid down next to Duke. He opened his mouth wide in a long yawn.

Chatty scurried back and forth on the screen. "What happened? We have been so worried about Oz. Preya is beside herself. And she just had four eggs, and..."

"Chatty, let them tell us what happened." Skamp put his paw on Chatty's shoulder.

Duke spent several minutes explaining how he had found Oz and convinced his master to bring him home. "I knew he wasn't dead!"

"Duke, if it had not been for you, he would have drowned in that pond. It rose two squirrel lengths from that storm," Skamp said.

"He still might die." Copper yawned again.

Duke growled at Copper and looked back up at Chatty and Skamp. "The nice animal healer lady came over, pressed him all over with her hands, and then wrapped him up. She gave him something in a tube, and he fell asleep. My master gave him more stuff in the tube later."

"What did they give him? Why can't he wake up and fly away? Are you sure he is going to be alright? They didn't poison him, did they?" Chatty scampered back and forth, trying to get a better view of Oz.

"OZ!" Chatty chattered as loud as she could. "Look! I think he moved. Duke, check and see if he is awake."

Duke poked his head in the box and sniffed at Oz, nudging him gently with his nose. Copper pushed himself up to peer into the box. The osprey seemed to be trying to move his shoulders as if he were in flight....

❖ ❖ ❖

Oz flew 500 feet over the lake fishing for mullet. He

flew up and down and did loop-the-loops again and again. An eagle, more enormous than he had ever seen, flew high above him. But what were those short, hot puffs of air? Second by second, he became aware that a dog was sniffing him. How could that be when he was flying, soaring, twirling in the sky? Why was that dog poking him? And a cat. Oz smelled a cat. And what was that chattering noise? Chatty!

Oz suddenly opened his eyes and, seeing the large dog head panting over him and the one-eared cat eying him, let out a screech and tried to fly away. He quickly realized he was still in that strange nest and still bound tight. Up above somewhere, he heard Chatty chittering excitedly.

"Oz! You're awake! You had us so worried. We didn't know where you were, and then you almost died and...."

Oz anxiously wondered if the dog would crunch him in his jowls and shake his life out of him or if the cat would sink his teeth into his neck. But they both just sat there. The dog panted and drooled a bit on Oz while wagging his tail. The cat yawned and laid down next to the box. Oz looked up to where he had heard Chatty and was blinded momentarily by a bright blue cloudless sky. Meeting her eyes, Oz could see her tail rapidly drumming the pool cage and her whiskers twitching.

"Duke found you yesterday and convinced his master you weren't dead. But you would have been if Duke hadn't saved you. You would have drowned in the pond. Yes, you would. We had a huge storm, and the kids were so afraid..."

Skamp took Chatty's tail and gently put it up to her mouth, earning a scowl. "Hey Oz, how are you?"

Yesterday? Oz had been gone a whole day? "I don't know; what am I wrapped in? Where am I?" Oz's head hurt, and he still felt like he was flying.

"You are at our house. My dad and the nice animal healer lady are taking care of you." Duke wagged his tail harder, smacking the chair behind him and making deep beating sounds.

"You might get better, or not." Copper licked his front paw and started to clean his ear.

Oz opened his eyes wider. Now, he recognized the cat. He was the one who had heard about the humans' edict.

As his head cleared more, Oz's thoughts magnified into panic. "Skamp, Chatty, how is Preya?" The last Oz knew was she was still in pain after laying her final egg yesterday morning.

Chatty and Skamp locked eyes. "She is resting. She is worried about you and will be so relieved to know you are alive." Chatty looked down at her paws and would not meet Oz's anxious gaze.

"Tell me what is wrong with her! How is Joey?" Oz struggled to get out of his wrapping. He had to get back to the nest.

"Oz, Preya is still in pain." Skamp took a tentative hop on the screen to get as close to Oz as possible.

"Get me out of this wrapping!" Oz commanded Duke, who sat down and just looked at Oz.

"I don't know how to. And my master and the nice lady would get mad at me if I tried to do that," Duke whined.

"You're such a daddy's boy. Want me to try and scratch it off?" Copper asked, stretching out his front paws and extending his claws.

Skamp squeaked a warning. "No Copper. I think Preya will feel better knowing Oz is alive and is being cared for."

"Skamp, I need to get to her! What about Joey? Is someone feeding him?" Oz tried to kick his feet but only accomplished getting his talons tangled in the white wrapping.

"We brought some grubs. They were really yucky, but we did it for Joey. One of them squished in my mouth before I could give it to him, and I almost threw up..." Chatty wretched, remembering the icky taste and sensation.

Oz struggled again and managed to roll over on his other side, now facing toward the wall where he could not see the squirrels, Copper, or Duke. He screeched in frustration.

"Chatty and I will go back and tell Preya and Huldah you are alive and where you are."

"I need to go!" Oz screeched.

Duke's whining was getting louder, punctuated with a few yelps.

Oz cried in anguish as he heard the two squirrels scamper away across the screen and skitter up the roof. Duke was now standing over the box and bellowing barks. Copper was still lying down but was smacking his tail on the ground in aggravation.

"Duke, settle down, what's wrong?" Jeffrey came out onto the lanai with Shannon close behind him.

Shannon knelt by Oz's box. "Poor thing, he is probably terrified. A few more minutes, and he would have ripped the bandage off. Good boy, Duke!" Shannon patted Duke's head. Copper strolled back into the house.

"I'm glad he is moving around as much as he is. That means he has a lot of fight in him to live, but I'll need your help to hold him," Shannon said. "An adult osprey is very strong, even in his condition, and wrapped up."

"Tell me what we are going to do." Jeffrey put on the leather gloves he had brought out.

"You hold him firmly around his body. I will give him one more dose of the antibiotic with the anesthetic. It will knock him out pretty quick, but not for long." Shannon reached into her medical bag to pull out the bottle of medicine and an oral syringe encased in a blister pack. Opening it, she filled it to the level she needed.

Oz heard the human voices and turned his head enough to see the man he had seen last night and a woman with hair the color of Duke's. She had those round glass disks over her eyes that some humans wore. Oz screeched a warning and ripped at the wrapping again with his feet. It was coming loose. If he had to defend himself, he would. Humans could not be trusted, no matter what Duke thought of them.

"Jeffrey, are you ready? We are going to have to act quickly. Where is the cage?"

"It is over there on the other side of the glider. Want me to get it?"

Shannon saw that the osprey was making good progress in destroying the wrapping. "No time. Quick, we have got to do this now."

Oz shrieked again as he saw the humans approaching him. The man tried to hold him, but Oz kicked harder, and the man backed off.

"Jeffrey, you have to hold him still."

The man again put his large hands around Oz, this time immobilizing him. Before Oz could shriek again, the lady grasped his head, put the tube in his mouth, shut his beak, and forced him to swallow the bitter liquid. Oz tried to kick his feet and move his wings in a weakening effort. In a few seconds, the scene around him started to melt into a fuzzy blue space. Duke's whining—or maybe it was the wind whispering in the trees—called to him, and he was lifted up and flew above the grove where his nest was. "Preya!" Oz called out as the sky around him grew dim and then dark.

CHAPTER 41

Oz's head pounded in rhythm with thumping nearby. Opening his eyes slowly, he saw Duke lying near him with his head between his paws, looking at Oz. His tail thumped up and down behind him. Oz realized he was no longer in the nest-like place but in an enclosure with metal wire on the sides and ceiling.

Oz rolled over on his stomach and tentatively braced his legs, trying to stand up. The wrappings had been removed.

Duke raised his head and perked his ears.

Still wobbly from the anesthetic, Oz's legs gave out, and he crumpled back down onto the purple cloth. He stretched out his wings and shook out the kinks. The enclosure only allowed him to extend his wings partially. Surprisingly, the intense pain he had felt from Obsolom's attack was gone. Even more amazing was the deep ache from his old shoulder injury was gone. Just a stiffness remained. Oz stood and slowly tramped around the enclosure, testing his legs and clicking against the metal floor with his talons.

"I knew my dad and that lady could fix you!" Duke stood and padded over to the enclosure, wagging his tail harder and panting.

"Maybe I'm fixed, but why am I in this prison? I need

to get home." Something felt funny on his right leg. He looked down and discovered a small metal band around his right leg. It was purple and had black markings etched on it. Oz kicked his leg repeatedly, but the metal band would not come off. He tried pecking at it but only managed to gash his leg with his sharp beak.

Duke kept wagging his tail.

Oz looked around his prison. In one corner was an upside-down bottle attached to the wire mesh with a bent tube protruding into the enclosure. Oz poked the end of the tube with his beak, and a drop of water dripped out. He realized how thirsty he was. He stuck out his tongue to the tube and lapped another droplet of water, and another, and another. Oz was also hungry.

Oz looked up. A ceiling was directly overhead, and he could see the bright sky just beyond. The shadow from the lanai roof reached about six feet to the small pond under the screen. Oz doubted there were any fish in it; it smelled sterile.

High up in the sky above, Oz heard a familiar voice.

"Fweep! Fweep! Fweep!"

"Huldah!" Oz called as loudly as he could.

Within seconds, Huldah swooped down and dropped a fresh mullet near the screen door at the back corner of the screened-in area.

"Duke," she cried, "come out your door and get this for Oz."

Duke bounded over to the door and slipped through a Duke-sized flap, retrieved the mullet, and returned through the flap door like he went out. Duke trotted over to Oz's enclosure and tried to shove the fish through, but the wire mesh was woven too tight for the mullet to fit through. Duke then found an area on one side of the cage where there was a long, narrow opening where he could poke the mullet through as Oz pulled it from the inside. Oz tore at the mullet.

Huldah perched on top of the pool cage looking down at Oz. "The Great One has answered our prayers."

Oz looked up at her sideways with a scowl and kept eating.

"Preya has not slept worrying about you. She is relieved, as am I."

Oz stopped eating. "How is Preya? Please tell me she is better."

"Preya is comforted and smiling again since Chatty and Skamp visited this morning and told us about you. But she is frail and still complains her belly hurts."

Oz swung his wings and jumped up, banging against the top of the enclosure. He tried again and again, his feet slipping on the metal floor. "I need to get to her. Huldah, get me out of here!" Oz crumpled on the metal floor, exhausted.

Duke whined and looked up at Huldah. "He is going to hurt himself again if he keeps that up."

"Oz, Duke is right. You can't do anything for Preya right now; you must heal. Between Skamp, Chatty, and myself, we are taking care of Preya and Joey."

Oz stood up and walked over to the side of the enclosure, looking up at Huldah. "Is Joey healing? What happened to Maria helping out?" Oz felt a pang of abandonment as he remembered Giuseppe leaving yesterday.

"Joey is healing slowly but needs fresher food. And more of it."

"Get me out of here, and I can get him more food! The mallards will give me food!" Oz pleaded and lifted his wings, banging against the sides of the enclosure.

"The mallards won't help you, Oz. Obsolom has ordered that no one associate with Preya, you, or me. They don't know yet where you are or if you are alive, but they will find out soon. Nor can anyone support or participate in the campaign to protect the muscovies under penalty of excommunication."

Oz hung his head. "Is that why Maria left?"

"No, Giuseppe came by and told us everything that happened yesterday. Giuseppe said you could not decide what to do, so he figured the campaign was over. Maria is not needed at the nest if there is no campaign."

"What is this campaign you are talking about?" Duke perked his ears.

"The muscovies. The humans posted an edict to take them away. Copper knew about it. We were trying to stop that man with the net. But, of course, failed." Oz looked away. "Probably shouldn't have tried."

"We saw that man in a boat the other day, and he had some baby muscovies. Dad yelled at him for making waves in the canal. We don't like him." Duke curled his lip and rumbled a low growl.

"Well, I guess it doesn't matter who likes him or not. He is here to stay. The campaign is over. All the volunteers went home. Even Chatty and Skamp ran off yesterday." Oz banged against the enclosure with his wing and brought it back sharply, shaking the sting out.

Huldah looked sharply at Oz. "Yes, Chatty and Skamp did run away when they saw the mercenary vultures approaching. But later, after the storm, they came to the nest, ashamed and apologetic."

"What good are a couple of squirrels anyway?" Oz shot back a look at Huldah.

"Oz, it seems like you need to think about a few things and pray. Those squirrels love you and have risked their lives for you and the campaign." Huldah took a few steps closer, leaving holes in the screen where her talons had been.

"Thinking is all I can do. I'm trapped. Just like the muscovies."

"I'm going back to the nest after I get another fish. I will pray for you and come back tomorrow." Huldah turned her head toward Duke. "Duke, please watch over that ornery bird."

Huldah leaped into the sky, and Oz was alone again with Duke, who sat looking at Oz with his brows furrowed.

"What are you looking at?" Oz screeched. "Do something useful! Go fetch a ball or something." Oz retreated to the enclosure's far side, sat with his back to Duke, and hung his head. After a few minutes, he heard Duke's nails clicking on the cement floor as he went back into the house.

CHAPTER 42

Pray. Huldah wanted Oz to pray. For hours, Oz had been hopping around the cage, banging his beak on the enclosure, looking for any weakness in the structure. A lot of good praying does, he thought. Oz poked at the side where Duke had given him the mullet. There were two horizontal openings, one at the top and one at the bottom. In between was a square section of mesh with a bar across the opposite side. Oz poked harder at it and discovered it had some movement. Oz jumped up and struck at it with his feet. While the section moved slightly back and forth, it did not open, no matter how much Oz banged on it.

Oz sat down, dizzy from the exertion and overwhelmed with worry. Something was wrong with Preya. She should have gained back her strength within a matter of hours after laying her last egg. And worse, Huldah had no idea what was wrong with her. Huldah. She was supposed to be the spiritual leader and healer.

Oz stood up and resumed circling the small enclosure. Four steps, turn. Four steps, turn. Four steps, turn. Four steps, turn. Again and again. The sound of his talons against the metal floor and the thoughts he could not turn off clanged in his head. The metal band chafed his leg, adding to his agony.

Everyone had deserted him. He wondered where

Othello had gone. And Cara had cowed to Carl. She was probably grounded at her nest, forbidden to leave. Is this why Obsolom had wanted Carl on the council? He knew Carl would march to his drum even if the beat was wrong. Petunia's betrayal hurt the most. Oz felt naive and stupid. He should have realized sooner her true alliance. A sour taste of acid rose in Oz's throat. He felt sick with foolishness. Some leader he was. Of course, Giuseppe had left. It was the smartest thing to do. Even Chatty and Skamp had run away in fear.

"Why did you ever want me to make a fool of myself thinking I could lead this campaign?" Oz shook his balled-up wingtip heavenward. He remembered the terrified cries of the captured muscovy in the trapper's boat yesterday, and a putrid feeling of uselessness nauseated him.

Oz's thoughts shifted to Tilly and Anton. Did they really think Oz knew what to do? Anything Oz did failed; anything he touched fell apart. Did the Great One care about any of this?

"You, YOU have caused everyone to ridicule and abandon me!" Oz turned his head upward, shaking both wings. "You have put me in this prison! Why are you angry with me?" Oz jumped up and down, screeching his lament. "Why?"

Oz heard Duke barking, and within a few seconds, he came bounding out and ran over to Oz's cage. Behind him, Duke's master and the lady with the golden hair walked over. Copper followed behind. Oz jumped up and down, banging his wings on the enclosure.

"Is he going to hurt himself?" Jeffrey questioned Shannon, wrinkling his brow.

"I hope not. I'm going to give him this fish paste.

Hopefully, he will eat some. I have a mild sedative mixed in that will make him drowsy. He needs to calm down and rest." Shannon pulled out a small plastic dish with some white paste that had a mild fish smell.

"You got a mullet for him?" Shannon looked up at Jeffrey.

Jeffrey looked in the cage where Shannon was pointing and saw a half-eaten fish. "No, I don't know where that came from. Maybe Sophie got it." Jeffrey doubted that was the case but couldn't think of any other logical explanation.

Duke looked up at Jeffrey, wagging his tail.

"Strange. That's good that he's eating; hopefully, he's still hungry. I want to get that out of the cage so he eats this paste. It also has another dose of antibiotics. I'm going to open the door just enough to slide my hand in to get the fish and put this dish in."

"OK, what do you want me to do?"

"Just be ready to help me keep the door firm. He might attack and bang against the door or try to bite me."

Oz had settled down a bit but was still hopping around in the back corner of the cage, looking warily at the humans.

Oz watched closely as the lady slid the bar across the square-framed section. This was his chance; the way out did have something to do with that section. When the lady swiveled the middle section toward her, Oz sprang at the opening but fell back as the man held the opening in place. The lady dropped the round dish and grabbed his mullet. She removed her hand before Oz could spring again, and the bar was pushed back in place. Oz bashed against it with his feet, releasing a loud, angry screech.

"He is definitely feeling better." Shannon inspected her

gloves, thankful for them, as she discovered a long gash from the bird's sharp talons. If that had been her skin, she would be on her way to the emergency room.

"How long before we can let him go?" Jeffrey felt his jugular vein pulsing fast. Shannon was a brave woman.

"Hopefully tomorrow. I wanted to get that last dose of antibiotic in him and give him one more night of rest. Let's pray he eats that." Shannon took off her gloves and repacked her medical bag. "Call me in the morning to let me know how he's doing. I have clinic hours till two, but I will come by later and help. I always love seeing the wild animals released after they are patched up."

Oz's heart thumped as he watched the humans go back inside the house. Duke and Copper remained and sat there looking at him. After a few minutes, Duke lay down, facing Oz, and put his head on his paws. Copper sniffed at the mullet that Jeffrey had taken out of the cage and, deciding he liked his regular food better, walked back inside.

"What are you still doing here?" Oz snapped.

Duke raised his head. "You have to eat what the nice lady gave you."

"I don't have to do anything," Oz hissed at the dog. He wasn't about to eat anything from a human. Probably poisoned. Even if he was hungry. Even if whatever was in the dish smelled scrumptious.

Duke stood up and plodded back into the house after sending a mournful look back at Oz.

Oz circled the cage for a few minutes. He paused by the dish. It did smell good, like fresh mullet. His stomach growled, and his mouth watered. He hopped to the back of the cage and sat on the purple cloth, looking out onto the deck. The shadows from the roof above had lengthened across the small pond. He desperately missed Preya. His head swam with grief and hunger. He looked back over his shoulder at the dish. Attracted by the smell of food, a fly had buzzed its way into the cage and landed on the edge of the dish.

Without thinking twice, Oz leaped over to the dish and devoured the paste. So what if it was poisoned? It tasted like the freshest spring mullet he had ever had.

Back now on the purple cloth, he felt full and sleepy. He didn't care about the campaign. He felt so weak. Was he dying? Maybe it would be better if he went to fly with his fathers.

CHAPTER 43

Mary Margaret heard a loud honking from one of the muscovies and turned toward the pond just in time to see the man scoop it up in his net. The muscovy was the female that had just laid a clutch of eggs last week. It irked Mary Margaret that the muscovies were so fertile; they seemed to have clutches twice as often and had more eggs than the mallards. The man wore the same filthy beige pants and the dark green sweaty shirt as the other day, but now one of the sleeves was almost torn off from the shoulder. His arm had a blood-stained bandage that was dangling loose. The man grunted up the bank toward his van while swiping dirty sweat from his chin with his shoulder. In one hand, he carried the net with the muscovy struggling inside, and in his other hand, he had the pole. The muscovy mom cried out again.

Just then, Mary Margaret heard another muscovy voice coming from the pond.

"Hronk, hronk, hronk!"

Swimming toward her was Girdie Green. Alone. As she got closer, Mary Margaret noticed Girdie's shoulder was gashed, and her wing dragged in the pond next to her.

"He took my babies, my Gunther!" Girdie cried out in an anxious chirrup.

Acting as if she had not heard the muscovy, Mary

Margaret turned to go back to her nest, where Peter Paul was watching their kids. She repeated in her mind that the exile of the muscovies was the right thing to do. They had become too many and had taken away their nesting areas. They were big and ugly and not uniformly beautiful, like the mallards.

"Mary Margaret, help me stop him!" Girdie honked louder.

Well, that certainly wouldn't be happening, Mary Margaret thought as she continued waddling away. The man is taking them to a better place where they can make a new life by themselves, away from here.

Mary Margaret heard a cry of pain behind her and turned to see Girdie walking toward her, dragging her wing.

"Mary Margaret, please! That man took my babies! Help me stop him. Please!" Girdie begged.

Mary Margaret looked down to avoid Girdie's eyes and, turning, continued to waddle away.

"Please!" Girdie honked.

Mary Margaret hesitated, straightened her shoulders, and resolutely kept walking. Passing a garbage can chained to a park bench, she stepped behind it, blocking her from Girdie's view. Something bothered her. She thought the man was only supposed to remove the muscovies, not hurt them.

Peeking out from behind the trash can, Mary Margaret watched Girdie. The muscovy's head hung low, and Mary Margaret could hear soft sobbing. This wife and mother had seen her whole family taken away and had probably gotten hurt trying to save them. Now, she was alone and injured.

It is for the best, Mary Margaret tried to convince

herself and ignore the thorn of sadness that had started to prick within her chest.

Behind Mary Margaret, the man returned to the pond from his van, where he tossed the crying muscovy. Mary Margaret scurried to get further away from the man.

"You safe lady. I ain't gonna take you. I don't get paid for mallards," The man said as he strode toward the pond.

"Hronk, hronk, hronk!" Girdie stood up straight at the sight of the man and extended her good wing. "Hronk, hronk, hronk!"

"Get away, Girdie!" Mary Margaret called out before she realized what she was doing.

"There you are, Mama; I comin' to get you. No gettin' away from me this time." The man began running toward Girdie with the net poised above his head.

Girdie continued honking and tried to work both wings but could only bat with her good wing. Mary Margaret noticed fresh blood oozing from the wound on the injured wing. She could only imagine the pain Girdie must be feeling.

As the man closed in on Girdie, she pushed herself off the ground, willing the useless wing to work. Amazingly, she lifted in the air and, avoiding the swipe of the net, stretched out her feet at the man's face, clawing a long, deep gash on his cheek. Swearing out in pain, the man punched his arm up, striking Girdie in the stomach and casting her to the ground.

Girdie tumbled several feet, scattering the leaves and dirt before she slammed into an oak tree trunk. Panting, she picked herself up to stand, only to fall back on her side. The man breathed heavily and walked slowly over to Girdie. Blood dripped onto his shirt from the gash on his face and merged with the other stains, sweat, and grime.

Girdie lay at the man's feet and, looking up, stared into his eyes.

"Say goodbye." The man pulled a pistol out of his pocket.

◆ ◆ ◆

The sound of the shot seemed to reverberate through the trees, across the pond, and back again for several minutes. Mary Margaret had watched the execution but could hardly believe what she had seen. Girdie lay at rest now. A puddle of blood pooled around her head, staining the oak trunk and seeping into the earth. Her dead eyes stared toward Mary Margaret. The man grabbed Girdie by the neck and dragged the lifeless body back to his van, where he threw the corpse on top of the pile of nets full of hissing, chirping, and squirming muscovies. Before speeding off, the man climbed into his van, waved, and tipped his sweat-drenched ballcap to a few humans who had gathered at the sound. Some were silent with their hands over their mouths while others spoke in alarmed tones to each other, but all wore bewildered expressions.

◆ ◆ ◆

A couple of squirrels chattered down the oak, briefly sniffed the crimson ground, and scampered away across the lawn.

◆ ◆ ◆

Mary Margaret ambled back to her nest, taking the long way home around the backside of the pond. She felt weak and disoriented. Sadness flooded her mind. Not looking where she was going, she tripped over a fallen palm frond and stumbled toward a patch of underbrush. Feeling foolish, she looked around to see if anyone had seen her. She noticed the underbrush had a path leading into it that only a duck could have made. Peering into the brush, she saw a muscovy nest with at least a dozen eggs. This must be that muscovy mom's nest, the one that was taken away just now. A thought briefly brushed her mind that the eggs looked very much like her own. Another batch of muscovy eggs that will not hatch and will die without their mother to protect them and keep them warm. Such as it should be. The thorn of sadness pricked her chest again.

CHAPTER 44

"Oz! Oz!" Chatty and Skamp ran panting over the screen, and stopped above Oz.

Since awakening a few hours ago, Oz had been sitting in a corner of the cage. There had been a new bowl of fish paste, but Oz was too depressed to eat. The man had just returned to the house after checking on Oz and putting a fresh bottle of water on the cage.

Duke came trotting out at the sound of the squirrels. Copper followed and stood beside Duke with his good ear bent toward the squirrels.

"That man killed Girdie!"

Oz leaped over to get as close as he could to the squirrels. "What?"

Duke barked and growled.

"She is dead, Oz, she is dead. That awful man took a black thing out of his pocket, pointed it at her, and made a loud noise. And then Girdie was dead." Chatty held her paws up to her face and wept; she had never seen anything so cruel and merciless.

In an instant, Oz's self-pity was vaporized and replaced with one clear call.

Lead them.

Born leader or not, fool or not, he had to do something. Oz knew the Great One would guide him.

"Duke, Copper! You saw how they opened the cage,

didn't you?" Oz frantically jumped up and down in front of the square section with the bar securing it.

Duke angled his head sideways. "Dad will be mad at us if we help you escape. Maybe Dad will let you out soon."

"Duke, you heard what happened; I must get out now. That man has to be stopped!" Oz tried to flap his wings. "Didn't you say your mom and dad didn't like the man?"

"Yes...but Mom and Dad..." Duke padded pack and forth whining.

"Let's help the bird escape. Honestly, sometimes you take that obedience thing too far." Copper walked over to Oz's cage to look more closely at the door. It looked familiar, like the door on that plastic box his mom and dad used to bring him to get poked and prodded by the nice animal lady. "Hey, I know how this works."

"Copper, can you open it?" Skamp called from above.

Copper clanged the metal bar up and down with his paw. "I know this bar has to move over, but I can't get it to budge. I'm not strong enough."

"Please, Duke, please help me stop that man."

Duke sat whining and panting. Oz slid onto the cage floor and bowed his head to his chest. "Great One," he prayed, "I believe this is your will for me to do something. Make it happen."

Several minutes passed. Oz fought the temptation to let despair close in again.

At the sound of metal scraping against metal, Oz turned around to see Duke with the protruding handle in his mouth, trying to pull it sideways. He managed to move it some, but the door was still latched.

Oz jumped over to the door. "Duke! That is great! Try again!"

Try as he could, Duke could not move the handle

anymore with his mouth; he could not get a good enough grip on it. As Duke whined and barked in frustration, Oz hoped the man would not come out and stop his efforts.

"Duke! Pounce on the metal thing with your paws from the side. Pounce like you do when you chase us up a tree!" Chatty coached, banging her tail against the screen.

With one more ecstatic bark and all his might, Duke jumped at the metal thing. The door clanged open and slammed against the side of the cage, sending the cage scraping backward. Oz leaped out of the opening and flew into the air, only to bounce off the top of the screened enclosure and fall back onto the pool deck. Duke was barking wildly, Copper was yowling, and the squirrels were chattering. Oz tried to fly again but hit up against the pool screen.

"Duke! What is ...." Jeffrey ran out onto the deck with Sophie close behind. "Sophie, get back in the house! Close the door and call Shannon. The osprey is loose!"

Oz was now on the other side of the pool, still attempting to fly and being stopped by the screen. Oz didn't know the man's intentions, and hoped no one would get hurt, but he had to get out of there. He had to save the muscovies.

"Easy, fella." The man's voice was calm. He crept slowly alongside one edge of the screen toward the back corner. "I'll open the door for you."

Oz's memory flashed, remembering the flapped opening Duke had gone out of yesterday to get Huldah's mullet. If Duke could go through that, so could Oz.

Suddenly, the osprey swooped over Jeffrey, brushing close enough to feel wing beats. The bird then burst through Duke's doggie door and, in seconds, was flying high above the canal. Duke ran out his door and stood barking up at the sky.

"Well, I guess I won't open the door for you." Jeffrey felt relieved watching the osprey fly away.

CHAPTER 45

Oz soared high along the updrafts. He was stiff from being cooped up but thankful his bum shoulder didn't have much pain. As he continued to his nest, Oz battled against a growing anxiousness over Preya's and Joey's conditions. As his nest came into view, his anticipation heightened. Preya was lying on her side with the four eggs visible, and Joey lay still on the other side of the nest. Where was Huldah? Diving toward the nest, Oz sunk hard onto a branch at the side of the nest, shaking it violently.

"Preya!" Oz leaped over to his wife and reached out his wing to gently touch her head. She was barely breathing. Her eyes opened and seemed to register on him before closing again.

Oz heard a slight peeping and saw Joey struggling to stand on his one good leg. The stump was covered in fresh sap-covered moss.

"Papa Oz." Joey's voice was weak. He wobbled and fell forward, then dragged himself closer to Oz.

"Joey, hey, little guy." Oz hopped to the duckling, righted him up with his wings, and drew him close. He would have to tell him about his mom, somehow, someday. "It's OK. I'm here." Oz felt a tear moisten his cheek.

Oz held Joey and looked over at Preya. He had not

thought they would be so close to death.

Oz's heart beat rapidly. In a vision in his mind, he saw himself in a mist high in the council snag. Obsolom was pointing and laughing at Oz. His jeering shouts pierced into Oz's head and chest like flaming arrows. *Failure! Fool! Worthless!* More faces appeared: Crete, Valafar, and other disfigured fiends with the heads of alligators, bodies of vipers, and wings of bats. They all lashed at Oz with forked tongues, whispering, hissing, chanting, cackling, screeching vitriolic incriminations of Oz's failure, mocking his fragile trust in the Great One and his frail intentions.

Suddenly, Oz felt a burning fury directed at the vapors poisoning his mind. "No!" Oz looked up and reached his wings skyward. "Great One, deliver me from these lies!"

Immediately, Oz felt like he was soaring high above. In his mind, he looked down at the scene of Obsolom and the other figures as they shrieked and cried in agony and shriveled to nothingness. Oz felt a solid peace guarding his heart and mind.

Oz hugged Joey closer and again looked over at Preya. He would trust that whatever did or did not happen, the Great One had Oz under the shadow of his wings where it would be well with his soul.

Just then, Preya stirred. Opening her eyes, she raised her head slightly toward Oz, trying to speak. Oz set Joey down and rushed to her side, cradling her head in his wing.

"Preya," Oz whispered into her ear, "I love you."

"Be—strong—and—courageous," Preya haltingly gasped out the words and closed her eyes. Her head relaxed in Oz's wing, and he laid it down carefully, letting her rest. Her chest rose and fell in shallow breaths.

"She gets her strength back in spurts."

Oz whipped around to see Huldah sitting on the opposite side of the nest. "Why do you always have to sneak up on me?" Oz's heart was drumming. "Huldah, she is so weak. Will she get better? And Joey, is he just hungry, or is something else wrong?"

"I see you got yourself away from the humans. I like your new bracelet." Huldah stepped over to Joey to check on his leg.

Oz looked down at the shiny purple band on his leg. Preya would like it.

"And," Oz pointed to the four exposed eggs, "what will happen to the eggs?" A tear slipped onto one of the eggs, the large one that had given Preya so much pain. They had waited so long to have a family.

"Preya is able to lay on them a few hours at a time. If needed, I can fill in. It's been a while, but I think I remember how." Huldah winked at Oz. "And Joey is getting fed." But for now, I think you have somewhere else to be."

Oz followed Huldah's gaze skyward as a large object blocked the sun over them. Looking up, far above in the upper stratosphere, an eagle soared. Oz felt a shock of amazement as he realized the enormity of the eagle to be able to cast a shadow in flight over the nest.

Lead them. Be strong and courageous. The eagle made no perceptible sound, yet Oz heard him clearly. As the eagle passed in front of the sun, Oz blinked, and the eagle was gone.

Oz burst off the nest, confident of what he must do. He flew higher and higher over the lake and above the canals. He could see the whole neighborhood beneath him. He held his wings close to his body and dove sharply for thirty feet, stretching out his wings and arching upward, lifting again.

"Fweep, fweep, ker-cheep!"

CHAPTER 46

"**A**nton! I think that's Oz! Is he calling us?" Tilly poked her head out of the water from underneath a dock where she had been hiding from Obsolom and his gang.

Anton stood on the dock, his wings wide open, drying from his morning fishing dives. He refused to retreat into hiding. He was in the military to obey orders for the right cause and would not desert his post.

"Yes, Seaman Tilly, that is affirmative."

"Fweep, fweep, ker-cheep!"

"Raise the sails! We have been given orders to meet at the peninsula. We are going to battle."

Oz continued soaring over the lakes and canals, rising and diving and rising again in figure-eight patterns. Once or twice, he thought he had seen another glimpse of the giant eagle, but it always disappeared when he tried to focus on it. Below, he saw a group of gulls and thought there might be a remote chance that Giuseppe or Maria was with them.

"Fweep, fweep, ker-cheep!" Oz hoped that if Giuseppe heard him, he would decide to rejoin the campaign.

Oz wondered if anyone would meet him at the peninsula to join him in stopping the trapper. He also turned over in his mind what Obsolom would do. He or his spies would have seen and heard Oz. Remarkably, Oz did not feel any fear over what Obsolom might do. A peculiar joy flowed through his veins that had nothing to do with what was happening around him. No, this joy was a feeling of release of the heavy burden of hopelessness, a sense of buoyancy of riding on the updrafts of the Great One's protection.

Circling down to the peninsula, Oz saw Skamp and Chatty bounding through the branches, chittering with each other toward the meeting place. Well, at least he had the loyal squirrels.

"Reporting for battle, sir!" Anton said as Oz landed in the meeting tree. Tilly had stationed herself at the base of the tree and was still panting from swimming as fast as she could and then plodding at full turtle speed up the bank and over to the others.

Oz winced and hung his head at the deep gashes the vultures had inflicted onto Tilly's shell that she would display for the rest of her life. The beautiful orange markings were now marred with blackish raking. "Anton, Tilly, I am so ashamed of how I spoke to you. You have risked your lives for this cause."

"Good soldiers carry out their duties knowing their lives may be in danger and are not offended by moments of frustration of their commanding officers. Apologies are not necessary." Anton stood tall and saluted.

"And I bear these battle scars as medals of honor," Tilly

pronounced as she stretched her head out of her shell.

"Thank you, both." Oz turned to the squirrels. "Skamp, Chatty, thank you. Many muscovies have been saved because of your bravery in coming forward."

"What's next, Oz?" Skamp asked. Chatty twitched her whiskers and held her tail, trying to keep it calm.

"We are being called to stop the man." Oz looked up as a shadow passed over him. "This mission is the Great One's and will be successful by his power."

CHAPTER 47

"That trapper shot a muscovy!" Jeffrey exclaimed.

"Are you serious?" Shannon scrunched her eyebrows together.

"The post just came over from the Havenport News site. It happened earlier this morning." Jeffrey handed his phone to Shannon so she could read the post. They had been standing outside on Jeffrey's back patio, talking about the osprey escaping, when Jeffrey's phone chimed.

Sophie crossed her arms across her chest. "All they were supposed to do was capture those poor ducks and release them in a wild refuge area."

"This says the trapper was attacked by a female muscovy who appeared to have an injured shoulder." Shannon looked at Jeffrey and Sophie. "I think this was Mrs. Green. I saw her the other day with a wound on her shoulder. None of the ducklings or Mr. Green were with her. I bet the trapper took them and injured her."

"I haven't seen the Greens the last several days. They usually come by in the morning for Duke to bark at them." Jeffrey scratched Duke's head.

"This is wrong!" Shannon cried.

"Fweep, fweep, ker-cheep!"

"Hey, isn't that our osprey?" Shannon pointed up to an osprey diving and rising. Duke joined her and ran around in circles, barking at the bird. The purple aluminum identification band that Shannon had attached to the bird's leg glinted in the sunlight.

Jeffrey and Sophie walked to Shannon's side and looked up, shading their eyes with their hands.

"Yes, I see the ID band. Well, look at him! He sure seems to have healed well." Sophie hugged Shannon.

"I'm surprised he is doing so well. He almost died. So, he flew out through Duke's doggie door?"

"Yeah, he shot through it like a missile launched from the USS Freedom!" Jeffrey stroked his beard. "Something must have made him eager to get away."

"Maybe he heard the shot. That would have alarmed him." Shannon adjusted her glasses, wiping sweat from under the nose pads. "Jeffrey, Sophie, we have to do something about this trapper. We can't let this continue. This is inhumane."

"Fweep, fweep, ker-cheep!"

"Mommy, is that Mr. Oz?" Mary Catherine peeped and pointed up to the sky with her stubby winglet to an osprey flying up and down. "Daddy said he was dead."

Mary Margaret knew it was Oz before she confirmed it with her eyes. Oz was calling everyone and anyone to meet him at the peninsula to launch an attack on the trapper. A muscovy had been shot.

And Mary Margaret had witnessed it and done nothing for Girdie. Nothing. But this is what the humans had decreed, and her council supported. Why, then, was she feeling such thorny sadness in her chest about this? Girdie and her were both ducks, and both had husbands and ducklings. They ate the same food and swam the same waters. But the muscovies should have left on their own; they knew they were not welcome. Then, maybe all this wouldn't have happened.

Peter Paul had also been listening to Oz, whom he thought was dead or at least seriously injured. A cold fear swept over him. Obsolom would be calling for Peter Paul any minute.

CHAPTER 48

"So, what do you want us to do, Oz? We could throw acorns at him or scurry above the tires in front of his van and chew some of those black tubes. They don't taste very good, but we would do it for you. Or we could..."

"Sweetheart," Skamp reached over to Chatty, "let's hear what Oz has to say."

Chatty scowled at Skamp but sat back on her tail to immobilize it.

Oz considered his small band of four volunteers. Though tempted to despair, he remembered the great eagle soaring above and the ancient saying: Those that wait upon the Great One shall renew their strength; they shall mount up with wings like eagles.

Oz bowed his head. "Let's pray for the Great One to lead us." Several moments passed, and Oz felt strength rising in him.

The sound of a gull calling overhead broke the silence. Oz looked up, happy to see Giuseppe landing on the branch near him.

"Giuseppe! I wasn't sure you heard me or that you would come." Oz hopped up to the gull and clapped him on the shoulder.

"How ya doin'? You know I'm a gull of action. And remember? We're family." Giuseppe hugged Oz tight and pecked him on both cheeks.

For the next twenty minutes, the small band of rescuers discussed strategies. The last any of them knew, the man had been riding up and down the canals in his boat looking for unsuspecting muscovies. A combined water and air attack was planned.

Suddenly, a pelican clonked to the ground with a loud squawk. Oz had to blink twice to make sure he was seeing straight. "Petunia?" Oz tensed his shoulders.

"What's that dirty rat pelican doing here?" Giuseppe braced himself to leap into attack.

Still trying to catch her breath, Petunia cried out to Oz. "Danger is coming this way. Now!"

Giuseppe dove down and stood before Petunia, jutting out his beak. "What are you blabbing about? Give us a reason to trust you."

"Yeah!" Tilly stretched her head fully out of her shell toward Petunia. "Why should we listen to you? You watched us get beat up by Obsolom and his gang and flew off with him!"

"Listen to me! You need to protect yourselves!" Petunia squawked, ignoring the accusations.

Oz felt calmness flow through him, removing the tension in his shoulders. Trust her, he sensed the Great One saying. "Everyone, let us hear what she has to say."

Petunia flailed her wings and shouted out. "A rowdy group of hellions led by Obsolom has gathered against you; they are at the Dead Marsh, where the vultures hang out. They will be taking flight any minute. Or maybe they already have." The Dead Marsh was only a five-minute flight away.

Oz leaned forward. "Petunia, tell us everything you know."

"When I heard you, I figured Obsolom would have heard you too. I waited for a call to a council meeting, and I knew when I did not get one, that he must have arranged with others to stop you for good. I'm sure he suspects I am not loyal to him. So, I eavesdropped."

Giuseppe poked his wing at the pelican, "Not loyal to Obsolom? Whudah you talkin' about, you're not loyal to us!"

Petunia leaned forward to the gull, "Giuseppe, can't you see? If I had not shone support for Obsolom, I could not stay in his confidence, and none of us would know of this impending attack!" Petunia then shifted to meet everyone's gaze. "Do any of you know what this has been like trying to appear devoted to Obsolom when his toxic superiority complex and injustice turns my stomach, and I see my companions of justice beat up and then have to act like I am deserting them?" All were silent as Petunia panted, regaining her composure. She turned first to Giuseppe and then to Oz. "I'm so sorry for what they did to you. I am loyal to you; I wish you would believe that."

"I do, Petunia, I do." Oz looked around at the others and then back to Petunia. "Who has aligned with Obsolom?"

"Crete and a bunch of his cronies, maybe fifty mercenary vultures led by Valafar, Cronan, and a flock of crows from his old neighborhood. About a hundred birds."

"Was Peter Paul there?" Oz questioned.

"No, at least I did not see him."

"Man the ships!" Anton cried out.

Chatty gasped and ran up the tree and hid behind some leaves.

"I'm not scared of them!" Tilly stood as high as she could on her stubby legs and stretched her head out.

"They are going to be on top of us any moment! What are we doing?" Petunia looked up at Oz with anxious eyes.

At the realization that they would momentarily be overtaken by a massive force intent on annihilating the group, Oz felt the cruel talons of fear threatening to tear at his mind and soul. Oh, Great One, he thought, help us! A shadow passed over, and Oz caught a glimpse of the great eagle, bigger than a human's vehicle.

Oz stood on the tip of his talons, looking up and lifting his wings. "O Great One, you are Lord of all! In your hand are power and might so no one can withstand you. You called us to protect those who could not protect themselves, and now Obsolom and his forces are coming to destroy us and stop us from carrying out your will. O Great One, defend your cause!"

Immediately, Oz was again aware of the eagle flying high above them. It was calling them to fly up to him. "Tilly, Chatty, Skamp, hold your position here. Giuseppe, Anton, and Petunia follow me."

As the four birds took flight, a roiling dark cloud of whirring wings approached from the west. What sounded like a swarm of enraged hornets swelled into battle cries of cawing, screeching, and shrieking.

Oz looked up at the eagle and felt it speaking to him. "Do not be afraid; the battle is the Great One's. They will come against you, but you will not need to fight. Fly onward and hold your position." The eagle soared higher until it disappeared into a cloud.

Oz called to the others. "Do not be afraid. The eagle will lead us."

"What eagle?" Giuseppe squawked back.

"I don't see an eagle!" Petunia cried, her voice almost drowned out by the deafening noise of the approaching mass.

Oz knew then that only he could see or hear the eagle. An emboldened strength surged through him and carried him along the updrafts toward the oncoming horde.

Obsolom and his massive regiment were now close enough that Oz could distinguish who was who. Oz met Obsolom's eyes and felt malevolence glaring back at him. Oz called to the others above the din. "Hold the course; do not turn back or sideways. Fly straight toward them!"

The four birds flew wing to wing into the midst of the onslaught. Obsolom flew directly at Oz and steeled his wing to give a death blow to Oz. With all his might, Oz resisted the urge to dive or turn. He tensed as Obsolom met him in the air, ready for the blow. But, instead, Obsolom struck against something else, something solid, something that made him spin out of control. Oz saw the great eagle chasing Obsolom as he spun toward the ground, uselessly beating his wings.

Then, hundreds of eagles appeared, flying toward them from all directions. They swooped, darted, and dove in and out of the massive air raid. Still, only Oz could see the eagles.

Confusion reigned. The vultures were screeching at the Great Blues for smashing into them, and the Great Blues were shrieking at the crows for flying directly under them and ruining their lift, and the crows were cawing at all the others for hitting them with their wings. From the corners of his eyes, Oz saw his companions observing the chaos with open beaks and wide eyes. They kept flying through the throng untouched, with their attackers reeling, spinning, and falling around them.

CHAPTER 49

Skamp and Chatty had climbed to the highest point on the pine to get a good view of the aerial battle. Chatty clasped her tail in front of her eyes, peeking through the thick fur every few seconds.

"Obsolom is heading straight toward Oz!" Chatty shouted over the din.

Skamp and Chatty put their paws over their mouths as they saw the collision, but Oz kept flying on like nothing had happened. Obsolom, however, spiraled toward the peninsula in a zig-zag pattern as if something was battering him on his descent. Down he came, crashing through trees and bushes.

The squirrels scampered down the tree to where Tilly was. "Did you see Obsolom fall?" Skamp asked.

"Yes, he fell head-first into that bougainvillea bush over there." Tilly pointed to the red-leafed bush about twenty feet away.

"Is that him making that screechy noise?" Chatty cupped her ear toward the bush. It was still hard to hear with the commotion happening above.

"Come on! Let's go check it out." Skamp leaped toward the bush. Chatty and Tilly hesitated at running into danger but then followed Skamp, leaving some distance between them.

Nearing the bush, they could see the grand osprey

hanging upside down and struggling. His long, thick pinions had become tangled amongst the thicket of thorny branches. As Obsolom fought to get loose, the branches locked to each other around him, forming an inescapable prison. "Get me out of here!"

The squirrels and turtle laughed at the arrogant bird striving and straining only to entangle himself more.

"I am ordering you to use your steely little teeth to chew these branches and release me or suffer consequences!" Obsolom tried to jut his head toward the group but only succeeded in getting his neck stuck in a brace of branches, immobilizing him even more.

"Why would we help you get out of that bush? You would want to hurt us; yes, you would! But we're not afraid of you! You're a bad leader!" With one hand on her hip, Chatty was shaking her other finger at Obsolom. Her tail slashed up and down and back and forth.

As the noise above intensified, the three moved further out into a clearing to get a better view of the sky show. The mass of attackers was flying out of control as if caught in a whirlwind. "Are they attacking each other? Look! Oz and the others are just flying through them!" Tilly said.

The four birds had glided through the mass and were almost to the edge of the bedlam. The crows, ragged from being attacked by who they thought were the vultures and great blues, were the first to give up. Oz heard Cronan crowing to them and they flocked to the other side of the lake. Seeing that Obsolom had fallen and the Great Blues had betrayed them, the mercenary vultures made a unison screech and headed toward their homeland several counties away. Most of the Great Blues were still being buffeted by the eagles and quarreled with each other. Some started to desert the fray.

"Fly toward them," the eagle whispered to Oz's consciousness.

"Bank around," Oz called to the others. "Fly directly at them."

"Reposition and attack!" Oz heard Crete scream out to the remaining Great Blues.

Oz and the three others now faced the oncoming herons. Crete led and stared directly at Oz with his orange eyes. The eagles flew above and below and to either side of the attackers but were not engaging with them. The herons picked up speed unhampered by the invisible eagles who had formed a tunnel around them.

Just as Crete was to make impact with Oz, an eagle swooped down and, with thick twelve-inch-long talons, grabbed Crete by his neck and shoulder. Oz saw the eagle drop Crete onto the peninsula. The other eagles were now clipping the herons with their wings and talons. The herons started attacking each other, thinking they had turned on themselves.

Meanwhile, Tilly, Chatty, and Skamp had been watching in amazement as the attackers fought each other. The crows and vultures abandoned the Great Blues, and now their friends were heading toward the herons.

Crete seemed to crumple above them in front of Oz, and then he fell, his body slamming to the ground near Tilly with a thud. Startled, Skamp and Chatty bounded up a nearby tree, and Tilly yanked herself into her shell as far as she could.

After a few seconds, Tilly heard a faint groaning. Wrinkle by wrinkle, she poked out her nose and then her eyes to see. Skamp and Chatty had come back down the tree and were creeping over. Crete was in a heap with one wing bent at a sharp angle across his back. Three large scrapes across his neck and chest were scarlet with fresh blood.

Skamp ventured closer to the bird, stopping a few inches away. Crete didn't seem as imposing lying there in that awkward position. Crete opened his eyes, blinked, and focused on Skamp. "Rat!" Like an alligator snapping, Crete lunged but immediately fell back to a lump, shrieking in pain. Rolling his eyes back in his head, he became deathly still.

"Chatty, quick! Help get some Spanish moss, lots of it! Tilly, don't let him get away!"

Tilly shrugged her shoulders, thinking about what she could do to stop Crete if he tried to escape. Maybe she should back up to him now and throw dirt on him with her back legs. Or snap at his beak with her powerful jaws. But Skamp and Chatty were soon back with armfuls of the greenish-gray moss that hung from the nearby oak. Together, they tightly wound several layers of the rope-like tendrils around Crete, securing his wings and legs against his body.

Oz watched as the herons flew away in every direction, one by one, to get away from each other. The sky was clear. Turning back around, he saw the eagles were gone, too.

"Back to base!" Oz called to the others.

CHAPTER 50

S uddenly aware of the absence of noise, Skamp looked up to see Oz and the others flying toward them and preparing to land. The Great Blues were gone.

"Is that Crete?" Oz landed and stepped over to see a sizeable mossy cocoon with the unmistakable beak of a great blue heron sticking out.

"Yes. And he is not going anywhere. He might be dead. But we didn't want to take a chance. He tried to eat Skamp." Chatty twitched her whiskers.

"Excellent work, soldiers!" Anton marched over to inspect the bindings, nudging Crete with his foot to see if he moved.

"Who's making all that racket?" Giuseppe looked over to where a shrieking noise was coming from.

"Obsolom. He is stuck in the bush and really angry." Tilly started trudging toward the bougainvillea bush while Skamp and Chatty bounded ahead, and the others followed.

"Well, if it isn't my treasonous baby brother," Obsolom snarled as the group drew near. "Get me out of here, and I might consider pardoning you."

"This looks like the work of the Great One. Who am I to set you free?" Oz marveled at how tightly the bush seemed to encase his brother. No matter how Obsolom struggled, it only increased the grasp of the thorny branches around him.

"You think your allegiance to a mythical god will save you? You are doomed to defeat! This bush cannot hold me. I will get out of these branches, and I will destroy you." Obsolom wriggled and writhed so that the branches strangled around his barreled chest and the thorns pressed into his flesh.

Oz stepped closer, keeping his eyes level with his brother's. "No, Obsolom. The Great One has delivered us from your clutches. And you are the one now at *his* mercy."

"Your laughable campaign has failed. You have been deserted. You are the joke of the community. I am the one the people listen to. The one they worship!" The long thorns were now extracting drops of blood along Obsolom's throat and chest.

"Obsolom, if only you could recognize the truth."

The massive osprey frenziedly tried to breathe as the branches gripped around his neck. "Truth! The truth is you cannot replace me as leader. You were a mama's boy from the day you hatched, and then Aunt Huldah coddled you under her wing. I am the strong one, the one who can lead with power. You are weak and will never be like me."

"I pray that is true." Oz turned around to the others. "Let's finish this. Let's get rid of that man."

The group looked up as a soft flutter was heard from a branch in a tree nearby.

"Othello!" Oz flew up to his nephew and wrapped his wings around him. Below, Obsolom's screeching turned into coughing as his neck became more constricted by the bush.

"Father!" At the sound of his father's coughing, Othello

flew down to where Obsolom was incapacitated in the bush.

Obsolom glared at his son. "If one drop of my blood runs through your veins, you will set me loose, and we will together eradicate these miscreant conspirators."

Othello stepped closer to the bush and held his wing out. "Dad, I love you but won't do that."

"Coward!" Unable to lunge, Obsolom hissed and spat at Othello.

Othello slowly turned away and stepped over to the group. "The man is at the back side of the pond by the park. He just returned from getting rid of the muscovies he captured this morning." Othello closed his eyes and put his head down. "I've been following him since I left the other day. I know where he takes them. And what he does with them." Othello looked back to his father, up at Oz, and then the others, and closing his eyes again, bowed his head to his chest.

"They have gone to fly with their fathers, haven't they." Chatty buried her head in Skamp's chest and wrapped her arms around him.

"We have to stop him. Now." Oz swooped down to join the others. In a huddle, they reviewed their strategy in hushed whispers. There was no taking chances that Obsolom, or one of his spies, might hear and try to stop them. Obsolom was trapped but still choking out threats.

The birds took off in a flourish of wings, and the squirrels bounded away. Tilly was left for only the minute it took to plod over to the water and dive in.

"You'll never succeed! The humans will prevail!" Obsolom's voice faded into gurgles and sputters as the thorns impaled deeper.

CHAPTER 51

The man tracked slowly around the back side of the pond, wading in the shallow waters in knee-high black rubber boots. Water midges buzzed around his sweat-matted beard and hair. Each step he took sucked a squishy sound out of the marsh as he pulled his leg forward. The imprint his boot left swirled fresh mud and smelled of rotting grass. He was having a good day. Ten ducks snagged this morning. No freakish birds attacking him. Except for that female muscovy. But he did get to use his pistol. The over-privileged people that lived here should appreciate him getting rid of the ugly muscovies. Maybe he would demand a bonus. He spat out a brown stream and wiped the spittle from his beard with his tobacco-stained sleeve.

Up ahead, underneath a cypress on the other side of some grasses, he heard faint rustling and the soft chirping of a female muscovy. There would be at least one, probably two or three. They seemed to always group in twos or threes. He could hardly believe his luck. This would be an easy start to the afternoon. Maybe he could start his drinking early at Belly Ups. That sassy blonde waitress better give him some respect with the fist of cash he would get from that stuck-up HOA president.

Rounding the corner of the pond, on the other side of the patch of tall grass where the ducks were, the man crouched down beneath the cypress. Carefully, he parted the grass so he could get a better view. Yup. Sure enough, he saw three shapes of ducks through the thick grass. One of them must be a juvenile, as it looked much smaller. The oversized male was brownish-gray, and the female was primarily black.

A pinecone hit and bounced off his back as he prepared to ready his net. Looking up into the cypress from where it had come, the man saw a couple of squirrels chasing each other through the branches and making rat noises. Varmints. He could get rid of those, too. Maybe that would be his next gig with this cash-cow neighborhood.

Standing up, the man took one measured step after the other to bring him around the patch of grass to net the muscovies. Above, the squirrels continued chittering and jumping up, down, and around in the tree. The man thought about what he would do to the varmints if they scared away the ugly ducks with all their noise.

Thwack!

Biting his tongue and swallowing his cussing to prevent alerting the ducks, the man reached his hand to his head, which a brick-sized chunk of wood had just clobbered. The squirrels were now looking directly at him from twenty feet above, squeaking and squealing. Shaking his fist at them, he continued around the corner one step at a time, carefully lifting his foot each step to avoid making a sound. With only a few feet more to go, he crouched again behind the last strands of grass to get a better idea of exactly where the ducks were.

There. Perfect. Still behind a lump of grass, he could see their backs and hear them chirping. He would aim for the large male and maybe get lucky and get all three at once. He was getting good at this; the ugly ducks were an easy target. Checking his net one last time, he raised it and sprang forward with all his weight, swinging the net down in front of him at the large gray muscovy. Success!

He tossed the pole net with the hefty bird on the bank and quickly grabbed another net. However, before he could get it into position, a seagull and anhinga emerged from the lump of grass and flew up at his head. Dropping the net, the man put his hands to his face as the zealous birds flew directly over him, depositing a shower of muddy pond water. Cussing, the man fell forward into the pond, where he met eye-to-eye with a turtle the size of a garbage can lid, who jumped at him and bit into his nose, gripping like a vice. The man screamed in pain, feeling his nose crack sideways. Using both hands, the man grabbed each side of the turtle's shell and pushed and rocked the turtle side to side until it finally ripped away from him and dove into the water with a chunk of his left nostril. Blood was streaming out his nose. He became aware that the squirrels were even more raucous as they seemed to laugh and make fun of his misfortune.

"Keep your yaps shut, you mangy varmints!" The man raged and shook his fist toward the squirrels. Just then, the anhinga and the gull flew together over the pond toward him, squawking and honking. As they drew near, the man faced the birds and took a long stick from the ground to defend himself against the possessed creatures.

"Come at me, and I'll kill you dead."

Suddenly, the man heard deafening screeching in his ears and strong wings beating against his head. He hit at the air with the stick, stumbling forward with force, and looked up to see two ospreys reaching fifty feet flying away from the pond.

"What the?"

Having looked away from the pond, the trapper was unprepared for the anhinga and gull who flew at the back of his head, grabbing chunks of the man's red matted hair and ripping it out amidst his shouts of pain. The two birds alluded the man's thrashing and flew up into the cypress, landing just above the squirrels, who were jumping up and down and appeared to be clapping their paws together.

Turning his head, the man saw the two screeching ospreys descending from opposite directions in downward spirals. They were both heading directly toward him.

"You devil birds ain't gonna mess with me!" The man growled and grabbed his pistol from its holster. Letting the birds get closer, the man aimed at the osprey with the purple tag on its leg and pulled the trigger.

CHAPTER 52

"This guy had better show up soon. I have to get over to the peninsula; I've been getting non-stop calls for the last hour about some huge flock of birds over there. Did you see or hear anything?" Jared had met Shannon and Jeffrey at the trapper's van so they could talk to the trapper about the shooting that morning.

Shannon turned to Jeffrey and back to Jared. "No, we haven't. Jared, that man is injuring the muscovies, and I highly doubt he is bringing them to a refuge. You know that he shot and killed one this morning right here in the park where people bring their kids. This has to stop," Shannon appealed to the HOA president. Shannon aimed to convince Jared to reverse the HOA's decision to remove the muscovies.

"I agree, Shannon. He's history. We will hire a more reputable capture and release contractor."

"Jared, you and I have lived here a long time. You know you can't remove the muscovies for good," Jeffrey reasoned.

"No, but several people have been complaining for a while about how numerous they are and the messes they make. We can at least reduce the numbers." Jared leaned against the filthy van.

"But you know they are no different from the mallards

in making messes. And they don't make as much noise," Shannon added.

"You two aren't telling me anything I haven't already heard. And your daily phone messages, emails, and texts aren't helping."

"They also eat tons of bugs. There are lots of other benefits...."

Suddenly, Shannon jumped at a blasting sound. "That's a gunshot." She pointed to the other side of the pond where it came from.

With high-pitched yelps, Duke bolted and strained at his leash, almost tearing it from Jeffrey's grip, and then pulled Jeffrey ahead toward the sound. Shannon followed close. Jared lagged behind, being careful where he stepped with his loafers. Behind them, they could hear the siren of a police car pulling up behind the trapper's van.

Jeffrey stopped short at the sight of the trapper aiming his pistol toward him. Between them, on the ground, was an osprey—their osprey with the purple tag on his leg—struggling to stand.

Duke barked wildly and, yanking the leash out of Jeffrey's hands, bounded at the man. With long leaps, Duke lunged his full eighty pounds at the man's chest, knocking the pistol out of his hand. The man fell back into the pond, where Duke pounced on top of him, alternately barking in his face and biting at his hands.

The trapper pushed against Duke but soon felt the large hands of two hulking police officers grabbing him by both arms and dragging him out of the water.

"You're under arrest," one of the officers said as he pulled out a set of handcuffs.

"For what? I ain't done nothin' wrong!"

"Shooting an osprey for one thing," said the second

officer.

"That bird attacked me." The trapper winced as the officer put his hands behind his back.

"Ospreys don't attack people," Shannon scolded as she knelt by Oz.

"And trapping protected birds," the second officer added.

"What are you talking about? I only bagged those ugly muscovy ducks," the man snorted as the officer tightened the cuffs around his wrists.

"Then these are some strange-looking muscovies!" Jeffrey pointed at two nets under the cypress where the second officer took pictures. One net trapped a brown pelican; in the other was a gull, an anhinga, and another osprey. Duke walked around sniffing at the nets, wagging his tail. The trapped birds were oddly calm.

"I don't know nothin' 'bout how those demon birds got in my nets. They attacked me!" The man sputtered.

"Birds only defend themselves against people who are trying to hurt them. What did you do to them?" Shannon demanded to know.

"And, officers, you can add trespassing on private property." Jared folded his arms. "I have received several complaints from residents."

"And, we'll add possession of a stolen firearm to the charges." The second police officer returned to the group with the trapper's pistol. He pointed to where the serial number had been filed away.

"I didn't steal that. I won it fair-and-square at a pit bull fight." Small tributaries of sweat were making their way down the man's face and arms, leaving trails through the grime.

"Maybe you better not say anything more." The first

officer started to walk back to the parked squad car, leading the trapper by the arm.

The trapper looked back at the HOA president. "You owe me five hundred bucks."

"No, we don't." Jared pulled out an envelope, removed some papers, and held them up toward the trapper. "Your contract with the Havenport HOA that you signed states that any illegal activity by you in carrying out the removal of muscovy ducks will render the contract null and void." Jared ripped the papers in half and then in half again.

The man spat at Jared as the first officer steered him away. "You bunch of uptight, overprivileged animal huggers!" The trapper could still be heard cursing as they rounded the corner of the pond toward the police cruiser.

"Ma'am, I understand you're a vet. Can you help me release these birds?" The second officer stood by the nets, eyeing the captive birds. The squirrels chattering above added to his unease. Animals, especially trapped ones, could be dangerous.

"Of course!" Shannon hurried over and strategized the best way to release them. "Let's release the pelican first since it is alone in that net."

Shannon and the police officer worked together to loosen the net and joined the others several feet away. Within a few seconds, Petunia pushed away the netting around her. She then walked over to the other net and tugged at it with her bill.

"What is that pelican doing?" Jared took a step closer to get a better view.

The three birds stood to their feet and, shaking off the net, walked out from underneath it.

"Well, I've never seen anything like that. And those birds are just standing there looking at us." Jared scratched his head.

"Me neither. Well, looks like I'm done here. Ma'am, are you going to take care of the osprey, or should I call the county animal control?"

Shannon walked over and knelt again in front of Oz. "I will take care of him." It looked like the same shoulder was injured again. She wondered what was going through the poor bird's mind.

"Sir, can you come with me to fill out some paperwork?" The officer looked at Jared.

"Absolutely. My pleasure. This one needs to be locked up." Following the officer, Jared paused by Shannon. "You say the muscovies have benefits. Write them up and present them at the next HOA meeting."

◆ ◆ ◆

Jeffrey squatted down next to Shannon and reached his hand out to the bird. "How is he, Shannon?"

Shannon wrapped a stray strand of hair behind her ear. "Thankfully, I don't see any bullet wound. It may have just whizzed past him, and he fell to the ground."

The lady with the red hair and glass disks on her eyes was carefully feeling all around Oz's body. Oz knew now that she and Duke's master wanted to help him, but he still struggled a bit. The same shoulder that had always given him a problem felt like sharp talons were digging into him. He couldn't move his wing, and it jutted out at a strange angle unfolded halfway.

"Shannon, look." Jeffrey nodded his head over to where the four birds were. They were meandering their way toward them. A giant turtle and the two squirrels making a racket in the cypress had joined them. Duke walked beside them, wagging his tail.

"It's as if they want to know what is happening with the osprey."

Jeffrey turned back to Oz. "What is wrong with him?"

"Same injury as before. Dislocated shoulder."

Without warning, the lady took firm hold of Oz's upper wing, pulled it straight out, and moved it sharply to the side. Oz shrieked as he felt intense pain and heard a sickening pop. He panted and felt light-headed from the sharp burst of pain but soon realized his wing was back in place, and he could move it again. The pain was still there but had dulled to a deep ache.

Jeffrey jumped at the sudden operation. "I can't believe you just did that."

Oz watched as the two humans stood and stepped away about ten feet. He rotated his shoulder and stretched his wings to work out the kinks. He stepped toward Shannon and Jeffrey, stopping less than a yard in front of them. The two humans met eyes and then turned their attention back to Oz. The osprey looked up at them and then uttered a gentle screech.

"I think he said thank you," Jeffrey said.

Oz then turned toward the others and, with a mighty leap, sprang into the air. The other birds followed him, and the squirrels scampered away. The turtle slid down the bank and dove into the pond. Duke barked and wagged his tail.

CHAPTER 53

"Meet me at the council tree." Oz led the others in flight away from the pond. He flew high, trying to ignore his aching shoulder. He looked around for the eagles, but they were nowhere to be seen. "I have to go check on Preya. Petunia, get the other council members. Anton, bring Tilly. Othello, tell Skamp and Chatty. Giuseppe, go to Cara's nest and convince her to come. Call to Maria to watch Cara's kids." Oz called out orders, and the four birds dispatched to their assignments, flying off in different directions.

Oz banked left and headed toward his nest.

Landing lightly on the edge, Oz hopped over to where Huldah stood over Preya, rubbing her back on the far side of the nest. Preya was crouched, and her chest was heaving with rapid panting. The four eggs lay exposed in their original spot. Joey sat beside the eggs, peeping softly and fluttering his stubby wing buds.

Concern struck Oz. "Huldah?"

"I think we finally know what is going on with Preya."

Preya gritted her beak and strained, letting out a muffled shriek. Huldah kept rubbing her back.

"What is wrong?" Oz paced back and forth, clenching and unclenching his wings.

Preya shrieked louder.

"Huldah! Help her!" Oz stepped closer to Preya,

reaching his wing to caress her head. Preya looked up at him and shrieked again in pain.

"Oz, she is doing just fine herself. Go sit on the side of the nest."

"But what is wrong with her?"

"Nothing, she is laying another egg." Huldah continued stroking Preya's back.

A fifth egg? Did he hear correctly? Ospreys don't ever have five eggs in a clutch. Ever.

"Another egg? Are you sure? Are you sure there is not something else wrong?"

"Oz, I'm positive. Now, go sit down with Joey and be quiet. Pray. Quietly."

Oz retreated to the side of the nest where the eggs were. A warm wave of relief washed over him. Preya was only laying her fifth egg. The realization then hit him. Five eggs? Heat spread through his body.

Joey limped over and sat close to Oz, nuzzling under his wing. Oz stroked his tiny head.

He was going to have five chicks?

Joey's bright yellow feathers were now interspersed with specks of brown. While still weak, Joey seemed better than he was this morning.

How were Oz and Preya going to raise five chicks all at once?

Joey looked up at Oz and peeped softly.

And a muscovy duckling?

"Push, Preya. Push now," Huldah instructed.

Preya expelled one long, loud shriek and strained hard.

"Excellent!" Huldah called out. "Oz! Come and see your new egg!"

With one leap, Oz was by Preya's side, cradling her tired head in his wing. The brightness had already returned to her eyes, and she smiled at Oz. Next to her was the largest osprey egg Oz had ever seen. "Are you OK?"

"I'm perfect." Preya shifted and sat up. Already, strength was returning. "Isn't it awesome?" Preya gazed at the egg that had given her so much suffering with eyes full of bliss.

◆ ◆ ◆

A flutter and a squawk announced the arrival of Giuseppe and Maria. "Another egg? Ma che bell'! How beautiful!" Maria clapped her wings.

"You've sure got your wings full." Giuseppe winked at Oz. "The council has gathered."

"Is Cara coming?"

"Yeah. She got one of the other crow moms to watch her kids." Giuseppe unloaded a few worms from his clutches for Joey. "How's the yellow ducky?" They bumped wings, sending Joey backward and giggling at Giuseppe's playful shove.

Maria revealed a catfish she had been carrying. "I'll stay with Preya and Joey."

"What is going on?" Huldah asked Oz.

"I'll tell you on the way." Oz looked over at Preya.

"I'm fine. Go. The Great One is with us!"

Far above, Oz heard the call of an eagle, but when he looked up, all he saw was blue sky.

CHAPTER 54

As the three birds arrived near the council snag, excited conversation met them. Oz landed on the snag with Huldah. Giuseppe perched near Othello in the branches higher above. Along with the council members, several residents had somehow heard of the impromptu meeting and were scattered amongst the trees and brush. Anton and Tilly were in the marsh below, and Oz could hear Chatty and see her tail switching in a tree nearby.

"Why are we here?" Cronan looked directly at Oz and then up. "And what is that criminal gull doing here?"

"I'd like to know why you are here." Peter Paul stopped preening and pointed up to Othello. "Obsolom banished you."

Petunia brushed a small branch out of her face only to have it return in front of her beak. "If you would all be quiet, maybe Oz can tell you. It will become obvious who the criminals are and who they are not." Petunia winked up at Giuseppe, who nodded back to her.

"Yes, Petunia speaks wisely. I am also curious as to why Obsolom is not here." Horatio rotated his head around to all as he discoursed.

"I will explain everything. Huldah, would you please pray?" Oz's words rose solid and clear. The voices calmed to silence.

"Oh, Great One, you are the author of truth and justice. You appoint and remove leaders according to your will. Lead us. Guide us. Give us your wisdom. Amen."

"A muscovy was murdered today. And many others have been injured and brought to a refuse site and left to die." Oz paused to meet eyes with each council member briefly. "And we could have prevented this."

Oz then directed his gaze first at Cronan and then at Peter Paul. "We are here today to make right what is wrong."

Cronan hopped from leg to leg. "What is wrong is you going against Obsolom's orders and protecting those muscovies."

Peter Paul glanced at Cronan, hesitated, turned to Oz, and finally lowered his head to look down at his shiny orange feet. He thought back to this morning when Mary Margaret told him all about what she had witnessed when Girdie was killed.

Cronan whipped his head around to Peter Paul. "Where were you this morning when these outlaws attacked us?" Cronan waved his wings toward Oz, Giuseppe, and Anton and ended with Petunia. "And you, pretending to be on our side."

"I am on the side of truth and justice." Petunia stepped forward on the limb, stopping and catching herself from tumbling down. "We did not attack you this morning. You and your crow friends, Obsolom, Crete and his cronies, and Valafar with his mercenary vultures attacked us."

"Crete and mercenary vultures? Petunia, do you know what you are accusing our leader of?" Horatio peered down his beak at Petunia.

"According to section J14Y3.47.012 of the Avian

Military Code of Justice, it is called Illegal Alliances with Known Criminals." Anton flew up to a branch to get closer to the group. "And Petunia is correct. I witnessed it also."

"And we were there too. We saw hundreds of birds come after Oz and the others." Skamp and Chatty had emerged from their hiding place and sat next to Huldah.

"Not these tree rats again. Is the council really going to put up with this?" Cronan crowed toward Horatio and Peter Paul. "I demand to know where Obsolom is!"

"Wait, something doesn't make sense." Peter Paul looked around at the others. "If there were hundreds of birds attacking this puny group of four birds and two squirrels..."

"And a turtle," Tilly called out from below. "Don't forget the turtle."

"Right. And a turtle. As I was saying, if hundreds of birds attacked this group, why would they all be here unharmed? Cronan is the only alleged attacker here. And he looks a bit ruffed up."

"Yeah, explain that!" Cronan cawed.

"Cronan, look at me." Huldah had flown down to the branch Cronan was on. She stood with the sun at her back, casting her shadow over the crow. Cronan avoided her gaze. "I said, look at me." Huldah lowered her head so her eyes were level with Cronan's.

Cronan slowly raised his head toward Huldah and gulped. The sun directly behind her created an aura of light around her head. He had never been that close to Huldah. He had this feeling that she could see right into him.

"I want you to tell us the truth. Did Oz and his group attack you?"

Seconds ticked by as Cronan's shoulders twitched back

and forth, grinding his beak side to side, seeming to wrestle with some internal personage. "No!" The word shot out, leaving Cronan breathless.

"Well then, what happened?" Peter Paul struggled with what was true or false and who he should believe.

Huldah still stood in front of Cronan, commanding his attention. "Cronan?"

Cronan squirmed and shuddered and tried to hold his wing over his beak but could not keep back the explosion of testimony. "We attacked Oz and his group. But instead, the Great Blues attacked the vultures and then blamed us for flying in their space, and the vultures attacked us crows and the blues." Cronan panted as if he had just flown a two-hundred-yard race. "Me and the rest of the crows flew off."

Peter Paul leaned forward to Cronan. "What happened to Obsolom and Crete?"

At that moment, the council snag was shadowed by a group of seven gargantuan eagles flying in a "V" formation. Two of them each carried a bundle and dropped their objects when they were directly over the snag. All gasped and stared in amazement as the eagles flew away, soon obscured by tall cypresses and pines.

Oz was thankful that the eagles had shown themselves to everyone so they could see the justice and deliverance from the Great One.

The objects fell and lodged in some mangrove trees growing over the marsh. One of the objects appeared to be encased in Spanish moss, and the other in thorny sticks.

"It's Obsolom and Crete!" Chatty and Skamp skittered down and bounded onto the mangrove tree.

"We tied Crete up all by ourselves in Spanish moss. Well, Tilly helped too. And Obsolom got stuck in thorns."

Chatty ran up and down and over the mangroves from Crete to Obsolom and back again.

The council members and a few others flew down and, muttering to each other, perched around the objects. They could see Crete's beak poking out of the Spanish moss. Obsolom was completely immobilized by his prison. The thorny branches tangled around and through his once beautiful pinions, which were now frayed, bent, and broken. Obsolom could only dart his eyes from one person to the next and utter faint gurgling noises. Even though he could not speak intelligibly, palpable hatred pulsed from his eyes.

Huldah stepped over to Obsolom, who attempted to spit at her but only managed to receive a new puncture on his cheek from a thorn.

"The Great One has allowed you to keep your life and is allowing you to explain your actions." Huldah looked over at the two squirrels. "Skamp, Chatty, can you please release him?"

"Are you sure about that? You know how mean Obsolom can be." Chatty wrung her tail with her paws. "He might eat us."

"He will not be allowed to harm you or anyone else here," Huldah's voice assured.

Skamp and Chatty inched over to Obsolom and began to chew at the branches. Soon, sections began to fall away, and Obsolom was able to break through with his great wings. All that remained was a clump of tight branches binding his feet and another woven section around his head. The squirrels scampered a safe distance away and chattered back at him.

Obsolom tried to lunge at Oz, causing many birds to jump back, but his bindings caused him to fall at Oz's feet.

"I should have killed you instead of just pushing you out of the nest."

People turned to each other with quizzical looks.

Oz felt a slicing twinge through his chest, and it became suddenly clear. He remembered now. At first, it was fuzzy and blurry, but then the puzzling memory started to piece together in his mind. Oz was so young then, but a clear image emerged of his older brother standing on the side of the nest, convincing Oz he could fly when all he had was wing nubs. And then Obsolom extended his great wings, knocking Oz out of the nest! All these years, he was told it was an accident. That is what his parents believed. Never could they imagine Obsolom wanting to hurt Oz.

"Why did you push me out of the nest?" Oz didn't feel anger; instead, he felt an abysmal grief from knowing his brother, whom he loved and looked up to, had wanted to hurt him.

"Because of her." Obsolom pointed at Huldah. "Have you ever told him about your vision when he was born?" The fury oozed through Obsolom's voice.

"Aunt Huldah?" Oz scrutinized his aunt.

Huldah shrugged and spoke calmly. "It was not my place to tell you, Oz. I was only instructed to tell your father with Obsolom present." Huldah reached out her wing to touch Oz.

Oz pulled back. "What was the vision? Tell me!"

"Oh, I suppose it doesn't matter now since it has come to pass."

Obsolom screeched, thrashed his wings, and tried again to lunge, but his feet were still fettered.

Huldah continued. "Before you hatched, we all assumed Obsolom would become the leader when your father, Otto, went to fly with his fathers. But the Great One told me you would be the protector and that Obsolom would contend with you and fail."

Everyone looked at each other with open beaks and wide eyes.

"I can still kill you." Obsolom glared at Oz.

"No, you will go quietly." Huldah peered into Obsolom's eyes.

"And what makes you so sure of that, oh phony prophetess?" Obsolom spat out.

"Look up. You will be escorted."

Everyone looked up and saw four of the giant eagles hovering overhead.

Huldah continued, keeping her eyes fixed on Obsolom. "When released, you will fly northwest over the Gulf and along the coast for three days. There, your wings will fail you, and you will live the rest of your days chasing sandpipers on the beach and begging them for food."

Obsolom glowered.

"You are now released." At Huldah's words, the branches around Obsolom's feet and head fell loose.

Obsolom sprang at Oz, but before his feet could leave the branch, one of the eagles dove down and snatched Obsolom up, a shoulder in each taloned foot.

As the eagle rose to meet the others, Obsolom's voice trailed off with them. "You will regret this!"

Everyone gazed skyward as the eagles became small dots and then disappeared.

A few moments of silence passed. All then turned their attention to the moss-encased Crete.

"Is he alive?" Oz asked. He had not seen him move since he had been dropped.

"Yes. Barely. But he will strengthen." Huldah pulled

back the moss to expose Crete's head and could hear deep, low breathing. She loosened a few strands of the Spanish moss around his neck and chest.

Crete coughed and sputtered. He tried to move, but the bindings held him tight. Opening his eyes, he looked around, trying to figure out where he was. He then made eye contact with Oz. Oz was glad the bird was still bound.

Suddenly, a whooshing sound was heard overhead. The other three eagles flew in circles until one swooped down, grabbed the moss-wrapped heron, and carried it to join the other two high above. Together, they turned toward the southeast and, in moments, faded into the clouds.

"Where are they taking him?" Oz asked.

"To the Everglades," Huldah answered.

CHAPTER 55

"Preya, you need to eat more. Come and finish your meal." Maria poked the half-eaten catfish into what she hoped was a more tempting pile.

Preya had regained most of her strength and was stretching her wings and legs on a branch above the nest. Below her, the five eggs reflected the sunlight with a yellow glow.

"And Joey! Mangia! Mangia! Eat, eat! My poor little skinny boy." Maria crouched down, looking at the thin duckling sitting and staring at nothing.

Preya cast a worried look and hopped down next to the muscovy duckling. "Joey, why don't you eat those worms Uncle Giuseppe brought you?" Preya picked up one of the limp worms and held it in front of Joey. "They sure look yummy to me."

Joey peeped soft, indiscernible sounds. Maria held her ear close to him but could not make out what he was saying, if he was saying anything. She stroked his yellow head as he closed his eyes and fell asleep.

The sound of branches and leaves rustling below diverted their attention.

"Oz is the new leader! Oz is the new leader!" Chatty and Skamp bounded up the trunk and over the branches to the nest.

"Five eggs? Oh, how wonderful!" Chatty's tail twitched, and her whiskers switched.

"Oz will be here soon. He sent us ahead to tell you all about it," Scamp said.

Chatty held her tail as it wiggled in her paws. "How are you feeling, Preya? How is Joey?" Chatty ran over to Joey and saw he was sleeping. She tried to lower her voice as she tiptoed back across the nest. "Preya, you look so much better! We were all so worried about you and..."

Maria cocked her head sideways. "Oz is the new leader?"

"Yes. And Obsolom and Crete are gone. The big eagles picked them up and took them away," Chatty chittered and jumped up and down, unable to keep her tail in check. "How are you going to take care of five babies?"

Preya and Maria exchanged curious looks. "The big eagles?" Preya asked.

"Yes, there were seven of them..."

Chatty interrupted Skamp. "They dropped them in front of us. The bush strangled Obsolom. We tied up Crete in Spanish moss. And Huldah banished them. And no one believed us but..."

"Please, slow down. Did you meet Oz this morning at the peninsula?" Preya asked.

"Oh yes. Skamp and I heard him calling and scrambled as fast as we could. There were hundreds of vultures and great blue herons and crows and...." Chatty continued chittering about all that had happened. Preya and Maria had to interrupt every few sentences to ask questions of both the squirrels to unravel the tale and so that Chatty wouldn't hyperventilate or pass out from excitement. Eventually, the recount of all the events was finished, and Chatty sat down holding her dizzy head.

During the story, Preya had positioned herself back on the eggs. She had to keep shifting around to make sure all five were covered at some point. How was she going to keep up with this? And then raise five chicks?

"So, let me see if I understand." Maria put her wingtip to her beak. "Cronan is off the council for good, and Peter Paul is suspended."

"Yes. Oz is making Cronan and his crow buddies that attacked us this morning sit on any orphaned muscovy eggs as community service. You should have seen Cronan cawing and crying, but Cara stood by his side. It was only because of her that he was not sent to who knows where, maybe back to his old neighborhood, if they would take him, and ..."

"Thanks, Chatty," Preya interjected. "I'm happy that Othello and Carmen are both on the council since Oz is now the leader and Cronan is off."

"Yes! Either one of them should have been chosen instead of Cronan in the first place," Maria said.

At the risk of more non-stop chatter, Preya asked a question. "While Peter Paul is suspended, who will fill his spot?"

Skamp spoke up before Chatty could jump in. "They are talking about that now. Before we left, Horatio and Petunia suggested that Anton fill in for Peter Paul. But Peter Paul suggested Mary Margaret."

"Mary Margaret? That haughty Matron of the Mallards?" Maria said disapprovingly.

Chatty switched her whiskers. "Well, I think Peter Paul thinks that if Mary Margaret takes his place, he has a better chance they won't kick him off for good. I suggested a muscovy should be chosen, but they all just stared at me like I'm some stupid rodent without a brain, and I don't think that is very nice because…"

A flutter of wind announced Oz's landing on the nest. Rushing over to Preya, he wrapped his wings around her and caressed her head with his beak. "How are you?" Oz sat back and looked into Preya's eyes.

"I'm fine. And so are your five eggs." Straddling the eggs, Preya stood briefly so Oz could see the clutch.

Oz hugged Preya, being careful not to put any weight on her. Oz felt a radiant relief surging through his body, almost like his chest would burst.

"So, Leader! Congratulations!" Maria squawked.

"Yeah, well, the Great One is The Leader, I just follow orders." Oz turned his attention to Joey. "He looks worse. Has he eaten anything?" Oz looked from Maria to Preya.

"No. He sniffed at the worms we brought but won't eat them."

Joey made faint peeping sounds, but Oz could not understand him.

"We told them all about what happened today, Oz, just like you asked us to. Yes, we did! They know everything about the battle and the eagles and…"

"Thank you, Chatty," Oz smiled.

"Did you decide who would fill in for Peter Paul while he is suspended?" Preya asked.

"For now, Anton. But only until we find someone else or decide that Peter Paul can return. Anton wants to return to his retirement and watch movies with Duke's master."

Both Preya and Maria gave Oz questioning looks.

Chatty swished her tail back and forth and up and down. "Duke is the dog that saved Oz and …"

Chatty was interrupted by the tree swaying. "Preya, how are you feeling?" Huldah said as she landed on the nest.

Still picking at the catfish, Preya smiled and stood so Huldah could check on the eggs.

Huldah gently nudged each of the eggs. "All five eggs are healthy."

"So, Huldah, when do they begin to hatch?" Oz tried not to flutter his wings and show his apprehension about raising five chicks at the same time.

"Each egg incubates for about five weeks. They will hatch in the same order they were laid."

"I laid the first one nine days ago. Oz, our first chick should hatch in less than four weeks!" Preya wrapped her wings around Oz.

Suddenly, there was a crashing sound two trees over. Bits and pieces of bark and leaves filtered through the branches and down to the ground.

"Who's there?" Oz jumped closer to the sound, putting himself between the intruder and his nest.

"It's just me. For goodness' sake. What are you so jumpy about?" Petunia stumbled closer to the nest and clapped her wings together, seeing the five eggs. "Congratulations, Preya and Oz!"

"Thank you, Petunia." Preya stepped back to the eggs and settled over them as best she could.

"I've never heard of ospreys having more than four eggs. The Great One has blessed you!" Petunia tripped over a twig and almost fell on her face but caught herself just in time.

Oz instinctively reached out to steady Petunia, who, ignoring him, acted like nothing had happened.

"How are you going to take care of five chicks? That is a lot of babies! I've just raised three, and they kept me scrambling constantly. Skitter, my oldest by two seconds, left the nest the other day, and Chatarina and Scatter are moving out tomorrow; I am going to miss them...." Chatty put her head in her paws and started to cry.

Skamp wrapped his arms around her and hugged her close. "Maybe we can go on that vacation we had been planning for so long."

Chatty pushed away from Skamp and burst into loud sobs.

"My Giuseppe and me, we only ever had three at a time. Once they start hatching, they are so hungry," Maria said, raising her voice to be heard over Chatty's lamenting.

"Little bottomless pits," Petunia added. "I only had two at once, and we could hardly keep up with them."

Oz could feel his temperature rising with each discouraging report of caring for two or three babies. How were they going to care for five? Preya and he could not continually fly back and forth with food, protect the babies, clean the nest, and eat and rest. He noticed Huldah didn't seem concerned.

"Oz, Preya, you do believe that if the Great One gave you five chicks, he would also give you the means to care for them, don't you?" Huldah turned from Oz to Preya and then settled her gaze on Oz.

Oz felt a prick of guilt. Was he ever going to trust the Great One?

Chatty jumped up and down on her hind legs. "I can help! I can help! I can clean the nest and bring new bedding. I know where the soft, spongy Spanish moss is. And pine needles; they smell nice."

"That would be very helpful!" Preya said. "Thank you so much. I have been starting to stress about how we would take care of the quintuplets."

Quintuplets. Oz was unsure if that sounded better or

worse than "five." Chatty's offer would help, but how would they continually get food?

"Giuseppe and I can help get fish." Maria looked down her beak at Chatty. She would not let the squirrel outdo her in being neighborly.

"I can, too," Petunia added. "I'll try not to swallow them before I bring them back here."

Chatty was still jumping around. "And I can babysit! I'll scare off any snakes or raccoons." Chatty jumped up, making a growling sound, and attempted a scary-looking face.

Oz chuckled, imagining Chatty trying to babysit osprey chicks who would soon be bigger than her or scaring off a snake or raccoon. "Thank you all." Thank you, Great One.

"You can call us the Quint Stint!" Chatty clapped her paws together.

Just then, Joey stirred and started making peeping sounds.

CHAPTER 56

Huldah stepped over to the yellow duckling's side. "Joey?" After getting no response, she took his head in her wings and stroked his brow. "Joey, tell Aunt Huldah how we can help you." Huldah held her ear as close as possible to Joey's beak and listened for several seconds to the weak peeps. "He needs to get food for himself. He can't eat half-dead worms and bugs anymore."

"He what?" Asked Oz.

"And how will he do that as weak as he is and stuck in this nest?" Asked Maria.

"He can't fly yet," Preya added.

The birds and squirrels looked from one to another and back to Joey.

Preya faced Oz. "Can't you take him in your talons to get food?"

"Me? How?"

"Othello brought him here in his talons, like a cage around him. Can't you do that?"

"He is bigger now, and Othello is much stronger than me." Oz hoped Othello would show up just then, but he knew he was back at the council snag working out details with the other members. "Aunt Huldah?"

Huldah stared back at Oz with a level gaze.

Obviously, Huldah thought Oz should do this. And

Joey could not wait much longer. Oz did not believe he was strong enough. Would he kill both Joey and himself trying to get him somewhere to get food?

"Oz, please try." Preya reached out her wing to Oz.

Oz thought he heard a far-off call of an eagle. Only with the help of the Great One could he do this. He thought now would be a good time for one of the giant eagles to swoop down and help.

Oz sprang up into the air flapping his wings to get a lift and, hovering over Joey, picked up the duckling, carefully wrapping his talons around him to fully cage him in. Flapping harder, Oz tried to lift higher, but Joey's weight and his weak shoulder prevented any gain in height. Oz looked down at the yellow duckling as he beat his wings.

Joey opened his eyes and, looking up at Oz, smiled slightly and peeped, "Papa Oz."

Oz felt a new swell of strength and pushed his wings back further and down lower, ignoring the intense pain that shot through his shoulder and back. Feeling the lift now under his wings he rose above the nest and out of the branches with Joey safely in his clutch.

Now, where to bring Joey? Of course, by the pond in the park where the mallards always could find food. Unable to fly too high, Oz buzzed the treetops, trying not to knock into them and drop Joey. The park came into view. But below was Mary Margaret with her brood and the other mallard moms and ducklings. He didn't want to bring Joey near them. They would likely ridicule Oz and know the bugs they had gathered before had been for a muscovy duckling. But Oz had no choice. His wings were giving out, and he would crash into a tree or fall to the ground if he didn't land now. Oz might survive, but Joey would not.

Oz banked slightly and descended, hoping to land unobserved by the mallards on the far side of the pond.

"Mom, look!" Mary Cathryn jumped up and down, pointing her winglet over to the far side of the pond.

Mary Margaret looked where her daughter was pointing and saw an osprey releasing something, then land awkwardly. Was that Oz? What was their new leader doing over there, and what had he been carrying? It almost looked like.... No.

"Come on ladies, we need to investigate," Mary Margaret called to the other mallard moms. In unison quacks and honks with their broods following closely, they trooped over to where Oz had landed.

As the mallards waddled closer, Mary Cathryn broke away from her family. "Joey!" Running over to the muscovy duckling, she wrapped her wing nubs around him.

"Mary Cath..." Mary Margaret started to call out to stop her daughter, but her words failed in mid-sentence.

The muscovy duckling leaned against Oz, hardly moving. Mary Margaret noticed that one of his legs was missing below the knee. All Mary Margaret could think of was what she had seen this morning—was it just this morning? Joey's mother was killed. For no reason at all, except for being a muscovy duck. A duck. Really, not much different than Mary Margaret. This little yellow muscovy duckling had no mother, no family.

Mary Margaret waddled over to Oz and the two ducklings, one loved and coddled by her, the other she had disdained. The other mallard moms and ducklings were a reserved distance away, unsure of what Mary Margaret would do. They would follow her lead as long as she stayed strong.

"Greetings, Leader Oz." Mary Margaret would respect the new leader. Maybe her husband would be allowed back on the council. Besides, Oz had always been fair.

"Er, hello, Mary Margaret." Oz didn't quite know what to do. It was too late to hide Joey, and he couldn't take him away. Oz had used up his strength and Joey probably would not survive another harrowing flight. Oz looked down at Mary Cathryn, hugging Joey, peeping over him, and pushing bugs toward him to eat. She was probably about the same age but was healthy and twice as big.

"What are you doing with Joey, and why is he so weak?"

Oz was surprised Mary Margaret knew the duckling's name and cared to even ask about his condition. "He needs to get bugs on his own."

It suddenly clicked in Mary Margaret's mind. She had seen Crete take Joey. Peter Paul told her about Othello stealing a yellow duckling from Crete. Oz had been trying to foster the muscovy duckling. And she and the other mallard moms had helped. Now, it all made sense.

"You used the mallards to feed a muscovy duckling unknowingly." Mary Margaret's level gaze matched her grave tone.

"Yes." Oz stood tall and looked Mary Margaret straight in the eye. "He would have died without your help. Thank you."

Mary Margaret looked down at her webbed feet. Oz was thanking her? She had helped keep Girdie's son Joey alive? Behind her, she could hear the other moms whispering to each other. They were probably discussing who would take over as Matron if Mary Margaret showed weakness.

Mary Margaret raised her head. "He needs to feed for himself. If he does not learn now, he will not survive.

Especially with only one leg."

"I know." Oz again looked directly into Mary Margaret's eyes. "Ospreys do not know how to catch bugs."

"That is obvious."

"Mom, I can teach him how to get bugs." Mary Cathryn ran over to Mary Margaret, wrapped her wings around her legs, and looked up into her eyes. "Can Joey come live with us? Please? Pretty please with bugs and snails on top?"

Joey peeped and hobbled on his one leg to get behind Oz. He had seen Mary Cathryn's mom get furious when she had seen Tina and Mary Cathryn playing together. He missed his sister Tina, his mom, and all his family.

"Mary Cathryn, you don't even know yourself all there is to catching bugs and digging for grubs and where to find slugs and snails."

"But Mom, Joey needs to get bugs so he can eat and grow big and strong. Like Daddy!" Mary Cathryn ran back to Joey.

Mary Margaret stood tall. "Like Daddy?" The other moms hushed as Mary Margaret's voice pitched higher. She then wrapped her wings around herself, falling on her side and kicking her feet in the air, laughing in loud hronking noises, shouting out every few breaths, "Like her daddy!"

The other mallard moms ventured closer, curious about what was wrong with Mary Margaret. Oz stood there speechless. The two ducklings were hiding behind him. No one was sure what was so funny or if Mary Margaret had just lost her mind, overwhelmed by all the tragic happenings today.

"Oh my," Mary Margaret calmed and caught her breath, "like your daddy."

Mary Cathryn peeked out from behind Oz. Joey stayed where he was. Everyone waited for what Mary Margaret would say or do next.

"Mary Cathryn, Joey is a muscovy duck. He will be bigger and stronger than Daddy in a few months." Mary Margaret stood, met Oz's eyes, and then turned to leave. "Come on now, kids. It's time to learn how to find snails."

Mary Cathryn glanced up at Oz, then toward her mom, and back to Oz.

Oz raised his wing and peered down to see Joey shivering and clinging to his side. Oz nodded to Mary Cathryn and gently nudged Joey toward her. Joey took a few tentative hops as Mary Cathryn took his wing in hers. Oz watched with a mixture of joy and sadness as the two ducklings left him, made their way over to Mary Cathryn's four siblings, and followed their mom.

"We will have to call him Peter Joseph," Mary Margaret called back over her shoulder to Oz.

Oz smiled. That would be fine, Oz thought. Just fine.

EPILOGUE

"**O**z, did you see that!" Preya jumped over from the side of the nest where she had been tidying up and pointed to one of the five eggs.

"See what?" Oz hopped over to take a closer look.

"It wobbled!" Preya's eyes sparkled.

"Isn't this the first one you laid?"

"Yes, that was thirty-three days ago. I think Otto or Prasha will be joining us tomorrow or the next day!"

Oz gathered Preya in his wings and kissed her cheek. "Is that a tear of happiness? You are so beautiful when you smile! The others will also then start to hatch."

Preya settled herself on the eggs. "Every two or three days in the order I laid them. We better get our Quint Stint lined up!"

Just then, they heard leaves rustling below, and Chatty and Skamp soon scampered into the nest. "Did I hear Quint Stint? Here I am! Should I get the others? We came to tell you about the mallards and the muscovy... Are you crying, Preya? What's wrong?"

Preya smiled again. "It's a wonderful thing, Chatty. One of the eggs has started wobbling!"

"Congratulations, Oz and Preya!" Skamp patted Oz on the wing.

"Oh! That is wonderful news! I better start gathering

Spanish moss. I can get Cara to help. What else can I do?"

"Chatty, thank you; we will figure that out later. What is going on with the mallards and a muscovy?" Since Peter Paul and Mary Margaret had adopted Joey, Oz had seen the mallards foraging and socializing with the muscovies. That was already three weeks ago. Oz wondered if some of the old prejudices were resurfacing.

"Well, we were gathering acorns by the pond, you know, the big oak that..." Glancing at Skamp, Chatty stopped midsentence and grabbed her swishing tail. "Alright already, don't glare at me, Skamp; you tell them then!"

Oz and Preya met eyes and shared muffled chuckles. They had grown to love the two squirrels and the unlikely relationship they shared with them.

"A group of mallards and crows surrounded a brood of muscovy ducklings. They were quacking and cawing at the same time; Chatty and I couldn't understand them. I asked what was wrong, but they ignored me."

"Those baby ducklings are really tiny; I think they just hatched. I tried to count them but they moved around so fast, probably scared sick, the poor little things, with all that arguing. There were fifteen or sixteen of them," Chatty added, scrunching her nose and twitching her whiskers at Skamp.

Preya turned to Oz, "Oh, Oz! Those poor babies must be from one of the orphaned nests; that man took their mom and dad!"

"I'm on it!" Oz called out as he launched himself into the afternoon sky.

He could hear the raucous even before the pond came into view. As he glided closer, he saw a group of mallards and crows encircling the brood of baby ducklings, just as the squirrels had described. Oz's crown feathers peaked in alarm. Were they going to hurt the hatchlings?

"Peoples!" Oz called out as he landed next to the group. The cawing and quacking hushed as Oz strode to the center and stood beside the restless ducklings.

"Can someone please tell me what is going on?" Oz looked around at the birds, relieved that he did not see Cara or Cronan. He did notice Peter Paul and Mary Margaret standing further off with a group of onlooking residents. That was strange; the couple was usually involved with any mallard issues.

A female crow stepped forward, wringing her wings. "These are my babies, and she is trying to steal them!" She said as she pointed a wing at one of the female mallards.

The female mallard's eyes were red from crying, and her feathers ruffled. "She's a crow. She can't raise ducklings. They will starve! Just like Joey was going to starve with you, Oz!" She sobbed as she turned to her mate, who put his wings around her.

The ducklings huddled close together, a clump of downy feathers peeping unease.

"Oh, Great One!" Oz prayed silently. "Give me your wisdom."

Oz turned to the female crow who was clasping and unclasping her wings. "What is your name?"

"Christine."

"Christine, why do you feel these muscovy ducklings are your babies?"

"I was doing my community service for participating in the attack. Each day for the past three weeks, I sat on these orphaned eggs and grew to love them more every day. When they hatched this morning, I was the first one they saw. They see me as their mother."

Oz turned his attention to the female mallard. "And what is your name?"

The mallard lifted her head from her husband's chest, "Mary Ruth."

"Why do you feel you should raise the ducklings, Mary Ruth?"

Mary Ruth balled her wingtips. "I already told you; they will starve with a crow as a mother! My husband and I can give them a good home and..." Mournful sobs broke her sentence short.

"Our brood of four fully-fledged a couple of days ago." The mallard held his wife close.

Empty nest syndrome, Oz thought. Most birds and many animals suffer from the disease at some point in their parenthood. Oz again silently prayed for wisdom. He glanced over to where Mary Margaret and Peter Paul were and recognized some of the other residents. At once, clarity filled his mind. "Oh, Great One, your wisdom reigns," he whispered.

Oz addressed the crow and mallard. "Christine, Mary Ruth, you both have worthy reasons to have custody of these ducklings, and I can see you would both love and care for them. It is therefore my decision to split the brood. Christine will raise half, and Mary Ruth will raise half."

Immediately, gasps of unbelief and shock waved through the crowd. The baby ducklings sensed something was very wrong and peeped louder.

"No!" Cawed Christine. "You can't separate the siblings!"

"That would be the worst thing to do!" Mary Ruth quacked.

It was true. All the birds knew that siblings needed each other to thrive. Those who did get separated for one reason or another often did not survive more than a few weeks. Oz looked over to the onlookers and nodded to Mary Margaret, who whispered in the ear of a muscovy next to her.

All watched as a pair of muscovies waddled up to the group of crows and mallards who, one by one, stepped aside until the muscovies were in front with Oz, Christine, and Mary Ruth. The couple stood close together and held their heads low, not meeting anyone's eyes. The ducklings settled down a few feet away.

"Klara, Klaus, how are you?" Oz reached out his wingtip and touched Klaus's shoulder.

"We get through each day and hope for the future." Klaus looked briefly up.

Oz looked out to the group, who all stared back at him, trying to figure out what was happening. "Everyone, this is Klara and Klaus. They just realized three days ago that the eggs Klara had laid last month and had been incubating were not alive. They had probably died weeks ago when a human reached into their nest and shook them."

Exclamations of shock and grief passed back and forth among the onlookers.

Klara looked at Christine and then at Mary Ruth. "We didn't want to believe anything bad had happened when that human scared us away from the nest. Not to my babies. They never got to see the light of day. They would have hatched yesterday." Klara looked back down.

The transformation in Christine happened instantly

as compassion for the bereft muscovy mother overwhelmed her. She sniffed and rubbed her wing across her nose. "I love these ducklings as my own. But Mary Ruth is right, even though I hate to admit it. I would have difficulty raising even one as it needs to be. I only want what is best for the babies."

But Mary Ruth's posture slumped, and she could not meet Oz's gaze. Her husband put his wing around her and looked into her eyes. Mary Ruth tried to control the shaking in her words. "I would like nothing more than to raise these babies. But I know they won't replace my four that are now on their own." She paused and looked over to the muscovy couple. "Klara and Klaus should adopt them." Mary Ruth relaxed in her husband's wings as he brought her close and kissed her cheek.

Klara and Klaus held each other's wings while keeping focused on Oz. The group hushed, waiting for Oz to speak.

"Klara, Klaus, would you be willing to give these orphaned ducklings a home and raise them as your own?" Oz asked.

"Yes! Oz, you know we would!" Klaus and Klara announced as they hugged each other.

"Then, by the power vested in me by the council, I give you full rights and responsibilities as the adoptive parents of this brood of muscovy ducklings."

The group cheered, hugging each other and clapping Klaus on the shoulder.

Ignoring the congratulations, Klara waddled toward the babies and chirped softly to them. Immediately, the downy ducklings came running and gathered beneath her wings. One by one, she nuzzled and tucked them in close to her.

Talking and laughing with each other, the mallards,

crows, and other onlookers began to disperse.

Oz watched the muscovy family waddle off, with Klara leading her new brood and Klaus following close behind.

Alone now, Oz mused over what had just happened, then thought back to all the events from the previous few weeks, to now take in his surroundings. In front of him, up on a nearby rooftop, a pair of mockingbirds sang their eclectic repertoire. Above him, an oak swayed and clapped its branches together as a gust of wind picked up. Oz felt joy and peace consume him.

Oz lifted his beak heavenward, "Thank you, Great One."

GLOSSARY OF CHARACTERS

Anton: Anhinga

Cara: Crow – wife of Cronan

Carmen: Cardinal

Chatty: Squirrel – wife of Skamp

Christine: Crow

Copper: Cat – owned by Jeffrey and Sophie

Crete: Great Blue Heron

Cronan: Crow – husband of Cara

Deborah: Human – wife of Douglas

Douglas: Human – husband of Deborah

Duke: Dog – owned by Jeffrey and Sophie

Girdie Green: Muscovy – wife of Gunther

Giuseppe: Gull – husband of Maria

Great One: God – appears at times as an eagle

Gunther Green: Muscovy – husband of Girdie

Horatio: Owl

Huldah: Osprey – aunt of Oz and Obsolom and sister of Otto

Jeffrey: Human – husband of Sophie

Joey Green: Muscovy – son of Girdie and Gunther

Klara: Muscovy – wife of Klaus

Klaus: Muscovy – husband of Klara

Maria: Gull – wife of Giuseppe

Mary Cathryn: Mallard – daughter of Mary Margaret and Peter Paul

Mary Margaret: Mallard – wife of Peter Paul

Mary Ruth: Mallard

Jared: Human

Obsolom: Osprey – brother of Oz, son of Otto

Othello: Osprey – son of Obsolom, nephew of Oz

Otto: Osprey – father of Obsolom and Oz, brother of Huldah

Oz: Osprey – husband of Preya, brother of Obsolom, son of Otto

Peter Paul: Mallard – husband of Mary Margaret

Petunia: Pelican

Preya: Osprey – wife of Oz

Shannon: Human

Skamp: Squirrel – husband of Chatty

Sophie: Human – wife of Jeffrey

Tilly: Turtle

Trapper: Human

Valafar: Vulture

ACKNOWLEDGEMENTS

I t is said that it takes a village to raise a child. From the conception of the idea for *Raptor's Realm: Protector of the Voiceless* to now, as it has fledged and I release it into the world, it has truly been a village effort.

First, I thank my husband, Paul, for walking with me on this journey. You persuaded me to take writing courses to grow my writing skills and boost my confidence. You listened to the early concept for this story. You read the first awful drafts before I let anyone else set eyes on them. You hugged me and dried my tears when things were not progressing as I thought they should—you did not let me hit the delete key. Thank you, I love you.

This book would not have come to fruition without my friend Susan. On our morning walks, you listened to my ramblings, counseled me on my worries, talked me off ledges, and rejoiced with me in triumphs. You have always been happy to read through the content and give me your honest opinions. When the book had laid dormant due to lack of publishing, you prompted me to self-publish so the story would be told. Thank you, my friend.

I thank my beta readers and reviewers: Alex, Dale, Karen, Meredith, Nancy, Rob, and Susan. Your thoughtful input helped craft *Raptor's Realm* into a story worth reading, and you kept up with my stringent review schedule despite your busy lives.

I sincerely appreciate my brother Skip and my sisters Barb, Dale, Patti, and Becky, who encouraged me every step of the way and were always willing to look at random excerpts. Thank you, family.

I could not have persevered without my Pastor, Dave Hubbartt, the congregation at First Reformed Church of Tampa, my Bible study groups on Sunday mornings, Monday mornings, and Wednesday evenings, and many friends and neighbors. Thank you for your kind words, for cheering me on, and especially for your prayers.

Thank you, *Gotham Writers*, for offering helpful online courses. Thanks to the instructors and students who gave constructive feedback when the book was initially being penned. Thanks to Sue, who gave me a primer on using KDP, and to Hampton for your gorgeous cover design; I could not have imagined anything better.

Thank you to Kandis and Kopper, my cats, for curling up next to me even when I was prickly with frustration and for forgiving me when I was late to treat time because I was heads-down working.

These acknowledgments would be woefully incomplete without recognizing my Father in heaven, who in this adventure has given me hind's feet when I needed to traverse rocky cliffs of impossibility, has shone His guiding light on my path when the way was shrouded by uncertainty, and who has carried me on His wings of love and grace at all times. To You be the glory!